Strung

Strung
Copyright © 2017 Victoria Ashley

All rights reserved. Without limiting the rights under copyright reserved above, no part of this publication may be reproduced, stored in or introduced into a retrieval system, or transmitted, in any form, or by any means such as electronic, mechanical, photocopying, recording, or otherwise without the prior written permission of the author of this book.

This is a work of fiction. Names, characters, places, brands, media, and incidents are either the product of the author's imagination or are used fictitiously. The author acknowledges the trademarked status and trademark owners of various products referenced in this work of fiction, which have been used without permission. The publication/use of these trademarks is not authorized, associated with, or sponsored by the trademark owners.

Cover Artist:
Jay Aheer

Photographer:
Wander Aguiar

Model:
Roddy Hanson

Editor:
Charisse Spiers

Interior Design & Formatting:
Christine Borgford, Type A Formatting

NEW YORK TIMES AND *USA TODAY* BESTSELLING AUTHOR
VICTORIA ASHLEY

Chapter One

Tegan
Arlington, Wisconsin

WHEN MY PHONE DECIDES TO vibrate across the bedside table for a fourth time within two minutes, I roll over and scowl at it, seriously considering breaking the darn thing against the wall.

I can barely even keep my eyes open this early in the morning, let alone manage to muster up the energy to reach over and read any stupid messages.

I wish my phone would get the damn memo, but apparently it doesn't, because it vibrates for a fifth time.

Annoyed, I growl out and reach for it.

There's only *one* person crazy enough to bother me this early in the morning.

One person, and that jerk is lucky he happens to be my brother. If I didn't love him so much I'd kill him. Especially since he *knows* how much my sleep means to me.

Alexander Tyler . . . I will break your pretty face!

I don't even bother reading his five messages before replying with an angry response. It's too early for me to give a damn right now.

After the party my friends threw for me last night, I needed every second of sleep I could get this morning to recover from my hangover, and he just ruined that for me.

My head hurts like hell and a wave of nausea hits as I press the send button.

Me: Piss off, Xan! I'm sleeping. STOP texting me!

Xan: Morning, Sunshine. And what the fuck did I tell you about calling me Xan?

Me: You told me not to do it. Now what the hell do you want, Xan?

I grunt as I look over at my alarm clock to see it's only ten past five. I want to reach through the phone and choke his annoying butt even more now.

With the way *every* little *part* of my body aches, I knew it was early, but I didn't realize it was the ass-crack of dawn.

"He is so fucking unreal," I grunt, while reading his next message as it pops up.

Xan: If you would read my messages then you would know why the hell I'm texting and we wouldn't be having this conversation. Scroll up, genius.

Trying my best to focus on the blurred words, I run my hand over my face and scroll up to the first message, before quickly replying.

I should've known.

That bar is his damn life now. I'm not sure anything else matters to him more than *Vortex*.

Me: Seriously? You won't be home when I arrive? You have a serious work problem, Xan. You couldn't even take the day off for your little sister's arrival?

Xan: Go back to sleep. You shouldn't be awake so damn early anyway. You don't have to be at the airport for another three hours.

Me: Asshole! It's your fault I'm awake. So how am I getting into the house?

Xan: The back. In the rock by the sliding door. See you tonight, baby sis. Oh . . . and enter the house with caution.

Me: Yeah . . . sure. Thanks for the warning. NOW BYE.

"Ugh!"

After I toss my phone aside, I close my eyes and try to force myself back to sleep, but all I can think about is the fact that in less than nine hours I'll be in California, chilling by the ocean and working on my new book, away from this small town and my overbearing parents.

My brother left as soon as he turned twenty-one and I've been waiting very *impatiently* to do the same. It's the only request that our parents had since they didn't want us running away on them so early.

They knew we'd both want out of this town eventually and they were right; although, I had to promise them I'd come back after the summer.

They still don't believe that I will, but I've decided to at least give it a few more years before I make the big decision of leaving Arlington for good.

I'm hoping this visit to California doesn't make me break my promise, because that's the one thing I hate doing the most.

The next hour is spent tossing and turning before I finally make the decision to crawl out of bed to shower and finish packing.

My roommate won't be awake for at least another five hours, so we said our goodbyes last night over two cases of beer between us and three other friends, which *feels* like a huge mistake now. Literally.

On another note, it sucks that my parents are waiting outside to drive me to the airport in Madison, which is at least a thirty-minute drive.

Once I hear the Acadia pull into the driveway, I pick up my two bags—being extra careful with the one my laptop is tucked inside of—and begin making my way through the small house.

I'm surprised when Whitney mumbles something from behind me and throws her arms around my waist before I can make it to the front door.

"Whoa. I didn't expect to see you again for the next three months. What are you doing up?"

"You didn't really think I'd let you walk out that door without me being up to say goodbye, did you? I may feel like total shit, but I'm going to miss you like crazy and wanted to see you one last time before you leave. I also wanted to remind you to have fun, but not too much fun, got it?"

"Got it." I turn around and give her a tight hug. "I'm going to miss you too. Try not to have too much fun while I'm away. I'm sure Ethan will be living here the whole time I'm gone anyways, so you'll have plenty of fun to pass the time."

"Ha Ha. Aren't we funny," she mumbles. "Tell your brother hi for me, and I better have a damn good book to read about from your adventures once you return. You hear me?"

I nod and look over toward the door as it opens.

"Ready, Sweetheart?" My dad doesn't waste any time before walking over and grabbing my bags from me. "We're cutting it close already, and as much as we don't want you to leave, we don't want you missing your flight either."

I quickly tie my hair back and follow my dad to the door, stopping before I can walk outside. As boring as this place is, I really am going to miss Whitney over the next three months, and possibly even this crappy little house that I've finally gotten used to. "Alright. I'll message you tonight sometime. Don't miss me too much."

She laughs. "Just get out of here before I make my roomie stay or either squeeze my way into one of your bags and tag along for the summer."

"Yeah, I don't think Ethan would appreciate that or else I'd shove you inside myself. Later, babe." I smile and shut the door behind me, quickly jumping into the back of the red SUV.

Even though my dad looks as tired as I feel, my mother somehow looks upbeat and energetic, as if she's been awake for hours.

"We better be picking you back up from an airport in three months or you'll be breaking your father's heart. We already have one child living too far away. We don't need our baby girl running away on us too."

I lean back in the seat and get comfortable. "I know. I said I'd be back and I meant it, Mom." I yawn and close my eyes, wishing I was already on the plane, because I plan to sleep the entire way there. "Can you wake me up when we get there? I just need to keep my eyes closed."

"Is your brother picking you up from the airport?"

I shake my head.

"Why not?"

"*Vortex.*"

She huffs. "I hope he plans on taking a break while you're there. He works too hard."

"I'm sure he will, Mom. And besides, I'm a big girl now and I can take care of myself. I'll figure it out."

"I know, I know . . . I'll be quiet now so you can rest, seeing as you must have had a rough night last night."

I open one eye to see her shaking her head in disapproval, but she doesn't say anything else.

I take this as an opportunity to end the conversation and get some peace and quiet while I can . . .

♪ ♩ ♪ ♩

Oceanside, California

EXCITEMENT COURSES THROUGH ME AS I toss my two bags into the first available taxi, before jumping inside and slamming the door shut behind me. The driver cusses under his breath, clearly not expecting me.

"Sorry," I say out of breath. "Take me here, please." I hold the small folded piece of paper over the front seat for the driver to grab.

He pulls it from my grip and opens it with a small, knowing smile. "Visiting Micah, I take it?"

I toss my bags beside me in the seat and crinkle my forehead in confusion. "Micah?" I question. "I have no idea who that is. I'm staying with my brother for the summer. This is the address he gave me, so I'm crossing my fingers that he wasn't dumb enough to give me the wrong one."

The man looks at me through the rearview mirror, before

changing his tone and becoming a bit more professional. "My mistake, ma'am."

He pulls out into traffic, before speaking again. "So, you're Alexander's sister?" he questions, while glancing at me in the mirror.

I smile. "His baby sister."

With Alexander owning a bar on the beach, the taxi driver knowing his name doesn't surprise me too much, but him knowing him by address . . . Yeah, a little weird.

"Is my brother a man-whore or something? Is that how you know his address? I know he doesn't go anywhere without his precious motorcycle, so I'm sure he has no need for a taxi himself," I say.

"Let's just say I've made a lot of early morning trips to his address."

"Gotcha," I say, grossed out. "No wonder he told me to enter with caution," I whisper under my breath.

A huge smile takes over my face when we finally pull up at my brother's beach house about twenty minutes later. I've wanted to visit him ever since he first moved here five years ago, but my parents wouldn't allow it, afraid that I wouldn't come back home. Xan had to come back to Wisconsin once every three months so we could see him and have family time.

Well damn . . . now I can see why.

"This is beautiful." I roll down the window and take a deep breath, taking in the salty air. "Oh my God. My brother is one lucky jerk."

The taxi driver smiles at me through the rearview mirror. "I don't disagree with you there, ma'am. What I wouldn't give to be in his shoes."

He stops the car and shifts it into park. "I hope you enjoy your summer here, ma'am."

"Tegan. Please don't call me ma'am. Makes me feel so old." I smile, grabbing my two bags. "No offense."

"It takes a lot to offend this old geezer." He shakes his head and pushes my hand away when I attempt to hand him money. "I can't take that. Your brother has been more than good to me. You just go and enjoy yourself."

"Thank you. That's nice of you . . ." I trail off, while searching for his name.

"The name's Tom," he says with a friendly smile.

"Perfect. Thanks, Tom." I toss him ten bucks as a tip and quickly take my bags, jumping out, before he can try and offer it back to me.

"Holy hell, my brother has been living the life while I've been stuck back home with my parents with nothing even remotely exciting to do."

Taking in the house, in total awe, I walk around to the back of the large house and I swear my breath gets knocked right out of me.

Hell, I even drop my bags, stunned.

There's a huge pool in the back, surrounded by a beautiful, lit up deck. Looking up at the house itself, I can see almost *everything*—huge sliding glass doors, large windows. There doesn't seem to be much privacy. Just a beautiful view, looking out at the oversized pool and beach.

"I hope my brother knows that I'm never leaving," I mumble, while picking my bags back up and making my way over to the door.

Just as I'm about to reach for the rock to get the key, a naked butt smashes against the glass in front of me and I scream, falling backwards.

"Oh my goodness! Holy shit!"

Placing my hand over my chest, I look up with squinted eyes to see that the tan butt is really there. It wasn't just my imagination playing a cruel joke on me like I'd hoped.

My eyes slowly ascend the site before me, watching, as a guy holds the butt in place while he shamelessly pounds into some girl right in front of my face.

I quickly scramble to my feet, my eyes meeting *his* baby blue ones as strands of long, dark hair falls into his face.

I expect him to stop screwing *her,* but instead, he just pounds into her even harder, while making sure to keep eye contact with me.

After a few seconds, he pulls his gaze away from mine and bites the girl's neck, causing her to slam her head back into the glass.

This gives me the strength I need to cover my face and turn the other way. "I'm going to kill my brother!"

Growling in frustration, I reach for my phone and start walking toward the beach to get away from the action.

This was not the action I was seeking by coming here for the summer. I didn't ask for a woman's naked butt in my face.

I call my brother and he answers it on the third ring.

"What the hell, Xan?"

"Shit," he mumbles. "I'm taking it Micah's there?"

"Oh! So, this Micah guy does exist. Good to know, dumbass. Especially since I just walked up on his dirty little screw-fest against the back door. Some woman's butt was in my face. Her *naked* butt. That's so not cool, Xan."

He laughs a little. He actually fucking laughs.

"Sorry. I didn't think he'd be back already, so I wasn't sure. That's why I told you to enter with caution. He wasn't supposed to be back home for another few days, but you never know with him."

Walking through the sand, I finally stop and take a seat, kicking my shoes off. "Why didn't you mention this Micah guy before? I didn't even know you had a roommate."

"Hang on . . ." The noise around him starts to die down. I

assume he's walking to his office so he can hear me better. "He has his own place, but I like him there to keep an eye on things since I'm not around much. He's the closest I have to family here and one of the only people I fully trust. He goes back and forth from my place to his. He's sort of made the downstairs area his."

"Then please tell me I'll be sleeping upstairs. I'm afraid to touch anything down there after what I just witnessed. I might even need to sanitize my eyeballs."

"Yes," he says firmly, all playfulness gone from his voice. "I want you close to me and *away* from Micah. He's my friend and I trust him, but not with you. Far from that shit."

I let out a relieved breath and stand back up, brushing the sand off. "Good, I'm sure there'll be no problem there. Now, when will you be home? It feels like it's been forever since I've seen you."

"Give me two hours or so and I'll be there. I'll call Micah and tell him to open the front door for you."

"Yeah . . . good, since I won't be going anywhere near that back door *ever* again. That might be best."

"Gotta go. Get settled in and I'll see you later."

"Later, Xan."

Hanging up the phone, I close my eyes and the first thing that takes over my thoughts is the way *Micah's* intense eyes watched *me* while he was having sex with another girl.

It sent chills down my spine, and almost turned me on, although, I'll never admit that to anyone.

I'm so embarrassed by it. I've never watched anyone having sex before and I wasn't planning on it anytime soon, that's for sure.

Giving Micah some time to finish his business, I stay on the beach for another twenty minutes or so enjoying the peacefulness, before walking back to the house and *praying* with everything in me, that there isn't a naked butt plastered to the door this time.

"Why the hell did I leave my bags around back?" I scold myself, realizing I'll have to go back to that stupid door to retrieve my things.

Once I get to the house I look around for my bags, but don't see them anywhere. I make my way around to the front of the house to see that the door is unlocked for me.

"Thank God." I push the door open and step into the house, surprised when I look over at the couch to see Micah naked with a guitar sitting in his lap.

He stops playing and looks over at me, not even bothering to act surprised that I just walked in on him naked. If I didn't know any better I'd say he stayed in the nude just to get another reaction out of me.

"I put your bags upstairs in your room," he says, before going back to relaxing and playing his guitar as if I'm not even here.

"I'm guessing you don't own any clothes?" I question sarcastically.

As hard as I try, I can't stop my eyes from taking in every inch of his exposed body. It screams trouble with every rock-hard muscle.

"Oh, I do." He looks up at me with a steeled jaw. "I just prefer not to wear them." He lifts a brow, looking my body over. "Want me to show you to your room?"

I let out an annoyed laugh. "No, thanks. Looks like you have a hard enough time finding your own."

My heart speeds up with unwanted excitement as his eyes continue to rake down my body. He slides his lip between his teeth, letting out a small growl.

God, that's a sexy lip . . .

Shaking my head, I clear my throat and pull myself together, before he can get any wrong ideas of what might be happening while I'm here for the summer. "Thanks for grabbing my bags. I'll be upstairs *alone* settling in."

Before he can say anything, I jog up the stairs and find the room with my bags in it.

It's huge. Much bigger than any room I've had back home, and even though I know I'm going to love it here, I can't help but to ask myself . . .

Why the hell does my brother have to have such a hot roommate?

Now he's really on my shit list.

Chapter Two

Micah

AFTER ALEXANDER'S LITTLE SISTER WENT to her room last night, *alone,* I went to *Vortex* for a few drinks, just to fucking get chewed out by my best friend for doing what I do best.

How the hell was I supposed to know she'd be coming in through the back door? And how was I supposed to know she'd be so damn hot, making me wish it were her against the door?

Alexander made it clear last night that I'm to stay away from his baby sister.

Good job, dude. You just found a way to make me crave having sex with her even more.

I'm in my office, getting things ready for the day, when Gavin knocks on the door, looking scared to take on his first day.

"Where do I start, Sir?"

Shutting down my computer, I spin around in my chair and look him over. "You can start by losing the damn shirt. You won't need one while working here."

"Right." He nods, pulling his shirt over his head. "I forgot."

"Follow me and I'll take you to Colby. He'll train you for a few hours and then you're on your own. Think you can handle that?"

"Yes, Sir."

"Don't call me sir, Gavin." I walk past him, motioning for him to follow me. "It makes me feel fucking old. It's Micah and nothing else."

"Sorry," he says apologetically. "Thanks for giving me this opportunity. I've had friends on the waiting list for over a year now. I was expecting to have to wait longer than five months to get in."

"You can thank your baby face for the job. Women go crazy for guys like you around here. We needed to replace our last baby-faced bartender. Now we just need to see if you can perform your job. That will determine whether or not we'll need a replacement for a third time, so don't mess up."

"Got it . . . uh . . . Micah," he stammers. "I won't let you down."

"Good to fucking hear."

Once downstairs, I spot Colby sitting on his knees on the bar, while some chick shoves money into the front of his jeans. "Are you a stripper or a bartender?" I question, causing him to cuss under his breath at being caught. "I can send your ass to *Walk of Shame* if you'd like, but you'd have to be willing to move to Chicago. I'm sure my cousin Slade could get you in."

"My bad. She asked for it." He smirks, while jumping behind the bar and looking Gavin over. "Our baby face replacement?"

I nod. "Have him ready to be on his own by five and don't teach him any of your half-assed shit. Train him by the book."

He looks him over once again. "I'll do my best, Boss."

I'm about to walk back up to my office when I spot Sebastian sitting at one of the tables drinking.

"That little shit . . ."

Angry, I throw my arm around Ryan and point at the kid. "Did you serve him again, Ry?"

Ryan swallows hard, while looking over to see who I'm pointing at. "Yeah. He had an ID. I checked—"

"Go home," I say firmly.

"But . . . how was I supposed to know it was a fake?"

Pissed off, I get in his face, causing him to back up a step. "Because it's the third fucking time you've been told not to serve him. Now get your shit and go home."

Walking away from Ryan before I lose my shit over his stupidity, I make my way toward Sebastian and drag him to his feet. "What the hell did I tell you about coming here, Sebastian?"

"Micah," he groans. "Come on, Man. I'm almost eighteen. Stop treating me like a child."

"You *are* a child," I spit out. "You should be worried about surfing and girls, *not* how many damn beers you can finish before I spot your ass in the crowd."

He attempts to reach for his beer as I drag him away from the table and out the door, but just ends up knocking it off the table instead.

Once outside, I drag him over to the sand and toss him down.

"Dammit, Sebastian." I grip my hair in frustration, while looking down at him. "I've been trying my best to keep my patience with you, but you keep testing my ass. Get your shit together, because I won't always be here to bail your ass out of everything. Got it?"

"Yeah . . ." He jumps to his feet and wipes the back of his shorts off. "I never asked you to bail me out of anything, and I definitely never asked you to act like you're my damn dad."

My eyes meet his as I step closer to him. "You want me to stop? Because I guarantee with the life you've been living that your ass would be *dead* in less than two weeks." I fix his shirt for him. "Now get your shit together, Sebastian. Get out of here."

"Whatever, Dude," he mumbles. "I'll see you later."

Worried about the kid, I watch as he runs through the sand and over to his little group of friends who high-five him and toss him something to drink. Most likely a beer.

"Fuuuuck. This kid never stops."

I really need to get him away from those little low-lives. They're no good for him, but they're all that he's had his whole life, since his parents have never given a shit about what he does.

I've been dealing with him sneaking into *Vortex* for two years now and I've been doing my best to help him get his head on straight.

The kid thinks I'll give up on him just like his parents did. He's wrong.

"Oh look. You do own clothing after all," a sarcastic voice says from behind me.

I'd know that sweet voice from anywhere, and I have to admit that I spent most of the night imagining what she'd sound like screaming from below me. Or on top . . . whatever she's in the mood for.

"I wasn't lying, babe." Smirking, I turn around to find Tegan sitting at one of the outdoor tables with her laptop. "This is just the only place I wear them. They're sort of required here." I tilt my head and watch as her eyes wander over my body. She's trying to play it off, as if it's not obvious she's picturing me naked, but the quiver of her bottom lip gives her away. "So, I don't own many."

"I'm sure that seems to work for you," she mumbles.

"It does; although, I usually get asked to take my clothes off here as well." I walk over to the table and peer over her shoulder, curious. "Still Breathing . . ." I smile as she stiffens. "Are you writing a book?"

Clearing her throat, she turns around and palms my face, pushing it back. "Do you mind? I can't think with you so close."

"That doesn't sound like a bad thing," I tease.

Grunting, she closes her laptop. "Yes."

"Yes?" I question. "That it's a bad thing?"

"That I'm writing a book." Her eyes wander over my body again, stopping on my chest. "Why are you wearing a shirt?"

"Would you prefer I take it off for you?"

She laughs sarcastically. "I think I saw enough of your body last night to keep my mind busy for a while, thank you." She smiles up at Gavin and thanks him as he drops a drink off at her table. "I asked because every guy here is shirtless, with the exception of you. Is that a thing here? My brother left that juicy little detail out. Shirtless, sexy bartender heaven. I have a feeling I'm going to like it here."

"All the bartenders are required to be shirtless, yes, but I'm not bartending or playing right now."

"Playing?" she questions. "Your guitar?"

"You can come watch me tonight if you want to know. I'm pretty sure that isn't against the rules."

Opening her laptop again, she looks up at me and laughs. "Rules?"

Letting out a small breath, I give her a serious look and pull my shit together, before I somehow manage to break these damn *rules*. "Your brother's," I say firmly. "Should you need me if my boys don't attend to you and take care of you like you deserve, I'll be upstairs in my office. Don't be afraid to tell me if they slack."

"My brother is funny," she says softly, watching me as I back away from her and turn around to leave.

Her words stop me. "How so?"

"For thinking he can control me while I'm here. Last time I checked I was a grown woman who makes her own decisions."

"Yeah," I mumble. "Well, good luck telling your brother that."

With that, I walk away, leaving her outside, *alone,* to work on her book. Something about leaving her alone here with shirtless men is bothering me. Maybe it's the fact that I know she likes it. Or the fact that I know they'll want her, and unlike me, they might have a chance of touching her.

Out of nowhere, a pair of hands press against my chest and begin feeling me up. "You're wearing too much clothing, Micah," Gwen says against my ear, as she trails her hand down to grab my junk.

Growling, I grip her hand, making her grab it tighter.

"Mmmm . . ." she moans. "Is somebody ready to play?"

"No," I whisper, just below her ear. "I'm reminding you of what you'll never feel in your mouth again." I push her hand away. "Now keep your hands to yourself or I'll have you escorted out."

"Micah," she huffs. "Don't act like you don't miss me. No one else will *ever* do the things that *I* do."

"Then they'll probably last longer," I say stiffly. "Now, I've got shit to do."

"Fuck off, Micah." She straightens out her skirt, seeming embarrassed. "You'll be back."

"Nope. I won't," I say, keeping my cool. "I'm needed in my office. Go cling to Colby. He actually enjoys it."

Without giving her a chance to respond I walk away, jogging up the steps to my office.

One time, over a year ago, and Gwen keeps coming back for more, thinking that I'll give her what she wants. She wants a man she can control.

That's not me.

Just as I'm opening my office door, Alexander walks out of his, closing the door behind him.

"Dude, have you been here all morning?" I question, looking his tired ass over.

He runs a hand through his messy, dark hair and yawns. "Yeah, got here bright and early to take care of some shit."

Opening my office, I enter, knowing that Xan will follow.

"Well, you look like hell."

Alexander smiles. "Thanks for the obvious, Asshole." He closes the door behind him and takes a seat in the chair across from me. "I saw my sister walk in. Will you keep your eye on her, Man? I need to get some sleep before tonight."

"You're trusting me to keep an eye on her?" I laugh and place my hands behind my head, lifting a brow to him.

"Fuck no," he grumbles. "But what other choice do I have? There's a lot of assholes around here that will try to pick her up. At least make me feel somewhat better that you'll be here."

"Yeah, Man," I say, while watching the cameras. "I'll keep the assholes away."

Alexander stands up. "Yourself included," he says sternly. "My sister is a good girl. She deserves a good man that will take care of her, not someone to just show her one night of pleasure and kick her to the curb. Promise me, Micah."

Hearing the worry in his voice causes me to look up and truly see how much this means to him. The last thing I want to do is piss my best friend off and lose his trust. He's had my back for years now. More than anyone else has.

"Yeah, Man. Myself included." I point at my door. "Now get the hell out of my office, Dick."

"On it. I'll be back in a few hours."

After Alexander leaves, I sit back and watch Tegan, ready to protect her from any asshole that tries to pick her up on my watch.

Myself included.

Shit, this is going to be harder than I expected . . .

Chapter Three

Tegan

HE COMES AT ME SLOWLY, *sweat dripping from his hard body.*
"No," I grunt, while hitting backspace.
He comes at me slowly, sweat dripping from every rock-hard muscle. His eyes trail over my bare flesh as if he's ready to taste every exposed inch of me.
"Whoa! Whoa! What the hell are you writing?"
My brother's voice scares me, causing my heart to nearly jump to my throat. I didn't have a chance to see him last night since he's been so busy, and he decides to choose the worst possible time to show up out of nowhere.

Figures.

"What the hell, Xan!" I slam my computer shut and spin around to face him. "Didn't anyone ever teach you not to read over someone's shoulder? You don't do that shit. I was in deep concentration. Now you just messed up the flow of the scene."

"My bad," he mumbles, while opening his soda. "Didn't mean to disturb the porn scene in your head, little sis."

"Oh, come on. That's gross. Don't ever let me hear that word come from your lips again."

He eyes me over his can, while taking a long drink of his soda. I almost think he's never going to stop for air. All that acid at once has to burn.

"What are you doing here, anyway? I thought you were writing at the bar."

"I was," I complain. "Until Micah sent me home."

Xan smirks, before finishing the rest of his soda off. "Oh yeah? Why?"

My brother looks entirely *too* happy right now. I'm guessing he had something to do with Micah popping by my table every damn time a guy showed up.

"Because the bartenders kept trying to pick me up. I wasn't getting anything done, apparently. At least that's what Micah said when he picked up my computer and sent me packing."

"Good boy," he whispers.

"What?"

"Nothing." He kisses me on the head and walks back over to the door, stopping to look back at me. "I need to get back to the bar. Micah plays in an hour and I need to take over the staff. Those boys are fucking trouble unless you watch them twenty-four-seven. No lie. I promise we'll do lunch or dinner soon and catch up."

The image of Micah playing his guitar, naked, takes over my thoughts, and suddenly, writing can wait. I need to be at the bar to see him play.

I came here for entertainment and I have a feeling that he's going to take the spotlight.

"I'll be there then," I say, opening my laptop back up. "I'll just finish this scene and head out."

"I thought you wanted to get your book done," he quips with amusement. "Instead, you'd rather stress my ass out by hanging around at my bar full of horny jerkoffs?"

I take a second to think his words over. "Yeah. Isn't that what siblings are for? Maybe you should've thought about that *before* you decided to open a bar full of hot, shirtless men serving beer. Just saying."

He grunts. "I was hoping to keep you away for as long as I could. Just bring Jamie with you so you're not alone. She's been dying for you to get here. Call her."

"Good idea. I haven't seen her since she moved."

"I guess I'll see you soon. Just don't fall for their stupid games. I'm serious. My guys are trouble." He waves his hand at me, before rushing out of my room and down the stairs.

After he leaves, I stare at my computer for a good twenty minutes, but the words won't come. "Damn you, Xan."

I shut my computer down and call Jamie, before changing into a pair of comfortable shorts and a tank top, with a bikini underneath.

The best thing about my brother's bar is that you can drink a few beers and get a little tipsy, before running down to the beach to get wet and play in the water.

You can't beat that . . .

ONCE JAMIE ARRIVES WE DO a little catching up on the last three years, before walking down to the beach and heading toward *Vortex*.

"I can't believe you're finally here. Do you have any idea how bored I've been without you?" Jamie asks, holding her blonde hair out of her face as the wind blows it everywhere, causing her to eat it while she talks.

Waving my arms around me, I laugh at her for even thinking she can trick me into believing that crap. "I'm sure you've been *so* bored without me; spending time on this beautiful beach, full of sexy, half-naked men. I have no idea how you've managed this long without me," I tease.

She grins as a hot guy jogs past us, chasing after a Frisbee. "You're right. I totally lied. Check out the abs on that one." She lifts a brow, inspecting him. "But seriously though, you're here now and we're going to have a blast. I'll make sure of it."

Her words have me smiling, but my mind drifts to Micah, and suddenly, I'm curious.

"Do you know this Micah guy that my brother hangs out with?"

She stops dead in her tracks and starts fanning herself. "Who the hell doesn't? He's the sexiest man to hold a guitar." When I turn back around, she's following me again. "He's pretty well known around here. For both his looks and his talent."

"Yeah? But what do you know about him personally?"

She shrugs her shoulders. "I don't know. Not much. Just that he's been friends with Xan for a while now and that he moved here alone from Chicago. From what I hear, he's saving up to open his own bar. One where live music is a nightly thing."

"Yeah, well my brother failed to mention him to me, and I can't help but wonder why. Especially the fact that he practically lives with him. What the hell is that about? We used to be close."

Jamie shakes her head. "I'm not sure, but I have a pretty good idea."

"Oh yeah? Why?"

"Look at you. You're gorgeous, talented and young. Then look at Micah. Also gorgeous, talented and young. And he gets any and every girl his little heart desires. I'm sure he just wanted to keep you at a distance, worried that you'd fall for him and get hurt." She claps excitedly once the bar comes into view. "Look at this crowd tonight. It's the busiest on the nights that he plays."

"Wow!" I look around in surprise at how much the bar filled up in such a short amount of time. It's a huge change from this afternoon. "This is pretty amazing. I'm excited now. He must put on a good show to attract this many people."

"Oh honey . . . his voice is orgasmic. Let's hurry and grab a few drinks so we can get a spot close to the stage. If there are any left."

While walking up to the outside bar, my brother spots me from the other side and nods to me, before continuing his conversation with a group of girls that are practically hanging all over him.

"Go over to Colby's side. He's faster," Jamie says, pulling me through the crowd. "And he's the hottest one here besides Micah and your brother."

"My brother?" I roll my eyes and stick close to her until we make our way up to Colby.

"Yeah, your brother. He's extremely *hot.*" She shivers. "Those tattoos and abs make me want to run my tongue all over every inch of his hard body."

"Gross, Jamie! I did not need to hear that."

As soon as Colby notices me, he leans over the bar and grabs my hand, pulling my attention away from Jamie. "You ready for that date, babe?"

Smiling, I pull my hand out of his. "Nice try, playboy. How about a beer instead?"

"Make that two," Jamie chimes in. "And can you get them from the *furthest* back?"

Lifting a brow, he walks over to the cooler and bends down.

"Mmmm . . ." Jamie moans. "Keep looking, stud. We want the coldest ones. Dig deeper. Much deeper."

A minute later, Colby turns around, holding two beers in his hand. "Did you girls enjoy the view?" he asks, smirking, while sliding our beers in front of us.

"Very much so. Your ass is fantastic," Jamie responds. She grabs her beer and tosses some cash down. "Thanks. Keep the change."

I don't even get a chance to throw down a tip myself, before she grabs my arm and starts pulling me back through the crowd.

The last couple of tables close to the stage are now crowded with people, but when we get past that crowd, I see Micah leaning against a table that sits right in front of the stage.

As our eyes meet, he nods, and mouths for me to come to him.

Watching those lips move and having to focus on them to see what he's saying only makes me notice more just how damn sexy they truly are.

"Over here." I tug Jamie toward the table Micah's leaning against.

With his arms crossed over his chest, he watches me the whole time. I do mean every single step.

"Your brother told me you were coming." He uncrosses his arms and pulls out the chairs for us. "I'll be keeping my eye on you."

Keeping his gaze glued to mine, he slowly yanks his shirt over his head, as if doing a strip tease, and tosses it down, before walking away and heading to the stage.

"Damn," Jamie says with wide eyes. "Can he keep his eyes on me like that, please? What was that about? And did he just strip for you?"

"No. That was not for me." I shrug my shoulders and take a seat, my heart still racing from the look in his eyes as he stripped his shirt off. "Him and my stupid brother are being overly protective, as if I can't handle a few horny bartenders. That's all."

She takes a sip of her beer while watching Micah take a seat and tune his guitar. The way his long hair flows over his shoulders has it impossible to take your eyes away. "I'm staying at your place tonight," she says, not bothering to look at me when she speaks. "I promise not to stare too hard at the boys."

Rolling my eyes, I tilt back my beer and set my eyes on the stage, then kick my sandals off. "You're not good at keeping promises," I mumble.

"Doesn't keep me from making them," she teases.

"Good to see you, Jamie."

Jamie looks up from the sound of my brother's voice close by, blushing.

He's standing right behind her, peering over her shoulder; so close that their bodies are touching.

She swallows, before pulling herself together. "Good to see you too, Alexander. It's been a few months."

"You're looking good. Glad to see you're back home." He walks over to me and hands me some kind of pager type thing. "Push this if you need anything. It's connected to Colby's buzzer. I don't want you fighting your way through the crowd every time you girls need a drink."

"Seriously?" I look down at the buzzer. "That's all we have to do?"

"VIP . . . little sis. I got you ladies." He rubs the top of my head. "Just don't fucking abuse it or I'll have to take it away. Got me?" Smiling, he backs away. "Enjoy the show."

I can't help but to laugh when the girls clearly check him out as he rushes past them to get some work done, or whatever it is that he's in a hurry to do.

"Dude . . . your brother is pretty awesome. You know that,

right?"

"I guess," I mumble, smiling. "It's a good thing I take after him then, right?"

Jamie shrugs. "Eh."

"Screw off!" Laughing, I toss my beer label at her and then freeze when Micah speaks into the mic, getting the attention of the crowd.

"Are you ladies ready?"

The crowd screams. Myself included.

"Damn," he smirks, before looking around, his eyes landing on me. "It's not often I make the ladies scream while still wearing my jeans. I can't imagine how loud it'd be if I weren't wearing these."

The girls start screaming even louder, yelling at him to take his jeans off.

I stay quiet this time, even though inside I wish they were off too.

"Sorry, ladies. We have rules here . . . unfortunately." He laughs into the mic and it's so damn deep and sexy that I shift in my seat and sip my beer to distract myself. "I'm feeling like some Shinedown tonight. Here's one of my favorites. It's called *I Dare You.*"

The crowd quiets down as soon as he starts playing and all eyes are on him.

I honestly can't pull my eyes away as I watch his fingers move, pulling the strings of his guitar.

The way the muscles in his arms flex as he plays has me completely zoning in on him. Every part of him.

Until his lips move and the most beautiful sound comes out, working me up and instantly causing me to sweat.

It's crazy just how good he really is.

"He's soooooo good," Jamie points out. "I feel like it's been forever since I heard him play. We need to come here every week together while you're here. You game?"

Needing another drink to hopefully calm my now racing thoughts, I press the buzzer.

A few times.

"You need another beer? I need another beer. Is it hot out here?" I say quickly. "I need out of this stupid shirt."

In a hurry to cool off, I pull my shirt off and set it down next to me in my seat.

"Better?" Jamie questions with amusement.

"Yeah." Micah is now watching me as he sings. There are probably a hundred girls in this damn crowd, yet he's looking right the hell at me, as if he can't look away. "No." I shake my head. "Not really. I think I'm having a heatstroke or something. I need liquid and fast."

Colby appears over my shoulder, nearly scaring the crap out of me as he holds out two beers. "You know . . . this is almost like calling me, which you can do later tonight."

"Oh, is it? I bet you say that to all the girls that hold this special buzzer," Jamie teases. "It's a shame we didn't get to watch you fetch these beers though."

"You're telling me, babe. I feel sorry for you both." He winks at me and then backs away when Micah glares at him from the stage.

It's easy to see who the boss is around here, because Colby instantly walks away and returns to work.

Micah's gaze lands on me for a few short seconds, before finally turning away to look down at his guitar.

Knowing that Whitney will kill me if she knows I watched a hot guy perform at my brother's bar and not capture it, I take a quick photo to send to her.

A text comes through from her a few minutes later.

Whitney: Holy-beautiful-long-haired babe. He is gorgeous. I wonder if Ethan would be pissed if I make this my screensaver. I guess we'll see . . .

I laugh at her response but tuck my phone away, not wanting to miss any of Micah's performance.

He plays three more songs, causing the crowd to fall more and more in love with him and his voice. He then says goodnight to everyone and hops off the stage to grab a water bottle and pour it over his sweat-covered body.

His eyes lock with mine as he rubs the water down his chest and arms, before reaching for his shirt and walking away through the crowd.

I swear he gets stopped every step that he takes. These women are ready to eat him alive. Literally. I think one even tried to lick him when he walked past her.

It's ridiculous.

"What the hell?" I finish off my last beer and stand up. "Are the women always like this around here?"

Jamie stands up and stretches. "Not always." She smiles. "They're worse sometimes. I swear you'd think this was a strip club the way they feel all over these boys."

"Interesting," I whisper. "I should just write about my brother's damn bar."

"You should," she responds. "Do you have any idea how much action goes on around here?"

"Nope. My brother doesn't tell me shit."

She grins like a madman. "Well, you're about to see some shit this summer. Let's get out of here." She tosses her empty bottle in the nearby trash. "I have to work for a few hours tomorrow morning."

"Yeah," I agree. "I need to get some writing done."

WHEN I GET BACK TO my brother's house, I grab my laptop and bring it out back by the pool.

I've been writing for a good hour, suddenly feeling inspired, before a splash causes me to jerk back and look up.

Standing up, I glance into the pool to see a hard, muscled back, swimming through the water.

My gaze stays glued to Micah's back, until he emerges from the water, exposing his toned, naked butt.

"Holy shit! Come on, Micah," I scream, as he climbs out of the pool while covering his junk with both of his hands. "Why are you naked . . . again?"

"A little warning," he whispers next to my ear. "Stay away from the pool after I get home from playing." He moves in closer, his lips brushing under my ear. "Unless you want to get *wet*."

My entire body quivers as I watch him walk away and let himself into the house.

Why does his body and hair being wet have to make him even sexier?

I'm angry that he treats me this way, yet so damn turned on by it.

Maybe I'm just angry at myself.

Angry at myself for wanting his body so damn bad, knowing that I can't have it . . .

Chapter Four

Micah

SHE JUST HAD TO BE out back when I arrived at the house after my show. I shouldn't have gotten naked and jumped into the pool to cool off with her being there, but I couldn't stop myself.

Having her around and knowing that I can't touch her is really fucking with my head, and it's only been two days.

"Fuck you, Alexander," I mumble, while walking to the bathroom to turn on the shower.

It's that asshole's fault that I've been thinking about his sister all damn day and imagining all the dirty things I could do to her sexy little body.

"Lay one finger on my sister and I'll kick your fucking ass. I mean it, Micah."

That's what the fuck he said to me.

He should know me well enough to know that if someone

threatens to kick my ass for doing something, it makes me want to do it even more.

Call me twisted. I don't give a shit.

Call me dirty. It's true.

Closing myself in the shower, I lean my head back and stroke my dick to images of Tegan in her red bikini top.

She just had to take her shirt off while I was playing my guitar, completely drawing my attention and thoughts her way.

I tried to keep my eyes away, but it was nearly impossible with her breasts on display. Apparently, Colby's ass noticed too.

Gripping the wall, my strokes become faster and harder, causing me to moan out as I release myself down the drain, panting as it washes away.

"Fuck me!" I growl out.

I've been needing this release all day. That shit was intense.

Washing off, I get out and dry off, before lying on the couch in the den and wondering what Tegan thought of me naked in the pool.

She's seen me naked, twice, in only two days since she showed up here. Her eyes have witnessed every muscle of my naked body, except for the most important one: my dick.

My eyes glance over toward the sliding door when it begins to slowly slide open.

Tegan thinks that I'm sleeping.

I don't blame her. It's completely dark down here. That's how I like it.

Closing my eyes, I listen as she walks through the den, slowing down once she's standing behind the couch.

Her breathing picks up and it doesn't take a genius to know that she's checking out my body, lying in this low hanging towel. It barely fits around my waist.

"Are you imagining me naked again?"

Fuck! There goes my mouth again.

She sucks in a breath and clutches her computer against her chest when I open my eyes and look up at her.

"Not a chance," she says teasingly. "I just wanted to tell you that you played really well tonight. Wasn't sure if you were still awake."

Lifting a brow, I grab the back of the couch and sit up. "Well, it's been a passion of mine since I was a kid. So, thank you." I smile as she begins to walk away. "But you were still picturing me naked. For your book?"

She laughs. "Good night, Micah."

I find myself smiling as I watch her disappear from the room.

A part of me hopes she gets a little inspiration from me for that book of hers. It'll probably be the best damn book she's ever written.

♪ ♩ ♪ ♩

I PULL UP OUTSIDE OF Sebastian's parents' apartment a little later than usual, to see Sebastian chilling on the porch with his friends.

"Over here. Now," I yell out the window, when I see one of them pass him a joint.

Rolling his eyes, he passes it back and tells them that he'll be right back.

"You're late," he mumbles. "I thought you weren't going to show."

"Have I ever stood you up? Get your ass in the truck."

He waves his friends off and jumps in.

Every Sunday I pick him up, take him to lunch, and bring him to *Express*—the bar I'm working on opening.

I don't have much time to be there for the kid, but any amount of time I can give him, I do.

After picking up some burgers, we head to the bar and sit down to eat.

"Where are your parents? Don't they get tired of those lowlifes hanging out on your porch?"

He looks up from his burger. "You tell me." He tosses his burger down and sips his soda. "I haven't seen them in a week."

Anger boils inside of me at the knowledge that his parents took off again without telling him where. Last time they took off they were gone for three fucking weeks, leaving him with an almost empty fridge and no money to survive on.

"What the hell, Seb? I told you to let me know the next time they take off." I rake my hands through my hair in frustration. "Is there food in the house?"

Standing up, he tosses his empty wrappers into the trash. "Yeah . . . enough noodles to last me for a damn month."

"I'll tell you what." I toss my garbage in the trash and push my chair in. "Help me clean for the next three hours and I'll take you shopping for a new pair of shoes and some groceries. I'm not letting you live on those shitty noodles for who knows how long. They're terrible for digestion."

His eyes go wide, before he smiles. "Really? A new pair of kicks?"

"As long as you promise me something."

He crosses his arms. "I'm listening, big man."

"I don't want to see you smoking that shit with your friends, and I don't want to catch you hanging around *Vortex* trying to get drunk. That's why I'm not giving you cash this time. *I'll* take you shopping myself from now on."

He lets out a long breath, before speaking. "Fine. You got a deal."

"Good." I toss him some gloves. "Now let's get this place

cleaned up."

Three hours later, as promised, I take Sebastian shopping for a new pair of shoes and some groceries that will last him at least a month.

Afterward, I drop him off at home and watch as he goes inside, locking the door behind him.

I always make sure he locks the door before I pull away.

The last time he left it unlocked when he was home alone, he got robbed by some homeless guy that hangs out at the liquor store across the street from the apartment building.

His parents came home two days later and his dad beat the shit out of him. He couldn't open his right eye for three damn days.

It took everything in me not to break that fucker's neck for placing his hands on Sebastian.

After he gives me the thumbs up through the window, I drive off and head to *Vortex* to check on the boys.

Sundays are one of the slowest days for the bar, so I'm not surprised to see that it's dead . . . maybe nine or ten customers hanging around.

I'm also not surprised to see that Tegan is hanging out here with her laptop again. For some damn reason this place gives her inspiration.

"How's Gavin catching on?"

Colby turns away from cleaning out one of the coolers. "Better than I expected." He stands up and drapes the towel over his shoulder. "The ladies have loosened the kid up. Look." He points to the table of girls that Gavin's surrounded by.

My eyebrows raise in surprise as I watch him smoothly flirt with the chicks like a pro.

"Looks like he'll fit right in as long as he can keep up. I'll be out back if you need me."

"Sure thing, Boss."

Walking out back, I can't help the small grin that occurs when Tegan looks up at me and then slowly scans my body over, before turning away.

"I guess you were right when you said this is the only place you wear clothes." She goes back to typing, but then pauses. "I thought Xan was here."

I pull out the chair across from her and take a seat. "He is."

She laughs. "Okay . . . so you both need to be here? It's a Sunday. There's like no one here."

"You're here," I say. "Someone's got to keep an eye on you while your brother sleeps in his office."

She shifts a little in her seat and clears her throat. "Is that jerk really sleeping?"

"Most likely," I admit. "He's a workaholic and a worrier. He spends time here even when he doesn't need to. He has to sleep sometime."

"So that's why you're here?"

"Yeah," I say with a nod. "Gotta have my boy's back. Always have and always will."

My eyes shift over to her computer screen.

He's so damn cocky and hot that all I can think about is slapping him and fucking him at the same time.

My cock twitches.

"Are you writing about me?"

"No!" She quickly slams her computer shut. "Don't you know it's rude to read someone's computer or phone without asking?"

I stand up and walk behind her, leaning in close to her ear. She instantly sucks in a breath and stiffens at me being so close to her. "So, you *haven't* thought about fucking me, Tegan?"

"You're a cocky asshole," she says tightly as I walk back around to face her.

"Exactly." I grin, knowing that I caught her in a lie.

As hard as she tries to hide it, her eyes give her away.

"Fuck you."

"Please do," I tease. "I'll let you slap me too."

Her eyes lower down my body, but she's quick to pull them away and clear her throat.

"You know . . . if you don't want to get caught checking me out, you can always just look at the photo you took of me last night on your phone."

She looks up quickly, her face turning red with embarrassment.

"That wasn't for me."

"You expect me to believe that, Tegan?"

Our banter stops once Alexander walks out back, eyeing us over suspiciously.

"Am I interrupting some shit?"

Tegan gives me a hard look and then turns to her brother. "Nope. Micah was just leaving." She huffs, while opening her computer back up. "What is it about you two with reading my damn work? Can I have some damn peace and quiet now?"

I lift a brow. "Your dirty words caught my attention. Maybe if you weren't writing about sexy shit then I wouldn't read it."

Alexander glares at me. "Yeah, you're the last person that needs to read her porn shit. You already think dirty enough."

"Enough," Tegan jumps in. "Both of you. Buh bye. Now."

Her being so demanding only turns me on more, and without thinking I let my eyes roam over her tight little body, before ascending to stop on her thick, pouty lips.

I must lick my own, because Alexander nudges me and mumbles shit under his breath, looking displeased.

"We'll be inside."

Pulling my mind out of the gutter, I follow Alexander inside and to his office, closing the door behind me.

"I need to leave. I have to go on a trip for a few days. I know I can trust you with my bar, I always have, but can I also trust you with my damn sister?"

Fuck . . . can he?

"I told you I wouldn't touch her," I force myself to say. "I'll keep my word."

He looks me over, probably noticing how I tensed when I answered him. "Don't make me lose my trust in you. Trust means everything to me."

"Me too, Man."

Me too . . .

Chapter Five

Tegan

MY BROTHER UP AND DECIDED he needed to leave for a business trip now that I'm finally here to spend a little time with him.

I could kick his butt for leaving me when I just got here. He's never around as it is and I was hoping we could grow close again over the summer.

It's already been two days since he left, and oddly, I miss him. So maybe we have grown closer in the five days that I've been here, even though he's been gone for two of them.

I guess I can't complain too much. With Xan gone and Micah watching me from a distance, I've managed to get close to eight thousand words written in just the last two days, and I'm giddy with excitement, because I feel good about what I've gotten done.

I've never been so excited to write a book before.

Taking a sip of beer, I close my computer for the night and

walk over to dangle my legs in the pool.

It's so beautiful and peaceful out here. I really could just stay out here all night.

With Micah at the bar I've had the entire house to myself all day. No surprise butts in my face. No naked guy walking around with a guitar and no sexy, smart-mouthed guy to make me think dirty as sin thoughts. My brother would kill me if he knew.

Smiling, I let out a breath of contentment and close my eyes, enjoying myself.

My perfect moment only lasts about a minute before it's ruined with Micah jumping into the pool and yanking my legs to pull me under the water with him.

Fighting him under the water, I kick him away and come up for air to see him looking at me with the biggest damn smile I've ever seen.

It's like he gets off on messing with me.

"Seriously!" I angrily splash him, but he doesn't seem to care.

Swimming over to me, he picks me up and grabs my legs, wrapping them around his waist. "Sorry, it's the asshole in me." Gripping my thighs tighter, he walks us over to the edge of the pool and stops. "I just wanted to ask you to come out with me tonight. One of my friends is having a party."

"Well, you have a funny way of asking me to hang out," I huff. "You could've asked without dragging me under the water."

He smiles when I slap his hard, wet chest. "I deserved that," he admits. "So, did my way work?"

A part of me wants to say no, but seeing that crooked smile sitting on his perfect, wet lips, I say the opposite. "Yes. Surprisingly so, but *only* because I could use a little fun to clear my head. I've been thinking too hard today and need a break."

Lifting his brows in amusement, he laughs under his breath and lifts me up and out of the pool. I'm surprised at how effortlessly he does it. "Get dressed. I'll be inside in a minute."

With that, he dives back into the water, leaving me standing here, trying to get over how turned on I got by him handling me in the pool.

My legs felt so good around his waist that I didn't even bother yelling at him for picking me up like I meant to. Hell, I sort of wanted to hang here all night and feel his body against mine.

What the hell am I saying?

"Oh boy, I have serious problems."

By the time I get dried off and dressed, Micah is waiting for me by the front door, dressed in a pair of dark jeans and a black V-neck shirt.

Holy shit, that shirt hugs his sculpted chest so good that it nearly takes my breath away. I might even choke on a little drool.

Well, not really . . . but a little exaggeration never hurt anyone.

Looking me over, he opens the door and motions for me to walk out first. "Nice boots." His eyes wander down to my favorite cowgirl boots. "I've always wanted to *fuck* a girl wearing only a pair of those."

"Wow!" I give him a shove. "Do you have a filter or is it broken?"

He opens his truck door for me. "Never had one, babe." He slaps my ass, hard, as I boost myself up to get into his truck.

"That hurt!"

He grins in satisfaction. "Isn't that what girls like to read about in books? Asshole heroes. You're fucking welcome."

Rolling my eyes, I slam the door shut as he walks around to the other side and jumps in. "And what do you know about books and the things us girls like to read about?"

He starts the engine and backs out with a cocky grin. "You

don't think I've read a book or two in my lifetime? My mother used to make me read books every night before bed when I was a kid. So yeah, I've read a few Romance books since I hit puberty."

I've always thought a man reading was a turn on. So, to hear that Micah is open to reading . . . well, hell. It just got about ten degrees hotter in his truck.

Trying to keep my very dirty thoughts in check, I keep my eyes out the window for the rest of the ride to the party.

"Think you can keep up with me tonight?" Micah questions, while parking the truck. "It's easy to get lost in the crowd here. Come on."

He jumps out and I quickly follow, stepping out and shutting the door behind me.

Running my hands over the front of my dress, I look out at the street to see that there are tons of cars parked on the block.

"How did you manage to get a driveway spot? Special treatment for being so cocky?"

He lifts a brow at me and chuckles. "I'd like to think so, but no." I suck in a breath as he steps up to me and reaches behind me to pull the back of my skirt down. He's so close that I can feel the bulge in his jeans against my body. "Showing me the goods already and this isn't even a date. Special treatment for me being so cocky?"

My face heats as I clear my throat and back up to get some distance between us. "No, apparently your truck is a dick too." I smile and walk away. "Let's go."

His laughter comes from behind me as he takes a few quick steps, catching up with me. "You're fun tonight. I like it."

"Like it too much and you may feel sore in the morning," I mutter.

I stop walking when I feel his body press up behind me. Breathing in my ear, he grabs my chin and pulls my head back to whisper in my ear. "I'd watch what you say unless you want me to throw you into the back of my truck and *fuck* you until my legs give out." He lets out a small growl and nips my ear, causing goose bumps to cover my entire body. "It's been a while since anyone's been able to keep up long enough for my body to hurt."

Oh. My. God.

"Wow!" I remove his hand from my chin, trying to keep my cool, even though all I can think about is him between my damn legs and wondering how long he really can last. "You become a bigger dick the longer I'm with you. Congratulations."

"You're right. My dick has become bigger. Now stop trying to get me naked again and let's go."

He grabs my hand, pulling me along behind him before I'm able to think of a comeback.

"Fucking dick," I mumble, as he fights his way through the crowd, keeping me close to him.

He doesn't release his hold on me until we're out back by the pool. The back of the house is lit in neon lighting and there has to be at least close to eighty people just out here alone.

Most of them are dancing to the fast beat of the music, while a few of them are pushing through the crowd on skateboards, doing tricks into the pool.

The way Micah acts so uptight and in charge at my brother's bar, I never expected him to be at such an insane party like this one. It's crazy here. I've gotten the impression that he usually likes to be in charge.

"I never expected you to hang at a party like this one?"

"Why?" he questions, while pouring me a beer.

I grab the plastic cup from him and lean in close to his ear so he can hear me. "You seem uptight at my brother's bar."

He flashes me a half smirk. "Good thing I get to show you

another side of me then. There I have to be."

As I'm in the middle of taking a drink of my beer, he wraps his arm around my waist and pulls me close to his body; then begins dancing to the music.

I nearly spill my beer on him when he does this sexy little grind against my stomach. "What are you doing?" I laugh and hold my beer away as he thrusts against me like a male stripper or something.

"It's called dancing." He grips my hair and tilts my head to speak next to my ear. "Loosen up your body and just move it with mine."

I'm almost embarrassed that he can tell I'm scared to dance. I've always been self-conscious about people judging the way I move my body. It doesn't come as natural to me as it does to others.

Gripping my hip, he begins moving my body with his, biting his bottom lip as he looks down at my waist to watch me begin to sway with him. "Damn, girl," he teases. "Don't show me up now."

I slap his shoulder and laugh. "Don't tease me. Dancing isn't my thing."

He smiles, and it's so damn cute that my heart jumps a little.

"The only thing getting teased right now is my dick. Trust me." He lifts me up a bit and begins grinding his crotch into me, dancing so seductively that I can't help but to get into it myself and move along with him. "Keep grinding like that and I might have to break my promise to your brother."

My face turns red with embarrassment. "You made a promise to my brother?" I stop dancing and place my free hand on his hard chest. "He'd probably kill you if he saw us dancing like this right now."

He backs up a little and reaches for his own beer now. "He never said anything about dancing, Tegan. We're just having a little fun. I know where to draw the line and I don't plan on crossing it."

I feel a little disappointed for some reason, and my whole mood seems to change. Dancing close to him is the last thing I want to do now.

"Let's just skip dancing." I back out of his arms and tilt my beer back, feeling frustrated with my damn brother. Looking around, I spot two guys playing beer pong. "Let's play."

Before he can say anything, I walk over to the beer pong table and watch as they finish their game.

"Are you challenging me?" Micah asks from close behind me.

"Maybe."

"I like a challenge," he whispers next to my ear. "What do I get if I win?"

"Doesn't matter." I smile and begin setting up the table when the two guys walk away. "You won't be winning. The question is . . ." I begin filling up some of the cups as he does. "What do *I* get for winning?"

He stops and lifts a brow at me. "Honestly? I'd give you anything you fucking wanted, but your brother might kill me." He looks me over as if he wants nothing more than to taste every inch of my body. It has me completely turned on and aching for his touch.

"My brother isn't here," I say softly.

His eyes widen as if he heard me, but he doesn't say a word.

Hell . . . I can't believe that I said that myself.

There's just something about Micah that makes me want one night with him. One night to let him do anything and everything that he wants. No strings attached, like the girl I walked in on him with. Just one night of his talented fingers and mouth on my body.

With my brother around that won't be happening, and I can tell how much my brother's friendship means to Micah.

By the time we're down to the end of the game, there's two

cups left on my side and one left on his side. I'm completely buzzed right now and living in the moment.

"You've been talking a big game the whole time," I tease. "When are you going to show me who's in control here?"

He smirks and holds his ball up. "Right about . . ." he tosses the ball and makes it in one of the cups. "Now. Drink up."

"Cocky jerk." I roll my eyes at him and grab the ball out of the cup, before downing the beer. "We still don't know what the winner gets."

"The winner gets to kiss the loser anywhere under the dress." He flashes a cocky grin at me.

I throw the empty cup at him. "You're not wearing a dress, jerk."

"Exactly." He tosses his ball, making it effortlessly into the last cup. "I'm ready for my prize."

He doesn't waste any time grabbing my cup away from me and downing the beer, before dropping to his knees in front of me and spreading my legs.

My heart speeds up as I grab onto his hair and pull him back. "What are you doing?" I ask in a panic. "There's hundreds of people out here."

He smiles up at me and slightly lifts my skirt up my leg. "Relax. I can't kiss you where I want to anyway."

I begin looking around me, but close my eyes and moan when I feel the softness of his lips press against the inside of my thigh. He kisses it a few times, moving higher with each one, before biting me right below my panty line and then licking the spot.

"What the hell!" I scream and jump away from him. "You bit me."

"I got excited." He looks up at me and shrugs, before standing up as if nothing unusual just happened. "I'd apologize, but I have a feeling you enjoyed it."

Did I? Most definitely, but I'm not telling him that.

"You scared me. Biting wasn't part of the prize."

He places his hand on the small of my back and walks me away from the table when a small group takes over.

"Sometimes I can't control myself. You're lucky I didn't do what I really wanted to do."

He gets distracted when some guy with dreadlocks calls his name and jogs over toward him. "You made it."

Micah grabs his hand and gives him a one-armed hug. "I told you I would."

The cute guy smiles when he notices me standing next to Micah. "Who's this beauty?"

I see Micah's eyes darken as he answers him. "Alexander's little sister. She's off limits."

"I'm not little," I add with a scowl. "The name is Tegan and my brother isn't my boss."

I smile as he looks me over with appreciation. He's extremely cute and those ice blue eyes have me wanting to stare at them.

"Glad you could make it to my party, Tegan. I'm also glad that your brother isn't your boss." He reaches out to shake my hand and winks. "I'm hoping I'll see you around."

He pats Micah on the back and then quickly takes off when some people start yelling for him.

I'm still smiling when I turn back around to face Micah. The look on his face says he isn't so pleased himself. "Kalon just got out of a five-year relationship. He's on the rebound so don't let his sweet talk trap you into something that won't work out."

"I'm not trying to jump into a relationship with any guy," I mutter. "You and my brother are going to drive me crazy this summer."

I walk away and pull out my phone to text Jamie.

"What are you doing?" Micah places his hand on my chin and pulls it up for me to look at him. "I'm sorry if I upset you. I'm just looking out for you."

"I don't need either of you looking out for me, Micah. I'm twenty-one now. I'm not the young girl he left when he moved away years ago." I hit send on my text. "I asked Jamie to come pick me up. We've both been drinking and I don't want you to leave the party early."

"I think I've had enough partying for tonight." He nods his head toward the side of the house. "Let's start walking and Jamie can pick us up when she finds us."

Without hesitation, I begin walking next to Micah, letting him lead the way.

Jamie texts me back a few minutes later, letting us know which way she'll be coming from.

"What did you do back home?"

I look over at Micah to see him watching me.

"I worked at my family's convenience store and wrote when I had free time. It didn't seem I had much though, so I was desperate to get away and stay with Xan for the summer. I just needed some peace and quiet and a little inspiration."

"I'm glad you came. The people I'm used to being around all seem the same to me. You're different and it intrigues me."

I smile. "How so?"

"I'm used to girls jumping all over me the second they meet me. You didn't. I like that about you, and if I'm honest, it keeps me up at night, thinking of ways to change that."

I catch myself laughing. "Is that where you get all your *charm* from? Late night thinking sessions?"

"I do my best thinking at night. Don't you, for your writing?

You probably lay in bed at night, the scenes flowing through your head, giving you ideas on what to write when you wake up. Is that how it works?"

I nod, finding it interesting that he really seems to want to know. "Most of my ideas come to me when I'm either lying in bed late at night, taking a shower, or listening to music."

"I wouldn't mind being around for two of those," he teases.

"Come on." I nudge him with my shoulder when he wiggles his brows at me. "I thought you seriously wanted to know."

"I do," he says, sounding serious now. "It impresses the hell out of me that you're able to write books. I write lyrics in my spare time and it's hard enough to finish just one song. I can't imagine writing an entire story for two characters made up in my own mind. That shit can't be easy and it takes one talented as hell person to be able to pull that off."

"You write lyrics?" I ask, amazed. "I'd love to hear—" I stop talking when Jamie starts honking to get our attention.

She pokes her head out the window and whistles as her car stops in front of us. "Damn, hot stuff. I'm going to want to borrow that skirt. Just a heads up."

Micah opens the back car door for me to get in. I figured he'd ride in front with Jamie, so I'm surprised when he scoots in next to me and closes the door.

He's so close that his muscled leg is practically on top of mine. It has my mind racing with extremely dirty things.

"I have to be up in the morning, so I'm going to just drop you two off and hit the road."

"Thank you, Jamie. I didn't mean to keep you up."

She smiles back at me. "You didn't. I was chilling at *Vortex*, watching the sexy men working it. I just wasn't drinking since I have to work in the morning."

When we get back to my brother's house, we say goodbye to Jamie and head around to the back.

Micah pulls out his key and unlocks the door.

"You coming in?"

He shakes his head and yanks his shirt off. "Nah . . . I need some exercise to clear my head. If I go inside right now . . ." He slowly undoes his jeans and pulls them down his thick, muscled legs. "I'll end up in your bed."

With that, he turns around and jumps into the water, leaving me standing here with my thoughts all over the place.

I have no idea how I'm going to go the whole summer without wishing that he would end up in my bed.

Shit . . .

Chapter Six

Micah

BETWEEN *VORTEX* AND *EXPRESS*, I haven't gotten a chance to see or talk to Tegan since last night. As soon as I left *Vortex* around eight, I went straight to my work in progress and spent the next three hours painting.

My shirt is practically covered in black paint and I'm so exhausted that I considered just sleeping in my future office at *Express*.

It was thoughts of Tegan that led me back here tonight. As much as I tried to ignore that I want nothing more than to touch her in all the wrong places, my body and mind wouldn't let me forget.

The place is completely quiet as I let myself in through the back. I didn't notice any lights on when I pulled up out front.

Yanking my shirt over my head, I make my way into the bathroom and scrub my hands for a good five minutes, trying to get rid of as much of the dried paint as I can.

By the time I throw on a pair of sweats and fall down on the couch, my mind is already drifting back to Tegan.

"Shit." Sitting up, I run my hands over my face and decide that I have no choice but to at least check on her.

Maybe then I'll be able to sleep.

Quietly, I make my way up the stairs and toward her room. Her door is cracked open, and the *horny bastard* in me can't help but to peek inside and get a glimpse of her.

Standing in front of her cracked open door, I hear something vibrating, followed by the sounds of her frustration.

My dick instantly hardens at the knowledge that she's trying to get off, not even ten feet away from where I'm standing.

"Come on," she groans. "Why won't you work?" She slaps the bed and then tosses her vibrator down next to her. "Thanks a lot."

"Need some help?" I finally poke my head inside to see her scramble to grab her sheet and cover herself up.

"What the hell, Micah? Why are you creeping outside my door?"

She looks completely tired and frustrated, and I can't help but to hope that it's because of me.

"I couldn't sleep," I admit. I walk inside her room and reach for her purple microphone looking vibrator. I don't know whether to try and use it on her or sing into the damn thing.

"Give me that!" She quickly snatches it from my hand and hides it under her leg. "Please go. The last thing I need right now is you giving me a hard time."

"Who said I'm here to give you a hard time?" Reaching for the top of my sweats, I drop them to my feet, before stepping out of them. "You sounded frustrated. All I want to do is help you."

She looks me over and swallows. Everything about her body language confirms that she wants me as badly as I want her right now, but we both know there's one thing stopping us: Alexander.

"We both know that Xan would kill you if you laid even one finger on me."

Smirking, I yank the blanket from her body and suck my bottom lip into my mouth as I take in her sexy little body, wearing only a small white tank top and black panties.

"Who said I have to lay a finger on you?" Dropping down to my knees, I reach under her leg for her vibrator. "Nice microphone."

"It's a personal massager from the Couture collection," she corrects me. "And what do you think you're doing?"

Gripping her legs, I yank her down to the edge of the bed and spread her knees apart. "Doing you a favor . . . *without* laying a finger on you. Now lay back and relax."

She hesitates for a moment, before lying back and relaxing her legs. "I can't believe I'm about to let this happen."

"I can." Raising up a bit, I grip the straps of her panties and get ready to pull them down her legs.

"No." She grips my hand, stopping me. "Through the panties."

"Are you serious?" I arch a brow.

"I'm not going to let you sit there and look at my vagina."

I smile, knowing that once I start she's going to wish that she were bare. "I can work with that."

Wanting to get her worked up, I stand and rub my hand over the top of my boxer briefs, squeezing my erection.

"Look at me," I demand.

Her eyes open and land on my hand that is now stroking my cock through my thin briefs.

"Does this turn you on?" I grab it with both hands, giving her a better view of its thickness. "You like watching me touch myself?"

Her bottom lip trembles as she lets out a small moan.

"Keep this image in mind and pretend that it's my cock rubbing against your clit instead of your vibrator. Got it?"

She nods her head quickly and then goes back to closing her eyes when I drop back down to my knees at the end of the bed.

Grabbing her personal massager, I turn it on and rub the round top in circles over her clit. Her black panties were already soaked before I started.

"Oh. My. God." Her voice comes out with a moan as she grips the bedsheet and spreads her legs more for me. "That feels so good."

My dick throbs as I continue to rub her with her vibrator. I want nothing more than to give her the greatest pleasure of her life, and I have no doubt that my cock is just the right thing to do that with.

If it was my choice I'd rip her clothes off and slam her against the wall, but it's not. I shouldn't even be doing this right now. Alexander has been nothing but good to me, but a man only has so much willpower when it comes to something he wants and knows he can't have.

I grip her thigh with my free hand and turn up the speed on her massager.

"Ohhh . . ." she moans out and grips my hand on her thigh. "Keep going. Right there. Right there . . . Ohhhhhh . . ."

My cock becomes so hard when she screams out her orgasm that it hurts. It actually fucking hurts, and I want to take it out on her body so damn bad.

"You're welcome," I say with a cocky smirk.

Looking embarrassed, she grabs the sheet and throws it over her as I stand up. "Don't say one word about this to anyone," she whispers. "I've never let anyone . . ."

"It's between us and my cock," I tease.

She grabs a pillow and tosses it at me. "Now get out so I can sleep, cocky ass."

There's a hint of a smile on her lips and I know without a

doubt that she enjoyed me getting her off just as much as I did.

"I expect the favor to be returned if you walk by and hear me trying to get off. Four hands are better than two when it comes to my cock."

She laughs as I smile and leave her room. It's cute seeing her sexually relieved, and I know by looking at her that I want more of this from her.

I just have to find a way of doing that without pissing Alexander off and ruining our friendship.

Fuck me. Good luck with that . . .

Tegan

I'VE BEEN AWAKE TOSSING AND turning for the last hour, surprised that I allowed Micah to use my vibrator on me. I never thought I'd let myself do that.

If I had been thinking clearly, I would've kicked him out of my room the moment he stepped inside, but I was too sexually frustrated to not take him up on his offer.

He was right. I took that picture of him for myself; although, I tried my hardest to convince myself it was for Whitney's viewing pleasure.

I realized that the moment I had it pulled up on my phone and was reaching for my vibrator.

His muscles and long hair had me coming within fifteen seconds the first time and thirty seconds the second time.

So yes . . . it's exactly what it looks like. Don't judge me.

I haven't gotten off in months, so I went for a third time, but my vagina wasn't having it.

Not until he walked into my room; so sexy and sinful, a look of intent on his face.

I sigh and shove another piece of cookie dough into my mouth, eating my frustrations away.

"You gonna share that with me or are you going to eat my whole stash alone?"

When I look up Micah is standing across the room in a pair of sweats. The way they hang low on his waist has my eyes lowering to his bulge, but I quickly avert my eyes before he catches me staring.

After the hard-on I witnessed earlier in those tight briefs, I'm not sure I'll ever be able to keep my eyes from going there whenever he's in front of me.

"I figured this was yours. Alexander used to hide the cookie dough from me when we were kids and refused to buy me any when he was out on a store run. Complained I was going to get sick from eating it raw."

"Nah." He bends down and eats the piece right out of my hand. "You'll be fine. It's not like you're eating the whole damn package. You're not, right?"

He lifts a brow and I toss him what's left of the package. "I might've gotten close a few times before, but my brother always snatched it from me and tossed it in the trash before I could consume the last quarter of it. Like that small amount is going to make a difference.

"I think maybe I should keep this safe then." He rolls up the end of the package and sets it down on the island in front of him. "What are you doing up? Too many words in your head?"

"Maybe . . . how about you?"

"I haven't been able to sleep much. Been thinking a lot about getting my bar up and running." He huffs and runs a hand through his messy hair. "I've still got to order tables and supplies and figure out staff and payroll and a lot of other things that exhaust me just thinking about them."

"I heard it's based around live music; like how you occasionally perform at my brother's bar, except it will be nightly. I've always wished we had a place like that back in Arlington. I've seen them in movies and TV shows growing up and those have always intrigued me. I love that idea and it's awesome that's what you wanted. I can see myself spending a lot of time there whenever I'm here to visit."

"You might not want to go home after the summer ends if you spend too much time at my bar."

"Maybe not, but I have to. I promised my parents I'd wait a few more years before moving away. They were really torn up about Alexander leaving at such a young age and I don't want to put my parents through that again. It may not be what *I* want, but it's what they want."

"And what about a boyfriend or even an ex who wants you back? He want you to stay too?" His eyes lock on mine, waiting for an answer.

I shake my head and laugh. "I haven't had a boyfriend in three years, and there's no one back home who even slightly has me interested, so, no."

"That's good to know." He takes a step toward me, his eyes lowering to my lips. I suck in a breath at his closeness, which results in him taking a step back and running his hands over his face.

We stand here in silence for a few moments before he releases a long breath and looks me over, as if he's about to say something important but decides against it.

"It's late. I've got to be at the bar early to make sure everything is running smoothly for when your brother gets back tomorrow." He grabs the cookie dough and reaches into the fridge for a water. "You should go lay down so your characters can talk, yeah?"

I nod, watching as he disappears from the kitchen.

I don't know what the hell that was about, but I won't deny that I almost wish he would've kissed me.

But I have a feeling Micah isn't the kissing type. Not from what I've heard from my brother . . .

Chapter Seven

Tegan

XAN SENT ME A TEXT this morning to let me know that he'll be home around two and wants to take me out to lunch.

As excited as I am about seeing him, I can't help but to worry about how he'd react if he knew what went down with me and Micah last night.

As far as I know, Micah is his closest friend here and one of the only people that he truly trusts. That's a *huge* deal for Xan, and as badly as I want to jump on Micah and take him on a test ride, especially after how hard he made me come with my vibrator, I know that it could possibly ruin their friendship and trust.

He's so damn hot and tempting, but I need to stay strong. I didn't come here to mess things up for my brother. The thought alone makes me feel sick to my stomach.

When I close the fridge, I look up to see Micah going through the cupboards. "Hey," I say while spreading out the ingredients to make a chicken quesadilla. "Xan will be home in about four hours."

"Yeah." He closes the cupboard and looks down at the stuff I just laid out, before bending down and pulling out a couple of pans. "He texted me a bit ago to check on you and the bar . . ."

I watch as he pulls out the butter and then opens the bag of frozen chicken strips, tossing some in one of the pans, along with some butter and seasonings.

"Yeah . . . and what did you tell him?"

"I told him that you were both in good hands and that I've been keeping a close eye on you. Then he sent me some knife emojis. Not sure how he got that shit, because they're not on my phone. Not those specific ones at least."

I can't help but to laugh at the face that Micah makes while glancing back down at his phone when it vibrates.

He holds it ups. "He sent another knife emoji for good measure."

"I'm sure he's kidding," I say with a slight laugh. "Maybe. Most likely."

"He's not. Trust me. I know him when it comes to you. He's been talking about you for the last five years and how protective he gets when it comes to you. You're still his little sister; doesn't matter that you're not so little anymore. He'd kill anyone who hurts you."

"You headed to the bar soon?"

It's best to change the subject. I'm sure it's getting uncomfortable for him, because I've seen Xan go off on more than one jerk in the past who's broke my heart and I've never seen him look more lethal. I don't want to see that happen to Micah . . . especially with how close they are.

He presses against me, pinning me against the counter as he reaches into the drawer next to me and pulls out a fork. His lips brush against my ear, sending chills up and down my body. "I'm heading there in a few."

I release a breath as he walks away and starts forking the chicken. "Yeah, well I might stop by after I get back from lunch to get some writing in before it gets too crowded."

He begins flipping the chicken with one hand and preparing the tortilla shell with the other. "Who are you going out to lunch with?"

"Xan." I toss him the cheese and then search through the cupboards for plates. "We're going as soon as he gets back."

Releasing a slow breath, he turns to face me. "About what happened last night . . ."

"Don't worry. Xan doesn't need to know you even set foot into my room. I'm not trying to come between you guys, and he definitely doesn't need to know what happens in the privacy of my bedroom."

He quickly looks me over, his eyes landing on my lips, before he turns away and flips the chicken again. "Good. The last thing I need is Alexander on my ass. That's the only reason I chose not to use my tongue last night instead. I don't want one of those knives through my chest."

I swallow hard as my body heats up with need from his words. There's so many things I want to say to that, but choose not to. Nothing good can come from it.

When he's done cooking the chicken, he makes one quesadilla and throws it on a plate for me. "I need to get out of here. I'm running late. Tell Alexander I'll catch him later."

I look down at the plate and smile. "Why didn't you say something? You didn't have to cook my food."

"I know." With that, he disappears around the corner, most likely headed back downstairs to get ready.

My mind stays stuck on Micah the whole time I'm eating. For

some reason I want another glimpse of him before he leaves for *Vortex*. I shouldn't, but I do. Despite my brother warning us to stay away from each other, we both seem to be fighting it.

By the time I'm finished eating and throwing the dishes into the dishwasher, I realize that Micah must've left out of the backdoor.

It's probably best if we don't get any more alone time before Xan gets home anyway. I guess Micah feels the same way.

Either that or he's actually scared of the knives that Xan probably has hidden to cut his throat out with if he betrays him.

♪ ♩ ♪ ♩

I TOLD XAN THAT I would just meet him at *Villy's* because there was no way I was going to jump onto the back of his bike and look like a dork behind my brother.

He used to ride me around everywhere as kids. In the beginning it was on his bicycle and then later on his first motorcycle. I felt cool back then, hanging with my big brother and all. Now . . . not so much.

When I walk in, I spot Xan in a booth at the back of the diner with two Pepsi's already ordered for us.

I smile and slide into the booth across from him. "What makes you so sure that I still drink Pepsi when I go out to eat, Xan?"

He gives me that look, as if I've lost my damn mind. "Because you're my baby sister. And no one knows you better than I do. Not even our parents."

"Thanks for that." I give him an appreciative smile and grab my drink. "And for always being nice to me. Not a lot of younger siblings had it as good as I did growing up. You've always looked out for me."

He smirks. "I had my moments. Not all of them good, but I tried."

"I know. That's exactly why I've missed you so much."

"I've missed you too and you know that. I tried getting our parents to let you come and visit me sooner, but they wouldn't budge."

"Because they're too set in their ways. Especially Mom." I take a sip of my Pepsi. "But I'm here now and I'm loving it so far. The bar, the beach, you and Jamie . . . I can't stop smiling."

He smiles, as if it makes him happy to hear how happy I am. "Good. I knew you'd fall in love with this place. But I don't want you getting too attached to being here if you promised our parents you wouldn't move yet. Remember that."

I nod. "I know."

We continue talking for a good ten minutes, catching up on things, before the waitress comes over and quickly takes our order.

We're close to finishing our lunch and not a single word has come up about Micah yet. He keeps giving me this look, as if he's waiting on me to confess or to tell him something before he brings it up.

I won't do it. I won't do it.

"How was your trip?" I ask instead.

He sets his fork down and begins stacking up the dirty plates. "Pretty good. Had a couple of late nights, but business got done."

I watch him as he reaches for his wallet and begins pulling out bills. "Want me to get the tip at least?"

"No. A man always pays for a woman's meal. Relationship type doesn't matter. That's how I was raised and you know that, so don't ask that shit again."

"Just seeing if living here has changed the sweet boy who practically raised me."

He stands up and gives me a confident smile. "Some things have changed, but things you don't need to know about."

"Ugh! Yes, I'm guessing not. Especially since I see the women practically throwing themselves at your feet at the bar. It's disgusting."

"None of them are *the one*. Might as well have a little fun while waiting for her to show up." He gives me a hard look when I smile at the memory of Micah and the excitement from last night. "That doesn't mean I want you doing the same. You're a girl. Which reminds me . . ."

He holds the door open for me. I quickly walk outside and over to my car as if I'm in a hurry. This will at least give me a few seconds to compose myself and pretend that what happened last night wasn't breaking the rules.

But even the reminder has me all hot and bothered.

"Hold on a sec." He grabs my arm and stops me from opening my car door. "Did Micah try anything with you when I was gone? Don't lie either. You know how I feel about that. I can't tell from his texts."

"He didn't lay a finger on me," I lie. Well, it's sort of a lie. His finger didn't do the touching that got me off at least. I'm doing my best to convince myself that I didn't just betray my brother's trust.

He looks me over. "Good. I'd hate to have to kick his ass before I even have time to settle back in. He knows the rules." He kisses me on the top of the head and then backs up to his motorcycle.

"Where's your luggage?"

"With a friend of mine at the airport. They're dropping it off for me later."

I watch as he hops on and straddles his shiny, black Harley. His muscles flex as he grips the handles and looks back at me. "Where are you headed?" I ask.

He winks and revs the engine. "Don't ask me a question when you don't want to know the answer."

"Eww. Well, I'll be at *Vortex* for a few hours, writing out back. Find me when you show up."

"Text me if you need me before that. Just not within the next two hours."

I roll my eyes and open the door to Jamie's car. She's letting me borrow it while she's at work. "I won't. I'm a big girl. Stop worrying. And don't *ever* tell me how long you will take. Shit, Xan."

He waits and watches me pull off, before he finally speeds out of the parking lot and past me, in a hurry to get to this chick's house.

"Shit," I mumble to myself, feeling my stomach knot up.

Why the hell do I feel so guilty?

Chapter Eight

Micah

I'M TRYING MY BEST TO keep my shit together now that Alexander is back from his business trip, but I'm feeling especially on edge today.

He warned me to keep my hands off his little sister, and even though I technically didn't lay a finger on her, I gave her probably one of the best orgasms of her life; at least that's the way it appeared.

Not to mention the fact that after I watched her come for me I went downstairs and jerked my shit, not once, but twice.

I have no doubt his threats were real and that he'd pull one of those knife emojis straight from his damn phone just to cut my heart out if he ever found out I was in her room, let alone what he'd do if he discovered what I *did*.

It's Alexander, so I'm sure he could find something worse to do to me.

Then, to top it all off, I got lost in her and almost kissed her, when kissing isn't something I'm usually into. It's always seemed too intimate for me.

But when she talks, I can't stop looking at her damn lips, wanting a taste.

"Boss . . . want anything else from me before I head out for the day?" Ryan is in the middle of slipping back into his shirt as he stops in the doorway of my office.

"Are all the tables clean enough that you'd lick them like you'd lick your girl's pussy? If not then I need you back downstairs." I look down at my watch to see that it's a little past five. His shift ended less than two minutes ago. "And while you're down there I need you to take drink orders if the guys have more than three people waiting at any time. Think you can handle that?"

He nods and yanks his shirt off over his head, getting back into the required work attire, which isn't much. "Sure thing."

"And Ry . . ."

He's just about to walk away, but stops and pokes his head back into my office. "Yes, sir?"

I grind my jaw at him calling me sir. I don't know how many times I have to tell the guys not to call me that. "If I catch you serving drinks to Dave, Kyle, Nate or any other name that underage kid comes in here with on his damn ID . . ." I steel my jaw at the thought and slam the paperwork down on my desk. "I'll fire you on the fucking spot and personally escort you out. Got it?"

He swallows nervously and nods his head, before walking away.

I've already given his giant ass two chances and that's all anyone will ever get from me. It won't be hard to find a replacement for his incompetent ass.

There's a stack of at least three hundred applications in the drawer next to me and I'll go through every single one if I have to in order to find someone that can be trusted.

Releasing a frustrated breath, I spin the chair around to check the monitors. You can only leave these guys unattended for a brief time or else they think they can get away with anything and everything.

Too bad for them I'm not in the mood to let things slide today.

The traffic is beginning to pick up. I sit back and watch the guys for a bit to make sure they're on their game so I don't have to strip my shirt off and jump behind the bar to show them how it's done.

It happens often, but today I hope that it doesn't, because my mind is all over the damn place right now. I need some time to get my thoughts in check and learn some restraint when it comes to a certain person.

It's never been hard doing what my best friend has asked of me, until now. If I lose his trust, I could be losing one of the only people I trust, and on top of that, this job.

I'm still not quite where I need to be to open *Express,* so if I fuck things up with Alexander, I fuck up everything I've been working hard for over the last four years.

I switch my view to the outside bar to check on Colby, and that's when I notice Tegan sitting alone at one of the tables.

She has her laptop all set up and she seems to still be working, completely ignoring everyone around her.

Knowing that she's here has me not giving a shit if the guys need help or not. I'm going to help no matter what now.

So much for restraint.

Standing up, I exit my office and make my way downstairs, through the crowd of people and out back to where Colby has four women lining up for drinks.

Without wasting time, I unbutton my shirt and strip it off; smiling as whistles and screams come from all around as I join

Colby behind the bar.

Even though I jump right into taking orders, I can't help but to notice Tegan looking my way occasionally, watching me when she thinks I'm not paying attention.

What she doesn't realize is that I'm always paying attention when it comes to *her*. It's kind of become my job.

"Over here, gorgeous!" One of the girls at the front waves her money at me to get my attention. "I'll take two Martinis and you in my bed." She winks and leans over the bar to watch me as I reach for two glasses and begin fulfilling her order.

"I think that might cost you more than that twenty you have in your hand." I look up at the sound of Tegan's voice. "Micah is expensive when it comes to the bedroom, and last time I had to ask for a refund. Totally wasn't worth what I paid. Just a heads up."

My lip quirks into a half grin as the girl's face drops with disappointment. "You're telling me a man who looks like *that* is bad in bed. Well, that's a dream killer."

"Tell me about it," Tegan mumbles. "Biggest disappointment of my *life*."

Just to see if Tegan badmouthing me has worked, I set blondie's drinks down in front of her and give her a charming smile. "Sixteen for the drinks . . ." I lean in closer and whisper. "And five hundred for me in your bed."

The girl gives me a sympathetic smile and throws down a twenty. "Keep the change you poor, unfortunate soul."

I arch a brow and watch as she walks away as if she can't get away from me fast enough.

"You're welcome . . ." Tegan laughs, clearly amused.

"What makes you so sure that I'm thankful you got rid of her? She was damn sexy and it's been days since I've gotten laid. Ever since you showed up, actually."

"Are you blaming the fact that your penis hasn't had any action for oh . . . what . . . five days now, on me?" She reaches for the beer that I slide in front of her. "That's pathetic, Micah."

Before I can say anything, she tosses a rolled-up bill at my forehead and disappears through the crowd and back over to the table to pack up her things.

I make the next drink as quickly as possible and escape from behind the bar as soon as I get the chance. I snatch my shirt from my back pocket and slip it on, not bothering to button it up as I rush over to the table she's at.

"How is my book coming along?"

She gives me an annoyed look and guards her computer, as if I'm going to open it up and start reading her work out loud. "It's not about you. Trust me on that. My character isn't a cocky, arrogant asshole who sleeps with a different girl each week."

"Why not?" Moving in close behind her, I lean into her ear. "You do know that's what sells, right?"

"I happen to like my character. If I make him into *you* then there's a good chance I'll gag at every scene I write. But thanks for the pointer."

"Alright. Well, at least tell me this . . ." I move around to the front of her and give her a cocky little smirk when I notice her eyes roaming over my chest as expected. "Does your character get his body from me? Because I've been seeing you check it out an awful lot since you've been here. I'm pretty sure every inch of it is etched into your mind now. Plus, the picture of me on your phone helps."

She's in the middle of taking a drink of her beer, but spits it out all over my neck and chest.

"I'll take that as a yes." Keeping my eyes on her, I slowly take my shirt off and reach for the glass of water that's sitting next to her computer and pour it over my chest to clean off. "Did you do that on purpose just to see me wet?"

"Oh my God! You're so damn full of yourself and it's sickening. You're nice for a few minutes then go right back to your cocky self-absorbed self as if you just can't handle it. You never quit, do you?"

"Honestly, no. I don't believe in quitting."

"No. No, he doesn't." Alexander's voice comes from behind me, causing me to take a step back from his little sister before I lose a body part. "It's part of the reason I've trusted him with this place. Don't give me a reason to change my mind about that."

I know what he's getting at without even saying it. And I have a feeling Tegan does too because she tilts back her drink, not stopping for a good minute. "Alright, well, you boys have fun." She tosses her empty beer into the nearby trash and clutches her laptop to her chest. "I've got some promoting to do on this upcoming release and I can't concentrate now that more people are coming in. See you guys back at the house."

She barely even offers me a glance as she takes off in a hurry.

That's probably a good thing, because the last thing we need is Alexander having any more reason to be suspicious of us.

He waits until his sister is gone before he turns to me and crosses his arms. "How was she when I was gone? Any of the assholes here mess with her?"

"Nope," I lie, because I'm included in one of those assholes. "She was fine, I guess. She spent most of her time writing as usual." I know I should mention the party to him, but I leave that little detail out. "Are you good here if I take off and head to my place for the night? I've got a lot of work to do there still."

He looks around the place and nods. "Yeah, we can handle it without you, Man." With a thankful smile he grips my shoulder. "Thanks for always having my back when it comes to this place.

I appreciate it more than you know, brother. If you ever need any help getting your place up and running just let me know. Any money of mine is yours if you need it."

"You know I can't accept any handouts, Man. I appreciate it, but I've gotta work for what I want."

Alexander and I grew up in two totally different lifestyles. He's always had anything and everything he wanted, with a family who loves him.

Not me.

My mother abandoned me when I was eight and I spent most of my childhood in and out of foster homes of people who didn't give a shit whether I came or left.

Everything I have owned since the age of fifteen has been because I earned it myself or at my lowest point, stolen. But those days are far behind me. Have been since I turned sixteen and got my first job. I had no one to take care of me or buy me food or clothes. I was on my own.

It might be easier for someone like him to accept money from others when offered because it's something he's familiar with.

"Well, the offer always stands if you change your mind. I just want you to know that you're basically family, Micah. You've had my back since I moved here and I'll always have yours."

"I appreciate that too." I smile and slip my shirt back on. "But I'm less than two months away from having everything I need to open up. I've done it all by myself thus far, so I might as well finish it myself."

Micah nods his head and laughs. "I figured you'd say that."

"Alright, I'm out then. I have Ryan staying back to clean. Keep him until this place is spotless. He's working to keep his job because he's damn close to losing it."

Alexander just nods as I walk away when some girl comes over to talk, instantly distracting him.

Tonight is going to be a long night at *Express*, which is probably a good thing. Because I have no idea what will happen if I give myself some free time.

If I'm going to keep my distance from Tegan, then I need to bury myself in as much work as possible and do my best to pretend that I'm not dying to get between her legs . . .

Chapter Nine

Tegan

*I*T WAS A TOTAL LIE when I said I couldn't get any work done at my brother's bar because the people there were distracting. I could care less about the crowd at the bar. In fact, I barely even noticed them.

It had everything to do with a shirtless Micah.

Everything was just fine and dandy before he decided to come down from his office and strip out of his black button-down shirt, showing off his perfect chest and abs.

Not to mention that he had his hair pulled up today and it was the first time I've seen him that way.

I couldn't pull my damn eyes away from him and it had me becoming angry with myself.

It's bad enough that he already knows just how sexy he is without me letting on that I find him to be attractive. Me getting caught checking him out only gives him more fuel to push me and aggravate me until I want to pull his stupid, sexy hair out.

The bad part of that is that I want to pull it out while riding him.

"Uggggh . . ." I growl out my frustration, before slamming my laptop closed for the third and final time tonight.

After spending an hour or so promoting the book I published six months ago, I decided to see if I could concentrate enough to finish another chapter in my current work in progress, but failed miserably.

Every damn time I write about the hero, he becomes more and more like Micah. Hell, I even accidentally typed his name out a few times and had to go back and search it just so I could make sure I deleted them all.

It's now close to eight, and knowing that Micah probably got off work a couple hours ago has had me wondering where he is.

Is he coming here tonight? Now that my brother is back does he plan on staying at his place?

I hate that I even care, but for some strange reason I do.

Before long, I find myself walking down to the beach and planting my butt into the sand to clear my head and breathe in some fresh air.

Instead of clearing my head, I'm thinking about the bar Jamie mentioned Micah's been working on opening and if he's there right now.

I can picture him shirtless and dirty from cleaning the place up. Possibly wet with sweat, and I find my heart beating with excitement at the idea of watching him work.

My brother won't be home for at least six or seven more hours and Jamie is at work until eleven. I'm completely alone.

I know I shouldn't consider what I'm about to do, but I try to convince myself it's because I don't want to be alone all night.

Thirty minutes later the taxi I called for pulls up in front of a little bar with a sign that reads *"Express."* I took a gamble, hoping that most of the taxi drivers around here either knew Micah or knew of him, and I was right.

All I had to do was mention Micah Beck and his bar project and the driver knew exactly where to take me.

After the guy pulls away, I walk around the small building, hoping that the front door is unlocked.

My heart jumps with excitement when I pull on the handle and it opens. I wasn't expecting it to be.

Now that I'm here, showing up unannounced at Micah's place seems like a bad idea. I'm suddenly feeling nervous.

A part of me is questioning if he'll be upset that I'm barging in on him, while the other part feels the need to push his buttons the way he pushes mine.

"Here goes nothing." I take a quick breath and release it, before stepping into the place. My eyes scan the mostly empty bar, trying to imagine what it'll look like once it's all set up.

Straight ahead there's a huge stage for performing, with various guitars hung up on the wall, and off to the right is the bar, which looks to be slightly unfinished.

After seeing the way Micah looks while performing, his tight body flexing as he strums his guitar, it's hard for me not to blush when my attention focuses back to the stage.

I take a few more steps inside, but stop dead in my tracks when I hear a noise come from behind the bar.

It sounds as if Micah is tossing tools around.

I swallow and walk around to where the noise is coming from.

My eyes land on a shirtless, sweaty Micah. He's lost in his work as if nothing else seems to matter at the moment, other than getting this place up and running.

I find that to be extremely sexy.

I like a man who's dedicated.

"Looks like someone might need a little help."

I catch the muscles in his back flex as he lifts his head and turns around to face me.

His eyes are intense as he scans me over, and I find myself wishing I never showed up unannounced.

"I'll just . . . I'll just leave." I turn around and get ready to walk away.

"No." His stern voice stops me, before I hear the sound of another tool dropping. I feel the warmth from his body pressed up behind me, before his lips touch against my neck. "We both know you should leave, but we both also know that neither of us want you to. Fuck, Tegan. Why did you come here?"

"I was bored." I sound pathetic as the lie leaves my mouth. "I didn't want to spend the night alone."

His deep growl rumbles against my neck, causing my heart to almost jump from my chest. "So you figured I could entertain you . . . Is that it? Because I can promise that you can't handle the kind of entertainment I bring afterhours."

"I think you're full of shit." I take a step forward, putting a little space between us. I can't think straight with him breathing down my neck. "And I also think you don't know half of what I can and can't handle."

When I turn around his gaze is trained on me, as if he wants to devour me. He's looking at me the same way that I made Kingston look at Harley in the story I'm writing.

But who knows. Maybe I learned that look from Micah before Kingston ever did it.

I can't tell anymore. The words have been flowing since I've been around him and I hate to admit that he's the reason.

"I know what your brother can't handle, Tegan, and that's me being this fucking close to you." He moves in closer, causing me to back up until I'm pressed against the bar. "You really should leave before I mess everything up."

I swallow and keep eye contact with him, even though it's hard to without giving away how I'm truly feeling at the moment.

I want him to mess everything up for just *one* night. I keep telling myself that my brother never has to know, but I have a feeling that one night with Micah wouldn't be so simple to hide.

"I'm not afraid of you, Micah." I stand up straight, pretending that his breath hitting my lips isn't making my knees weak. "You can't boss me around like you do all the guys at *Vortex*. I'm here and I'm going to help, so tell me what the hell I can do, because I'm not going anywhere."

His eyes harden as they lower to my lips, and I can't tell if it's because I've pissed him off or turned him on by standing up to him.

"Well, fuck," he growls. "I warned you."

Before I know it my legs are wrapped around his waist and he's slamming his lips against mine so damn hard that my breath gets knocked out.

His taste alone is enough to leave me breathless, but the movement of his perfect lips as they capture mine is enough to keep me that way.

His tongue slips between my parted lips, sending a shockwave through my body that has my nipples stiffening with sensitivity and my stomach feeling fluttery.

My senses are all over the place right now and I can't seem to get a grip. All I can do is kiss him back while burying my hands into his thick hair.

I never expected Micah's kiss to be so damn powerful.

It takes his hands gripping my waist after he sets me down on the bar to come out of my little haze and realize that his erection is rubbing between my legs.

The more he grinds his body into me and the deeper his kiss becomes, the more sensitive it gets between my legs until I'm on the edge of an orgasm, about ready to come from his body.

As soon as that realization hits, I press my hands against his chest and shove him back, before I can manage to get too wrapped up in him. "Micah . . ." I pant. "I need you to back up. Now."

An animalistic growl leaves his lips as he releases my hips and runs his hands through his hair in frustration. "Shit. I should've never done that." He backs up and turns away from me.

I grip the bar, my heart racing as I watch him walk away and press his hands against the wall, bowing his head. He's breathing just as heavily as I am, his muscles tight with each breath he takes.

He knows as much as I do that Alexander would hate us both for going behind his back and disobeying his wishes.

I didn't think Micah cared before now, but clearly my brother's trust means a lot more to him than I originally thought.

It makes me wonder if there's a different side of Micah that I haven't had a chance to see yet. A side of him that puts others before himself and isn't selfish just because he knows he can get whatever and whoever he wants.

"It's just as much my fault as it is yours," I admit. "I could've pushed you away as soon as you kissed me, but I didn't." I jump down from the bar and wipe my sweaty palms down my shorts. "I also could've kicked you out of my room instead of allowing you to use my vibrator on me, but I didn't."

"Why not?" he asks stiffly.

"I don't know . . ." I swallow and watch as he turns around to face me. The guilty look on his face has me wanting to wrap my arms around his neck and tell him it's okay, even though it isn't.

His guilt confirms that we both care a lot about the same person. "You're not easy to say no to. Haven't you figured that out? Has anyone ever said no to you before, Micah?"

He runs his hands through his hair, before shaking his head.

"Exactly." I turn away, needing to look at anything in this room other than him, before I end up naked against every surface in this place. "I'm going to call for a taxi and head back to my brother's. I should've never come here to begin with."

I reach into my pocket for my phone, but right as I'm about to place it to my ear he grabs it from me and shoves it into his back pocket. "Stay and help for a bit and I'll take you home when I leave. I don't want you getting rides from strangers. Some of these taxi drivers are real pricks."

"I can handle that as long as we can order a pizza while we work." I look up at him and reach out my hand, wiggling my fingers to show him I want my phone back. "I think I'll need my phone for that."

Keeping his gaze on me, he reaches into his pocket and pulls my phone out. He steps in close, as if testing my body's reaction to him, before he hands it to me and flashes me a playful grin. "Be sure it has pepperoni. I'll go grab the mop bucket for you."

His smile leaves me smiling as he walks away and disappears somewhere into the back of the bar to fetch the cleaning supplies.

Even though we're both deep into cleaning I can't help but to look his way every time I feel his eyes on me. And every single time he catches me watching him, he seems to move in slow motion as he runs his arm across his forehead wiping away the sweat.

It's driving me crazy, because I can't tell if he's moving in slow motion to tease me or if my eyes are just playing tricks on me and he's in fact moving at a normal pace.

All I know is that I notice every single hard muscle flexing each time he does it, and it's making it extremely hard to look away and pretend I don't notice him.

I do my best to make small talk as a distraction.

"Is the stage for you to perform each week like you do at my brother's bar? Tell me about this place."

He nods and tosses down the rag he's been using on the walls. "Yeah. But it's not just for me. It's for anyone who wants to perform. If it happens to just be me then I'm okay with that too."

I look away long enough to push the mop bucket against the back wall and out of the way so the floor can dry. "Does anyone else perform at *Vortex* or are you the only one?"

His lips curl into a small smile as he meets me by the bar. "I'm the only one your brother trusts to play at his bar. *Vortex* was never meant to be a place where artists could perform. It happened one night when I decided to play my guitar out back to keep my mind off a few things . . ."

He pauses long enough to dig into a small fridge and pull out two cold beers. I must say that the view is much better than the one Colby gave us a few nights ago.

I think I just said "damn" aloud, instead of inside my head, because he let's out a small laugh, before continuing his story.

"It was dead that night, but a small crowd began gathering around and it slowly grew with the more songs I played. Apparently some of the customers were tweeting about my performance and letting their friends know that some *hot* guy was playing guitar and singing shirtless. A lot of things changed that night for *Vortex*."

"Your voice is amazing, Micah." I reach for the beer he slides in front of me and lift it to my lips. "I'm sure the fact that you were hot and shirtless wasn't the only thing bringing in the customers that night."

He smiles as he watches me down half the bottle in one drink.

"Thanks . . ." He takes a drink himself, before setting his beer down when the pizza guy walks in and knocks on the wall to get our attention. "For admitting you think I'm hot." He lifts a brow and winks, before walking away to pay for the pizza.

"You didn't have to pay," I say as he returns to set it down on the only table in the whole place.

"It's on me for you helping me out tonight. Hell, I owe you a few of these for the damn good work you did. I haven't had a chance to mop since I redid the flooring."

I quickly wash my hands, before joining him at the small table. Somehow, for the most part, I was able to keep my mind off Micah's lips on mine as we worked. But now that we don't have anything keeping us busy, but this damn pizza . . . all I can think about is our kiss and how good it felt.

"I'll remember that the next time I'm hungry."

It's quiet as we both eat, and I can't help but to wonder if he's thinking about the same thing I am.

From the bulge in his jeans I'm going to guess he is, because occasionally I catch him adjusting himself and cursing under his breath as he eats.

It's making it impossible not to think about how amazing it felt to have his thick erection grinding between my thighs not more than an hour ago.

I don't think I've ever been that close to an orgasm from a guy rubbing against me through our clothes, but just the thought that it was *him* had my body going crazy.

"Eyes on your pizza," he says teasingly. "Don't make me tell your brother that you're using me as a muse for your book. I won't leave out that you practically jumped on me tonight and took advantage of me."

"Oh, you're such an ass." I finish off the last bite of my pizza and jump to my feet, towering over him with narrowed eyes. "You only wish I would take advantage of you. If I remember correctly it was your lips that found their way to mine." I tighten my jaw in annoyance and that's when I'm reminded just how much of a pain he really is. "And the kiss wasn't anything memorable, trust me."

He stands up and pushes in his chair, before stepping into my space and placing his hand on my chin. With just a small tilt of my chin and a bow of his head, he has my bottom lip quivering with need. "If it was nothing memorable," he whispers, "then why is your body leaning into mine, waiting for me to kiss you again?"

I gasp as he slides his hand around my waist and pulls me against him. "And why is your heart racing?" he asks against my lips. "Because we both know you want another taste, regardless of what you say. But . . . you're going to have to learn some restraint, babe."

With that, he grins and backs away, making me want nothing more than to rip his stupid lips off.

"You're an ass. I'll be in your truck waiting." I give his chest a little shove, before I hurry my way outside and *away* from Micah.

I'm angry as hell, but mostly because we both know he's right.

One taste of Micah Beck is not enough, and he knows it . . .

Chapter Ten

Micah

I KNOW I SHOULD PROBABLY keep my mouth shut when it comes to Tegan and not push her any more than I already have, but I can't seem to control my actions when I'm around her.

The whole point of me spending my night here at *Express* and burying myself in work was to get away from the one person who decided to show up without a single text or call.

The moment I looked up and saw her standing there in her little shorts and tank top, I just about slammed her against the closest wall and buried myself between her thighs.

I wanted to make her scream and show her that I want to fuck her just as much as I know she's been wanting me to.

She tries to fight it, but I can read her better than she thinks.

It took every ounce of power I possess to hold back before I did some severe damage that I can't take back.

But then like the idiot that I am, I got too close and allowed myself to kiss her.

I didn't expect her lips to feel so good against mine, and I sure as hell didn't expect them to taste as good as they did.

Her taste alone was almost enough to make me blow my load inside my jeans because I desperately needed more. That's how fucking excited it made me.

If she hadn't stopped things, there's no telling how far I would've allowed myself to go.

And now that she's alone with me inside my truck, all I can think about is pulling over on the side of the road and lifting her onto my lap so she can ride me.

Being around her is only getting harder with each second and I feel as if I'm close to cracking.

We're sitting in silence, both of us most likely lost in our messed-up thoughts, so I turn the radio up when I hear *Hurricane* by Thrice come on.

Music has always been the best distraction for me. I learned that at an early age when I realized I was alone in this world.

Even though my mother did things with me before she abandoned me—like reading and singing to me at night—the druggie in her realized loving me wasn't enough to get her through anymore.

I still remember the day she dropped me off at school and never came back for me. My life imploded that day and I turned to music as a distraction to help get me out of my head.

I can feel Tegan watching me as I sing, but I keep my gaze straight ahead because I have a feeling the look on her face as she watches me will only make me want her even more.

It was days ago, but I clearly remember the overwhelming look of awe on her face as she watched me at *Vortex* that night. It was as if she was seeing me in a different light.

And we both know how she sees me on the daily—the asshole I pretend to be around her. Maybe I truly am an asshole.

I won't deny that I like the idea of her seeing the best part of me. The only good part.

"I've only heard that song a couple of times, but I don't remember it sounding so . . . I don't know . . . powerful."

I look over at her as I shift my truck into park. Her soft green eyes give away how she's feeling right now and I can't help but want to *feel* it.

So, I do something stupid.

After yanking my keys out of the ignition, I step out of my truck, walk over to her side, and pull her down into my arms.

The moment our gazes lock, I know there's going to be no stopping what I'm about to do.

I press her back against my truck and frantically reach for her shorts, ripping them down her legs, before I wrap them around my waist and kiss her again.

The little moan that leaves her lips the moment my tongue swipes across them, tells me that she's just as desperate as I am at the moment.

With one hand I work on undoing my jeans, so she can pull my dick out, while I struggle with moving her panties to the side with the other one, attempting to hold her up with my hips alone.

The moment her hand strokes along my thick length, I moan out, while biting her lip.

"Condom?" she asks against my lips. "Please tell me you have one."

"Back pocket." Having her pussy exposed and waiting for me has me losing my shit. I can barely contain myself right now. I just need to fucking be inside of her.

She rocks against me, while digging into my back pocket and

pulling out the condom I've been carrying with me since the night she showed up at her brother's house.

Before ripping the wrapper open with my teeth, I yank my shirt off and toss it aside.

I'm standing here shirtless with my jeans undone, my dick fully erect and my best friend's little sister wrapped around my waist, with no fucking clue how we got here.

A small wave of guilt passes through me, but the moment Tegan leans in to suck my bottom lip into her mouth as if she needs me inside of her, I quickly roll the condom on and slam into her so hard that she yanks my head back by my hair and screams.

"Holy shit, Tegan," I growl against her lips, before running my finger over the bottom one. "You're so fucking wet for me." I pull out, before slamming right back into her. "Scratch me or pull my hair if you have to, because I'm anything but gentle."

She nods her head and digs her nails into my arm, scratching me hard as I begin moving in and out of her.

Keeping my lips on hers, I grip the bottom of her tank top with both hands and lift it above her head.

Her hands immediately reach for my arms again, gripping onto me as I grind my hips between her legs, finding it hard to take it easy on her.

I want her to feel every hard inch of me, because we both know this will be the only time we can allow this to happen.

It may be a selfish, dickhead thing of me, but I want her to remember me filling her deeper than any other man has, so anytime she's with someone else she thinks of *me*.

The harder her nails dig into my back, the harder and deeper I take her until she's screaming so loud that it's beginning to hurt my ears.

Fuck, how that only makes me work my hips harder.

"Micah . . ." she moans into my mouth, before biting me. "This can never happen again."

Her words make me thrust as deep into her as I can and stop. "I don't want to fucking think about that right now and you shouldn't either." I grip her hair and yank it back, exposing her neck for my tongue to run across it. I work my way up her slender neck, stopping below her ear. "Let's just enjoy tonight."

"Okay . . ." she says, while fighting to catch her breath. "Okay . . . I can do that."

She slams her lips against mine, biting and yanking as if she wants me to be rougher with her.

So, I am.

I pull back on her hair even harder, while I fuck her up the side of my truck, not stopping until her muscles are clenching my dick as she screams out her orgasm.

All it takes is two hard squeezes from her pussy and I'm busting my load into the condom, not bothering to pull out like I usually do with women.

I can't.

If this is the only time I'm going to be inside of her, I want her to feel what she does to me.

I'm in the middle of growling my release into her ear, when she begins moving again as if she likes the feel of my come in the condom.

My dick is sensitive as shit, but I place my hands against the truck and allow her to move, until she's shaking in my arms for a second time as another orgasm rocks through her.

We're both sweaty, fighting to catch our breath, but neither one of us make an attempt to get away from each other.

I'm not going to lie . . . I like the way it feels having her in my arms with her face buried into my neck.

We stay like this for a bit, before I gently set her down and pull out of her.

"Holy fuck . . ." I groan from the sensitivity of moving my dick.

"Holy fuck is right . . ."

We both stand here looking at each other, our breaths mingling together, until my phone begins ringing from inside the truck.

Panic sets in because I know right away from the ringtone that it's Alexander. "Fuck! Fuck! Fuck!"

I back away from Tegan and quickly reach for her shorts and hand them to her, before I put my dick away. "It's your brother."

Tegan's eyes widen with worry as she quickly throws her shirt and shorts back on. "Oh shit. Answer it before he thinks we're doing something."

"We are doing something, Tegan. Fucking shit."

I'm angry with myself as I reach into the truck and grab for my phone.

I'm angry because I just betrayed my best friend and angry with myself because I enjoyed it just as much or more than I knew I would.

And from the look on Tegan's face as she watches me answer the phone, she's as mixed up about what we just did as I am.

"Hey, Man," I answer out of breath. "Everything good?"

"Not really." His voice sounds angry and it has me wondering for a second if he's had cameras installed outside his house since his sister came to stay for the summer.

"Okay, hit me with it." My heart races as I wait for him to chew my ass out. But this is on me and I'll take what he dishes out.

"What's wrong?" Tegan mouths.

I shake my head as Alexander yells at Colby for being a dumbass. If he's taking the time to yell at someone else while he has me on the phone, then chances are he has no clue what just went down here at his house.

I relax.

"Sorry. Damn, that asshole is pissing me off tonight. But that's not why I called. The kid is back and he's drunk off his ass. I figured you'd want to come take care of him."

"Fuck!" I'm pissed that Sebastian is there drunk, and even though I'm not sure I'm ready to walk away from Tegan after what just went down, I need to get to him and make sure he's okay before he gets into some shit he can't reverse. "I'll be right there."

I hang up the phone and turn to face Tegan. The sight of her standing there, covered in my sweat, has me wanting to claim her all over this damn house.

Shit, this is going to be harder than I thought.

"I have something to deal with at the bar. I don't think I'll be coming back tonight. But call me or your brother if you need us."

She nods and takes a step away from my truck. "Is everything okay at the bar?"

"Just some kid I take care of from time to time. He's drunk off his ass, so I'll probably let him stay at my place tonight and sleep it off." I pause to run my hands through my hair and cuss to myself. "If I don't take care of him no one else will."

"I'm sorry to hear that."

"To hear what?"

"That no one is there to take care of him." She offers me a genuine smile. "But it's really nice that you're there for him. He's a lucky kid to have you."

"Yeah . . ." I take a step toward her, as if to give her a kiss, but stop when I think it through and end up asking her something else instead. "Tell me a band you like?"

"A band?" she asks, looking slightly confused that I'm asking.

"Yeah. A band."

"I've been listening to *Amber Run* a lot lately. Have you heard of them? They have some beautiful acoustic versions that I can't stop listening to."

"I have now." I move in closer and lock eyes with her, fighting back my urge once again to kiss her. "Goodnight, Tegan." I turn around and jump into my truck, before I can make that mistake again.

The damage has already been done tonight. There's no denying that, but I'd be a dumbass to turn it into anything more than just a one time slip up.

Kissing only complicates things. Everyone knows that . . .

♪ ♩ ♪ ♩

WHEN I PULL UP AT the bar, Colby is standing outside taking a cigarette break, smoking it fast as if he's in a hurry. He looks beat but gives me a nod as I walk past him.

"How bad is it this time?" I stop to ask.

He pulls the cigarette from his mouth and shakes his head. "He's puked a few times and keeps trying to get away in between tossing his cookies. I'm pretty sure the kid thinks he isn't done partying yet."

"Shit." I rush inside and upstairs to Alexander's office when I don't see them anywhere downstairs. That proves right there that it's a fucked-up situation if he needs to be hidden from the public.

Steeling my jaw, I make my way up the stairs and shove Alexander's door open to see Sebastian leaning over a small garbage can, puking his guts out.

Just from a glance I can see he's covered in his own damn vomit. The sight makes me sick, because there's no telling how often he takes things this far.

"Sorry, Man. I'll have your carpet shampooed tomorrow." I

walk past Alexander who just nods and exhales. "Just give me a few minutes and I'll get him out of here. I'll take him to my place and let him sleep it off before I have a talk with him."

"Alright, Man." Alexander pushes away from his desk and heads toward the door. "I would stay and help out more but the guys need me downstairs. You gonna be good getting him to your truck. I can help with that first."

"I've got him," I say stiffly. "I'll drag his idiotic ass to my truck if I have to. I don't know what to do with this kid. He's pushing his fucking luck with me. Pretty soon I'm going to have to kick his ass myself."

"I've got your back if you need me for anything. I know it's hard work, but just remember that this kid most likely wouldn't be alive right now if it weren't for you. His parents don't do shit to protect him or keep him in line and never will. It's all you. Anything you need just ask."

I bend down and reach for the garbage can to help steady it as he begins another round of puking, before giving Alexander a nod. "Thanks, brother. That means a lot. But I can take it from here. The guys looked busy down there. Colby was just rushing back inside when I walked in."

"That dickhead took another cigarette break?" He takes a second to run a hand through his dark hair, while cussing to himself. "Call me if you change your mind. I need to get these assholes in check."

"I won't need you. Just take care of your business."

A few seconds after Alexander exits his office, Sebastian sits up and laughs uncontrollably. I don't know what this kid thinks he's laughing about, but I can promise he won't be laughing come morning.

I reach for one of the fresh water bottles lying next to him on the floor and open it, placing it to his lips. This will at least help hydrate him a bit.

He struggles with drinking it, but I make sure he gets a good amount before I close it and set it aside.

"You need to get your shit together, kid. You're going to end up in the hospital or jail if you keep this shit up."

He looks at me but doesn't say anything. It's hard to tell if he's comprehending anything I just said to him.

"Do you fucking understand me, Seb?"

"Dammit." When he still doesn't respond, I stand up and begin looking for anything I can take with me to keep my truck clean of this kid's damn stupidity.

Otherwise, he'll be spending the next week shampooing my shit until every last hint of his vomit is gone.

The best option will be to empty out the small trash in my office and bring that. I grab it and place it in Sebastian's hands and force him to hold it, before I pick his skinny ass up and carry him outside to my truck.

As soon as I go to reach for the door to set him inside, he pukes all over the side of my vehicle.

Annoyed, I stand here and wait for him to let it all out, before shoving him inside and taking him to the one place I know he'll be safe.

It takes him an hour to finally stop puking enough to pass out. Once I know he's good for the night I find my way to my bed and lay down, putting on some music to sway me from my thoughts.

As much as I fight to keep my mind off Tegan, though, she seems to be the only thing on it. Not just how good it felt to be inside her, making her come undone for me, but also the fact that I just fucked my best friend's little sister when I know I shouldn't have.

That makes me a piece of shit, and even recognizing *that* doesn't stop me from wanting to fuck her again.

I guess that makes me a special brand of asshole.

Chapter Eleven

Tegan

IT'S BEEN A FEW HOURS since Micah took off to take care of the kid he mentioned. Since then, what we did outside . . . against his truck . . . has been running through my mind non-stop.

My legs are still shaking and I can't seem to stop sweating, because I keep replaying it over and over in my head, despite the fact that I've been trying to think of anything *but*.

The way he slammed me against his truck and stripped me out of my shorts, as if he was desperate to have me, is quite possibly the single *hottest* moment of my life. I seriously thought I was going to *die* if I didn't have him inside of me right then.

That's how turned on I was and I hate it.

My whole body felt as if it ignited into flames the moment he slid that condom on and slammed into me. It was like he owned me.

He didn't take it easy on me like the men I've been with in

the past. He didn't treat me like he was going to break me in half if he moved too fast or too hard.

No, he *owned* every single part of me with just one thrust of his hips. And now I'm sitting here screwed because I allowed it to happen, and I know without a doubt that I'll only want to *feel* that way again.

How the hell can I not? Any woman breathing wants Micah Beck and having him once isn't enough.

How am I supposed to be around him every day and pretend like nothing happened when it was *the best* sex of my life?

I thought maybe . . . just maybe . . . one night with no strings attached would be enough, but I was wrong.

So damn wrong.

I let out a frustrated breath and exit out of *Word*, before turning on some *Amber Run*. I'm not getting anywhere tonight with where my thoughts are.

The words aren't flowing like they have been lately and all it's doing is giving me a massive headache.

When I look over at the clock and realize that it's past two, I get nervous, thinking about my brother coming home soon.

I haven't kept anything from him since we were kids, and knowing that I have to do it now has me feeling like a shitty sister.

All he wants to do is ensure I don't get hurt, and instead of listening to my brother I went and slept with the one person he warned me not to.

My brother seems to be closer to Micah than he has been with anyone for as long as I can remember, and the last thing I want is to mess up their friendship. For some reason Alexander has a hard time trusting people, which has always made it hard for him to have close friends.

So, I just need to remind myself that it's okay to think about

Micah but not to touch him *ever* again, no matter how badly I want to.

The sound of my brother's motorcycle has me shutting my laptop and sitting up, anxiously looking out the window.

I know it's bad, but for some reason I was hoping to see Micah's truck pull in as well, even though he told me he wouldn't be back tonight.

But my brother is alone.

My stomach twists into tiny knots when I hear my brother's footsteps coming up the stairs a few minutes later, because I have no idea what went down at the bar once Micah arrived.

I remain sitting here in the dark, my heart pounding as I listen to his footsteps stop in front of my opened door.

Please keep walking . . .

"Are you awake in there? It's really late." He pokes his head inside my room, squinting as he tries to adjust to the dark. I consider hiding from him, but I'm pretty sure he's already seen me at this point. "Tegan?"

"Yeah, I'm awake." I reach over and turn on the bedside lamp, yawning as I sit back and get comfortable. "I'm just thinking about my book and what I'm going to write in the morning. Sitting in the dark usually helps me think. How was work? Everything good?"

He laughs and nods his head, which relieves me. "Yeah, just tiring is all. I think I may need to have Micah hire more staff soon. I had to jump behind the bar to help my guys most of the night because they couldn't seem to keep up."

"That's a good thing though, Xan. You should be really proud of your bar. It was a smart business decision for sure. I mean . . . shirtless men serving drinks on the beach. That's genius."

He smiles proudly and takes a sip of his soda. "Appreciate the compliment, little sis. It definitely took a lot to get *Vortex* to where it is now and I have Micah to thank for the most part. That's why it's going to suck when he leaves to open his own bar. Don't get me wrong . . ." He runs a hand through his hair and exhales. "I'm proud as shit of him; he's my best friend, but it's going to be hard not having him there when he's been there pretty much since the beginning."

My heart is still pounding inside my chest from the first time he mentioned Micah since he's been home, but somehow the mention of his name for a second time has my heart beating even harder.

It's pounding so hard that I'm almost afraid my brother will hear it from across the room. Talk about being paranoid.

I begin fidgeting with the blanket on the bed when he looks down at his phone, as if to read a text. "How is the kid doing?"

My brother looks up from his cell and gives me a weird look. "How did you know about the kid?"

I swallow, just now realizing me asking about the kid gives away that I was with Micah when he called. Might as well tell him the truth. Well, most of it at least. "I was bored earlier, so I went to *Express* and helped Micah clean up the place a bit. He repaid me by ordering us a pizza and we just got back here when you called him."

His face hardens as he squeezes the door frame. "That better be the only way he repaid you, Tegan."

"It was," I lie. "Jeez, Xan. You don't have to worry about Micah getting to me. I'm a big girl. Now, are you going to answer my question or not?"

He flexes his jaw as if he's worried about me now, and I hope with everything in me that he doesn't question me further. "Sebastian showed up at the bar pretty wasted, but I kept him inside my office before he could get into any trouble. At least I hope. The kid is only seventeen and Micah has taken on the responsibility of taking care of the troubled little shit because his parents are never around for him. They could care less what that kid does and Micah is afraid he'll get hurt or arrested. He's been coming around for two years now and he hasn't given up on him yet."

My heart melts at the knowledge that Micah has been taking care of him for two years now. Micah can't be much older than I am and I can't even imagine having the responsibility of keeping someone else out of trouble. "How old is Micah?"

"Twenty-five. But Micah knows what it's like not to have a parent around who cares about him. His mom abandoned him at a young age and he spent most of his childhood bouncing from group homes to different foster families. He's pretty much been on his own since he was sixteen or something."

My heart drops hearing something so sad and personal from Micah's past. When he mentioned his mother to me and how she used to make him read before bed, I just assumed she's been around the whole time.

Knowing now that she abandoned him and made him feel so unloved and unwanted makes me feel sick to my stomach.

"Then it's a good thing he's been there for this Sebastian kid. He sounds like he needs someone who cares about him."

"Yeah." My brother nods his head and slaps the door. "Well, I should probably get some sleep. Micah is playing tomorrow night and you saw the crowd he drew in last week. It's like that every week and sometimes it's even crazier."

"Well, he's got a pretty amazing voice." One of the best I have ever heard, but I leave that part out.

"That he does," he says, while looking hard into the room, as if he's thinking. "I forgot to tell you that Parker Wright is stopping by the bar tomorrow and I thought maybe I'd introduce you two. He seemed interested when I mentioned you to him."

I give him a surprised look, because usually he wants to keep me away from his friends. The last thing I expected was for him to want me to meet one of them. It's a little odd and makes me wonder what he's up to. "Who's this Parker Wright person and why did you mention me to him without letting me know first, Xan?"

"He used to work for me. Once Micah leaves to open *Express*, Parker's coming back as management. The girls think he's cute and he's respectful when it comes to dating. I just thought you'd be interested in him, and if you're going to *date* anyone while you're here I figured he was the best choice."

"Are you telling me that you're setting me up on some kind of blind date or something? What the hell, Xan? I don't need your help finding a damn date." I try my best not to sound nervous, but the idea of going on a date with some other guy after what just happened with Micah has me feeling anxious.

It's definitely too soon.

"Parker is the only guy around here that I'd trust you to go out with, so yeah. This is me setting you up. If you guys hit it off then I can stop worrying about all the dickheads at *Vortex* trying to get with you. Micah included. I see the way he looks at you when he thinks I'm not watching. That shit isn't happening. When it comes to women he's nothing but trouble and I've already told you this."

It's already happened and it's the only thing I can think about now. It's completely taken over every single thought. "Dammit, Xan. You don't have to keep warning me about Micah!" I wave my hands at him and motion for him to leave. "Now go. I'm tired and don't feel like discussing this right now."

"So . . . can I count on you meeting Parker tomorrow? I already promised him and it would mean a lot to me. Help a big brother out so I can get some damn sleep."

I huff, while reaching over and turning the lamp off. I don't even want to look at my brother right now, because he'll only see how angry I am with him. He and I both know I've never had a problem wanting to meet a cute, respectful guy before, so I need to play this off as just being tired and cranky. "I'll think about it. I need some sleep. I'm really stressed right now."

"Fine. Text me in the afternoon and we'll figure it out?"

"Fine," I say annoyed. "Now go away, Xan. You're making my head hurt even more and I'm close to throat punching you if you don't walk away soon."

"That's what big brothers are for, but I'm tired as hell so I'll let you sleep."

"Oh, how nice of you, big brother. Lucky for me you're tired."

Once he walks away, I roll my eyes and punch my pillow to make it comfortable.

I lay back and try to imagine what this Parker guy must be like if my brother actually trusts him with me.

But all I manage to do is toss and turn for hours, thinking about Micah's hard body and cocky mouth and how badly I want them both on me again.

Micah has a body that screams trouble with every rock hard muscle.

He's wrong in every way according to my brother . . . yet it's him that I'm thinking about when I fall asleep.

♪ ♩ ♪ ♩

IT'S WELL INTO THE EVENING and I still haven't messaged my brother like he asked me to last night.

I'm dreading it because I don't know how to tell him I'm not interested in meeting this Parker guy without him putting it together that it's for a certain reason.

Once he realizes it's because I have another guy on my mind, he's going to question me and all of the guys who work for him until he figures out who it is he has to hurt.

I don't want that.

So, the only other option would be to meet this Parker guy to make my brother happy and then later tell him that we just didn't hit it off.

Agreeing to go on at least one date with him will give my brother reason to believe there's nothing to worry about when it comes to Micah or any of the other guys at the bar.

At least that's what I'm hoping for.

After taking a quick shower and getting dressed, I shoot my brother a text and he asks me to meet him at the bar.

It's getting close to sunset, which means Micah will be playing soon, but I'm hoping maybe he's not there yet. I'm not sure I'm ready to see him again so soon.

My brother is waiting for me to show up because he wants to sit down and talk to me about this Parker guy, so Micah being there would only make this situation weirder.

My nerves are all over the place the second I step foot into *Vortex* and I can't seem to stop wiping my sweaty palms down the front of my dress.

Seriously, how could one person's hands sweat so damn much?

I nod and say hi to Colby as I pass through the bar to go out back where my brother told me he'd be at. This place is already packed, so it takes me a good minute to spot my brother out here.

I freeze in place, causing someone to bump into me, because the last thing I expected is to see Micah and some other guy sitting at the same table as him.

As hard as I try I can't pull my eyes away from Micah looking so damn hot.

My heart instantly speeds up at the sight of him, sitting there dressed in a white button-down shirt and a pair of slim, black dress pants. The top two buttons are undone on his shirt and his sleeves are rolled up below his elbows.

But it's the messy hair blowing in the breeze that has me feeling weak in the knees. It reminds me of how I had it in my hands last night, pulling on it while he was *inside* of me.

Micah was inside of me less than twenty-four hours ago.

The reminder has my body reacting in a way it's never reacted before, and I have to clench my thighs to get rid of the sensations between my legs, making me sensitive.

Erase it from your mind. Don't think about Micah's hard body. Don't . . .

"Shit. This isn't working." I begin to panic, about to back up and turn around, but my brother waves at me before I have the chance to escape.

He's the first one to spot me and it's not until he stands up and says my name that Micah and who I'm assuming to be Parker stands up and looks at me.

Micah's blue eyes harden the moment he sees me and he slams back the shot in front of him. It's as if he's just now realizing why Parker is here and doesn't like it one bit.

I swallow back my nerves and finally set my attention on the third person at the table, before I can get too lost in Micah.

He's tall and fit with short, blonde hair and one of the cutest smiles I have ever seen.

He's handsome, whereas Micah is sexy and breathtaking.

But as good looking as he is, it's hard to appreciate the fact that he's cute just as my brother promised he'd be with the way Micah is looking at me, as if he wants to *bite* me and be rough with me again.

"Parker . . ." My brother grips the tall guy's shoulder and gestures toward me as I finally find the courage to walk up to them.

"This is my little sister Tegan; the one that I've been telling you about. She just turned twenty-one a few weeks ago and is visiting for the summer. I thought you two would get along well."

From the corner of my eye I catch Micah's jaw flex as he watches Parker reach out and grab my hand, pulling me closer to him.

"Oh wow. You're even prettier than I expected." He shakes his head and flashes me an apologetic smile. "I'm sorry. I don't mean to be rude. It's great to meet you. I've heard a lot about you. But wow."

I offer him a smile as he leans in to give me a quick hug. "Thank you." My attention sways toward Micah, but I'm able to quickly catch myself and focus on the cute guy in front of me before anyone takes notice. "It's nice to meet you too. I've . . . well . . . not heard much about you."

I can't tell if Micah has totally forgotten that my brother is here watching us, but he hasn't pulled his eyes away from Parker. It's as if he's watching his every move and is ready to rip his throat out if he does or says anything he doesn't like.

And from the annoyed look on my brother's face he's noticed it too.

"Micah," he says stiffly. "I need you to help me with something in my office before your show. We should leave these two alone to get to know each other."

"Wait . . . what?" I grab my brother's arm and yank him out of earshot. He's an asshole for setting me up like this. "What the hell are you doing? You're just going to leave me with him?"

My brother flashes me a small smile. "He *is* your date, little sis. That's how it's works, in case you've forgotten."

"What the . . . right now? Right here?" I begin to panic at the idea of being on a date in front of Micah. Not that we plan on being anything more than what we are, which is two people who need to stay away from each other, but still, I don't feel right about it. "Why not tomorrow or next week or . . . I don't know. A time when I'm ready. You tricked me and I'm pissed."

"You'll be fine. You may be pissed now, but you'll be thanking me later. Trust me. Now go talk to the guy."

Before I can say anything else, he smiles and gives me a little nudge toward Parker, which has Parker looking me over with a smile.

"Parker," Micah says in a deep voice, while reaching out to grip his hand. It's pretty hard to miss the tight squeeze he gives it as he leans in close to Parker's ear.

I stand here awkwardly and watch as Micah backs away from Parker with a scowl, his blue eyes locking on me momentarily, before he walks away without a word.

"I'll be back you two. I've got some shit to take care of," my brother says, before walking away after Micah, who's now being stopped by almost every girl he passes.

I hate the way they all smile and flirt with him, batting their stupid eyelashes to show him how much they want him.

It has me wishing I had my own shot to slam back now.

"I'm guessing Micah has taken on the role as your second big brother?" He gives me a somewhat nervous smile and takes a seat across from me as I sit down. "Hell, he seemed more concerned than Alexander did."

Definitely *not* a second brother role. "Yeah, something like that I guess. You can say he's taken on the role of being responsible for me it seems. I'm pretty sure Xan has been making him keep an eye out for me around here."

He messes with the buttons on his slick, blue shirt, unbuttoning the top two as if he needs some air. "Well, you definitely don't have to worry about me trying to kiss you on the first date with those two around. I'm afraid I'll break something valuable."

I'm not sure if I should laugh at that, but I do. He's afraid of my brother and Micah and I don't blame him.

Poor guy.

"Yeah, it could end up being a bit painful for you," I tease. "Everyone around here seems to be afraid of my brother and Micah. They're a bit intimidating when they want to be."

"I think it's mainly Micah everyone's afraid of. He's only intimidating about ninety percent of the time."

I find myself laughing, because from what I've seen it's true. It's one of the things that sort of drew me to him in the beginning.

Watching Micah demand orders and intimidate all the men around him is sort of hard not to find extremely hot.

Maybe I'll at least get a good laugh out of this little "date".

"I hope you like beer," Parker says as Gavin appears at our table and sets two bottles down in front of us. "Your brother said you did. Not a Martini girl like most of the girls who come here?"

"Yes, please." I nod and reach for a bottle, placing it to my lips, before I answer his second question. "Sometimes, but not often."

I have a feeling I'm going to need a few of these to get through this awkward situation. It's nearly seven, so that means Micah will be coming out to start his set soon.

Parker watches me with a smile and pays Gavin before he walks away. "Hey, I'm a little nervous too. It's been a while since I've been on a date. I wasn't really prepared for tonight since your brother only gave me a few hours' notice."

I set my beer down and look across the table at him. "A few hours?"

"Yeah." He takes a drink and nods. "He called me a few hours ago to ask what I was doing."

"Is that right?" I ask stiffly.

That asshole . . .

"I had plans to meet up with him soon to talk about the management position, but I had no idea what day exactly that would be, until today."

"I see." I take another drink, biting my tongue before I end up going off on my brother.

He made it seem like he had it planned beforehand and it wasn't just a last-minute thing; otherwise, I would've declined.

"So, you're a writer? How long have you been publishing books?"

I offer a tight-lipped smile as I set my beer down. I'm annoyed with my brother right now, but that doesn't mean I should take it out on this guy. He seems nice. "I started writing about a year ago, but just recently published my first book; a little less than six months ago. I'm currently working on the second."

"That's pretty great. My sister has always wanted to publish a book, but doesn't know where to start. Maybe you could give her some pointers on how to go about that."

I nod. "Yeah, sure. I'll be sure to give you my number before the end of the night and you can pass it to her."

"That would be awesome. She'd really appreciate that. Thank you."

"Not a problem."

There's an awkward silence for a few moments, so I look around and watch as everyone around me talks and gets excited about Micah's show.

It feels really strange that I'm here with a "date" about to watch him perform. I didn't expect tonight to go down this way and now that it has, I'm not feeling good about it at all.

"So . . . my brother tells me you used to work for him. Were you the old babyface?" I ask, attempting to keep the awkward silence to a minimum.

"For two years . . ." he pauses to take a quick swig of his beer. "I left for a bit to help my dad manage his restaurant when his assistant manager quit. I stayed on for a while and helped him find a replacement. That's when I got a call from Alexander asking me if I wanted to take over for Micah once he leaves."

"You sound pretty excited about that."

"I love this place," he says with a huge smile. "Who wouldn't love it here? It's amazing."

"I agree. I'm not sure I'm going to want to go back home once summer is over."

"I'm sure no one will be complaining if you decide to stay." He flashes me a flirty smile as his gaze lowers to my lips.

I tilt my beer back and chug it. He's extremely cute, but the idea of him wanting to kiss me has me on edge.

"I'm going to toss this and order us a couple more beers." I get ready to stand up, but Parker stands up and puts his hand out to stop me.

"Please, let me handle all the drinks tonight." He grabs my empty bottle, before downing the rest of his drink. "I'll be right back. Want a shot?"

"I'll take two. Doesn't matter what."

As soon as he walks away, I look over toward the door, as if knowing Micah would be exiting it at this very moment.

The sight of him walking out with his guitar, his shirt open and blowing in the wind, steals the air straight from my lungs.

Everyone around me begins screaming and whistling as he walks past their tables to get to the stage, but he keeps his gaze locked on me the entire way.

I wish I had a beer to chug at the moment, or a bag I could breathe in to catch my damn breath.

I don't know how his stare alone can cause this kind of reaction from my body, but there seems to be so much intensity behind his eyes.

He doesn't even look away as he adjusts his microphone and acoustic guitar.

"That took a little longer than I hoped. Sorry about that."

I manage to pull my eyes away from Micah long enough to smile up at Parker and snatch up one of the beers. "Thank you."

I can feel both of their gazes on me as I chug back the beer, wishing I could disappear from this messed up situation right now.

He fucked me hard last night.

The man on stage.

Right in front of *us*.

Of me and my *date*.

If it weren't for trying not to upset my brother, I'd get up right now and walk away. I'd take this beer and two shots with me and walk out onto the beach and listen from a distance as Micah sings.

Because I don't want to miss that.

Not after hearing and seeing what it's like when he's up on that small stage.

I get so lost in watching Micah prepare that I almost forget that I'm with Parker until he speaks.

"Have you heard Micah play before? He has a great voice."

"Yes. He has an amazing voice. One of the best I've ever heard."

"I take it you find that to be hot."

My eyes widen as I look across the table. "What would make you say that?"

He laughs and places his beer to his lips. "The way you just said it is all. It's cool." He pauses to tilt back his bottle. "Every single girl who comes here thinks it's hot. I don't think there's been one girl who's come here and hasn't wanted Micah to take them home and sing to them in *bed*."

I swallow, trying not to imagine that in my head, but it's too late, and I find myself getting extremely hot and nervous. "Not *every* girl, I'm sure."

"Right. Good thing he's taken on the role as a second brother figure to you. Or else I'd have problems getting a second date."

"Yeah . . . good thing." I let out a nervous laugh and jump into changing the subject. "Have you lived here your whole life?"

"I have." He flashes me this cute little charming smile that I can't help but to somewhat like. "Since you're asking me personal questions . . . maybe I can assume I'm doing okay so far?"

I smile back, feeling a bit more comfortable. "You're better than most guys I've been on dates with. The fact that you haven't texted another girl to flirt gives you some bonus points."

"Oh man." He lets out a small laugh. "Someone did that to you?"

I nod. "More than one guy, actually. What does that say about me?"

"That they couldn't handle a woman as beautiful as you." He winks over his bottle before tilting it back. "Good thing I'm man enough."

As awkward as this whole situation is, I have to admit that Parker is a really nice guy and I like his company.

Everyone seems to be quieting down, so I turn my chair toward the stage, giving Micah my full attention.

"How's everyone doing tonight?" Micah asks the crowd with that confidence he has that I love so much.

Everyone screams out their answers, but all I can focus on is Micah's fingers as he plays with the strings of his guitar while he talks.

I love how confident he is with them . . . as if he knows exactly what to do with them without even looking.

"Good. We're going to start the night out with one of my favorite bands: *Kaleo*. So, just tilt back a few drinks and relax."

His voice instantly has me mesmerized just like the last time I heard him sing, and I find myself lost in his voice all the way up to the very last word.

Everyone takes a few seconds to clap and whistle for him, but the crowd is quick to grow quiet again as Micah begins strumming his guitar, ready for the next song.

I know I should be focusing most of my attention on Parker, given the situation, but I can't, no matter how hard I try.

Micah's performance has me completely lost in him right now . . .

Chapter Twelve

Micah

FUCK, THE FACT THAT TEGAN hasn't taken her eyes off me since I began playing is messing with my head.

We both agreed last night that we shouldn't have slipped up and had sex, and we both agreed not to ever let it happen again.

But the way she's looking at me now has me wanting to pull her up on this stage and fuck her on this stool right here in front of everyone.

I don't care who's watching, but I have to keep my asshole thoughts under control. So, I do what I came here to do and try my best to get lost in my performance.

Realizing Tegan was here for a date with Parker almost made me want to skip my performance so I could keep a closer eye on them, but then the thought of her possibly liking him only made me want to get her thinking about me even more. I remember the way she looked at me the last time I played and I want that again.

Parker may be a good guy. He may know how to treat Tegan better than I ever could, but it doesn't mean I want that shit to happen.

Seeing that she was the *girl* Alexander had coming for Parker to meet had my blood boiling.

Especially seeing how damn sexy she looked standing there in that little dress with her dark hair blowing around her face.

I wanted nothing more than to walk over to her, pull her hair back and crush my lips against hers to show Parker that she's mine.

But the fucked-up part is that she isn't mine and never will be, and the fact that he trusts Parker with his sister and not me bothers me. It has me wanting to give him a reason to trust me with her.

I know more than anyone that's going to take a lot, because he knows my track record with women. He knows I've never been on a second date, or hell, even a first one.

It's always been straight to the bedroom and then straight out the door.

But I can't fight this feeling in my gut that she's different than the rest.

She didn't drop at my feet from the sight of me like most of the women I've met.

Hell, no. It took me pushing and teasing her to even get her to want to spend a little time with me. Usually words aren't even needed when it comes to me getting what I want.

I look up and catch her zoned in on me as if she's so lost in me she can't look anywhere else. It's like I'm the only guy out here, and I can't deny that it has adrenaline pumping through me, working me up.

It's not until Parker grabs her arm and leans in close to her that she finally shakes out of her zone and turns to face him.

Whatever he's saying has her laughing as if it's the funniest thing she's heard.

The fact that he can make her light up like that has anger and jealousy swarming through me, because all I can think about is how he could possibly make her happier than me.

What the fuck am I thinking?

Giving a shit about a woman I've slept with isn't something I do, and it wasn't something I planned on doing anytime soon. Especially when it's my best friend's little sister.

So, why the hell do I want to break this guitar over Parker's pretty face right now?

Every muscle in my body is tight as I continue to play, not missing a beat.

That is until Parker pulls Tegan's chair closer to his and rubs his hand over her arm as if he has the right to.

It's hard to miss the anger in my voice at the sight. It even has Tegan backing away from Parker and giving me an odd look.

She may be able to tell I'm pissed about her being so close to Parker, but fuck it. It's been pretty obvious I'm not thrilled with their little date since the moment she showed up.

I'm not going to pretend that I approve of it.

At the end of my set, I stand up and take my guitar off, not missing the fact that Tegan slides a little piece of paper across the table to Parker.

With a clenched jaw, I set my guitar down and reach for the water beside me, pouring it over my face to cool off.

When I open my eyes again, Tegan is standing alone at the table, watching me hard.

She's looking at me like she wants to come over and say something, but changes her mind and walks away instead.

That's probably a good thing with the way I'm feeling right now.

My head is fucking with me tonight and what I really need is to hurry and get out of here before I can cause a scene.

When I make it upstairs to my office to change into a fresh shirt and a pair of jeans, Alexander is stepping out of his.

"Great performance, Man. I've never heard you sing Kaleo before. I'm impressed."

I slip into my jeans. "I figured Kaleo would be a good choice for tonight." I button my jeans and reach for my t-shirt, slipping it on. "Did your sister leave with Parker?"

"Fuck no," he says quickly. "There's no way in hell I'd let her leave with any guy after the first date. She went home to work on her book, alone. She mentioned sitting outside by the pool for a bit."

Relief fills me, knowing that she at least didn't leave with Mr. Perfect. "Good. I was going to kick your ass if she did."

He steps into my office and crosses his arms as he watches me log out of the computer and reach for my keys. "I'd be kicking my own ass. Parker may be a good guy but that doesn't mean I fully trust him with her. I just trust him more than I would most guys with her."

I look up and lift a brow, already knowing what his answer will be. "Like me?"

"Especially you, Micah. Have you met you?"

"I've had the pleasure," I mumble. "I'm sort of an asshole. I've never denied it. But only because I choose to be. I don't have to be."

"Dammit, Micah." He runs a hand over his face and I can feel his frustration. "Don't ruin our friendship over my sister. You're not a long-term type of guy. We both know you'd get bored within a day. So, push my sister far from your dirty fucking mind before I have to kill you."

"Hey, I didn't say she was on my mind." It's bullshit and even I know it. "Just wanted to see if you still don't trust me with her.

That's all."

He doesn't say anything as he watches me head for the door. He just moves out of my way.

That's probably a good thing right now.

"I'll be at *Express* if you need me. It may be a long night."

"You look like you need to unwind a bit, so I'll leave your ass be. We'll be fine here. We're going to have to learn to be soon anyway. Go to your place."

He flashes me a proud smile that has me feeling guilty as shit about last night. "Thanks, brother."

Before long I'm pulling up at *Express,* needing some time to play and think.

I grab a few beers and head up to the stage, taking a seat on the black stool.

It's been a while since I've played my own music. I always told myself that the first time I play it for an audience will be on my own stage.

Not on someone else's.

It's crazy to think it'll be happening soon.

Relaxing and thinking with a few beers has the music flowing. I'm sitting here, lost in my performance, when I look up and see Tegan standing in the doorway watching me with her small laptop clutched to her chest.

My heart speeds up at the sight of her, because I didn't expect her to show up here tonight, but then again, I didn't expect her to show up the other night either.

"As much as I hate to admit it to someone as narcissistic as you, you're really talented. And music helps me write. I figured you'd be here playing and thought maybe I could write. I hope you don't mind."

I watch as she walks over to the table in front of the stage and takes a seat. She doesn't say anything else. She just sets her laptop down in front of her and opens it, giving me a small smile. "And don't get too cocky up there. It's your voice that relaxes me and gets me lost in thought, not your good looks."

I arch a brow when she looks up at me. "Are you sure? I can lose the shirt if it helps." I can't help the cocky little smirk that takes over when I catch her looking my body over, as if she's trying to picture me shirtless. "And the pants too. Anything you want."

"I think you losing your pants is the last thing we both need right now. So, how about you stay dressed for once." She shakes her head, as if she's surprised by my offer. "My brother is already giving me dirty looks whenever your name is brought up. Which reminds me . . ."

"What?" I sit forward and run a hand through my messy hair. "This should be good. Does this have anything to do with your hot date tonight?"

"It wasn't much of a date. Trust me," she says quickly. "It was all Alexander's idea. My brother isn't stupid. He knows how you are with women and he knows I'm a sucker when it comes to men who look like you. He's trying to distract me."

"Then why the hell are you here?" My words come out harsh, but it doesn't seem to faze her like it would most women.

"I told you. For some inspiration." She looks up at me, her eyes softening. "So, will you please play something? I don't care what. I just need the words to flow and they seem to do that when I'm listening to music and also when I'm around you, even though I hate to admit it. So, what could be better than you playing music for me?"

I exhale and reach for another beer, tilting it back.

Tegan has no fucking clue how hard she's making it to be a good friend to her brother.

She doesn't get that I can't be around her right now, but now that she's here I don't want her to leave.

Especially since she came here because she needs me.

It makes me want to be the hero in her damn book. Or maybe I want him to be me.

Either way, I find myself playing for her.

But I choose not to play my own music, because I'm not sure I'm ready for that just yet.

When she finally hears one of my original songs, I want it to hit her in the heart. I want her to *feel* my words so she can see why this place is important to me, because I have a feeling she'll understand more than anyone else does.

Words are her passion too, and that's another thing that has me so drawn to her when I shouldn't be.

I play for close to an hour, neither of us breaking concentration.

It's just the two of us, alone, in this room, lost in what we love to do. I find something oddly comforting about it.

We're connecting in a way I've never connected with anyone before and I find myself wanting to learn more about her.

I set my guitar down and run to grab two more beers, placing one down in front of her, before I take a seat on the stool again.

"Tell me something about yourself."

She looks up from her laptop and laughs. "What?"

I sit up straight, saying the words firmer this time. "Tell me something I don't know about you. You tell me something and I'll continue to play. Unless you don't want me to, of course. I can stop anytime."

She keeps her eyes on me while reaching for the bottle in front of her and taps the side of it, lost in thought. "Well, when I was five a neighbor's dog bit a small hole in my face and I had to get six stitches. I'm pretty sure I cried for two days straight."

I don't like the feeling I get inside when I picture her as a small girl hurt and crying. All it does it make me wish I were there to protect her.

"Tell me something else. Something happy. I don't want to picture you hurt while I'm playing."

A small smile forms on her face, but she quickly hides behind her bottle as if she doesn't want me to see it. "I don't know. I used to write these cheesy love poems when I was like twelve and one of them got published in a book. I remember being so excited and thinking that someday I'd be a famous writer. That's what made me want to become an author. It took me a while to get brave enough to self-publish one of my recent stories, but I finally found the courage last year and so far it's the happiest I've ever been. I love everything about it."

The proud look on her face has me smiling. "Has your family read your first book?"

"Oh god, no!" She turns red in the face. "I can't allow them to read the stories I write. They're . . . uh . . . I don't know . . ."

"Dirty and erotic," I answer for her. "That's not something to be ashamed of, Tegan. Everyone loves a good dirty book once in a while."

"Even you?" she asks.

I keep my eyes on her as I tilt back my beer. "Even me. Words are sometimes better than pictures, because then you can imagine the person you want to do those things to."

My answer seems to have her squirming a bit in her seat. She's likely getting where I'm going with this. Yes, I've jerked off to my fair share of erotic books and I'm not afraid to admit it. The thought that she likely has too has me hardening.

"Is that right?" She reaches for her beer and takes a quick swig.

"When was the last time you read a book?"

I wipe my arm over my mouth, absorbing the excess beer, before tossing the bottle into the trash beside me. "The night I came into your room and helped you relieve a little frustration. You weren't the only one needing a release."

"How did I know this conversation with you would turn into something sexual?" She shakes her head and shuts down her computer, showing me that she's done writing for now.

I jump down from the stage and grip the table, moving in close enough to almost kiss her, wanting to see what me being close to her does now that she's had me inside of her. "Because everything turns sexual with me. You know this, yet you still came here, Tegan. We both know that was a mistake, yet I let you stay."

Her breathing picks up against my lips and I know without further confirmation that my body still has the same effect on her as before. Maybe even more now.

Shit, how that turns me on.

But being the asshole that I'm supposed to be to keep her at a distance, I decide to push her and see if I can piss her off.

"How was your little date? Did he make you want him inside of you as much as I do? Is that why you gave him your number?"

"You're so full of yourself, Micah." She palms my face, pushing it away. "I've already had you inside me once and that was more than enough."

"That didn't answer my question." I walk after her as she tries to get away. Before she can reach the door I back her up against the wall and brush my lips over hers, causing her eyes to close and her heartbeat to race against my chest. "Did he?"

"It's none of your damn business," she breathes. "We're not supposed to give a shit what each other wants, so let's stick to that. From what I've heard it's something you're good at."

She opens her eyes, allowing them to lock on mine for a quick second, before she pushes me away and walks out the door.

I'm not sure why hearing her say out loud how much of a piece of shit I am when it comes to women has me all worked up, but it does.

I haven't touched another woman since the day she walked through her brother's door. Well, at least not since I sent Denise home as soon as I was finished with her.

"Shit." I run over and grab my keys, not bothering to clean the place up, before I rush outside and lock up behind me.

There's no way I'm letting her walk away from me in the middle of the night.

She's barely made it through the parking lot before I pick her up and begin carrying her toward my truck. "Put me the hell down, Micah."

Even though she continues to bark orders at me, I don't set her down until I'm standing beside my truck. "I'm sorry I'm an asshole. We don't have to talk on the way home, but I need you to get in so I can drive you."

She looks me over, hesitating for a moment, before she climbs inside and slams the door shut behind her.

I guess being an asshole to keep her away is going to be harder than I expected, because I hate the way it felt just now watching her want to get away from me.

Everything inside of me was screaming to go after her, and that's exactly what I did. Now I have to manage this drive home, pretending that I don't want anything more than to kiss her and make sure she wants me and not Parker.

I want to be inside of her, reminding her of how it felt to have me take her.

Parker will never be able to make her feel the way I can, both mentally and physically.

He's the good guy who will open doors for her and buy her flowers to make her smile.

I'm the asshole who will fuck her good and hard to show her how much I want her, and I'll kick another guy's ass for getting too close.

That's exactly why I'm the one she should be staying away from.

A few minutes into the drive she looks over at me and speaks. I can tell from the tone of her voice that she's trying to stay mad at me. "Why don't you play any of the songs you've written when you perform? Or have you?"

"Just doesn't feel right performing them anywhere other than a place I put a lot of heart and dedication into. I thought about playing one for the audience at *Vortex* during my first real performance way back, but the thought had me too anxious, so I chose a few random songs to get me through the night."

"Understandable. Tell me about Sebastian."

"You sure are asking a lot of questions for someone that's pissed at me," I say with amusement.

"Yeah, well, oddly I need to know. I'm not sure why, so please don't make me feel like an idiot."

"Okay." I grip the steering wheel, because I hate talking about Sebastian's problems. Mostly because he reminds me a lot of myself when I was younger. "He came into *Vortex* about two years ago, looking like a tween with an ID that said he was twenty-one. I took one look at the shit-job some idiot sold him and tossed him out on his scrawny ass. He kept coming back and eventually I started looking out for him because I knew no one else would. He's seventeen going on eighteen now and I'm still kicking him out of the bar weekly. He's got some balls. That's for sure."

"Where are his parents?"

"Not taking care of him like they damn well should be. The kid doesn't even know where they are right now."

"That's sad and entirely messed up. No kid that young should have to be on their own."

Just as expected, she doesn't speak to me the rest of the ride back to Alexander's, but that doesn't mean I didn't catch her looking over at me whenever she didn't think I would notice.

It seems I bring out her creeper tendencies and I can't deny that it gets me somewhat excited.

The fact that she feels the need to look at me whenever she can means that I'm most likely on her mind just as much as she's been on mine.

Fuck me, I need to get out of here.

That shit is messing with my mind, and I'm two seconds away from pulling her into my lap so she can ride me long and hard to show her I've been thinking about her too.

And now that she's showing interest in my bar and Sebastian it's only messing with my head more, confusing me.

"Goodnight," I say as she's opening the truck door.

She's about to jump out but stops to look back at me. "You're not staying here tonight?"

"No." I grip the steering wheel and give her a quick glance. "I'll wait here until you get inside. Lock the doors so I know you're safe."

Without another word, she jumps out of the truck and shuts the door behind her, walking away.

Just as I do with Sebastian, I wait until she gets inside before I drive off and head to my small apartment.

It's not much, but it's the best I could afford while putting all my money into *Express*.

Once I get upstairs and pour myself a drink, I text Sebastian on the phone I picked up for him earlier today to check on him.

As soon as I get the confirmation that he's home safe in bed, I allow myself the pleasure of drinking until I pass out, because I know that's the only way I won't make the mistake of changing my mind and ending up inside Tegan's room.

Chapter Thirteen

Tegan

IT'S BEEN THREE DAYS SINCE Micah has come around the house, and even though I want to see him I've been avoiding *Vortex* because I know it's the best thing to do.

It seems whenever he's around I can't control my mind or body and all I want is for him to touch me. I want him to push me with his dirty mouth like he always does, because it's become exciting and something I crave now.

As much as I hate to admit it, being around Micah is a rush and he makes me feel things I've never felt before.

I just haven't figured out if that's a good or bad thing yet, and maybe it's best if I never do.

"There you are!" I sit up at the sound of Jamie's voice and open my eyes to see her running through the sand toward me, dressed in a white bikini top and a pair of cut-off shorts. "I've been calling you all day. What the hell have you been doing?"

"Sorry." I reach for my sunglasses and remove them, before laying back down on my towel and looking up at my friend as she hovers above me. "I just needed some peace and quiet for a bit so I could think. I left my phone on the charger in my room because I didn't feel like dealing with it today. My parents have been calling nonstop to check on me, as if they think I'm not coming back when I already told them it's only for the summer."

"Because they're right and we both it. There's no way you're going back home once the summer is over. Not after seeing what it's like here. Oh, and by the way, I went to the house looking for you there first and your brother answered the door, wet, only wearing a towel. Ooh wee." She begins fanning herself, before throwing a towel down beside me and taking a seat. "He offered me this towel once I told him I was looking for you. I was hoping he'd give me the one he was wrapped up in, but he totally gypped me by giving me this clean one."

"I haven't made any plans past summer, so please don't be like my parents. And stop it, I'm completely disturbed by that," I admit with a scowl. "Please tell me you didn't come here to blab about your fantasies in regards to my brother, because if so you can find somewhere else to lay that is nowhere near my immediate vicinity. My ears can't handle that mess today."

She laughs and lays back, getting comfortable as she reaches for my bottle of water and takes a drink. "I wasn't planning on it, but I am sort of having fantasies after seeing the way he looked in that towel. It was hard to keep my eyes away from his . . ."

"Don't even say it, Jamie."

She sits up and smiles down at me playfully. I hate that smile because I know it well, but unfortunately, I'm not quick enough to cover my ears before she can say it. "Bulge."

"That's so gross." I sit up and give her a dirty look, wishing

I could slap her for that one. "You've ruined my whole day with that one little word."

"Oh, it wasn't little, sweetie."

"Okay, my whole damn week! You've ruined my whole week now. I did not need to know that."

"You act like you haven't had bulges on your mind lately. I'm pretty sure I caught you checking Micah Beck's out last week during his performance."

"His guitar was covering it," I say defensively. "I couldn't check it out."

"Exactly," she points out. "But you looked for it and that's how you know it wasn't visible."

"I'm here to relax, so let's not talk about my brother or Micah please. Can we move on from bulges now, sheesh?"

She shrugs and lays back at the same time I do. "Alright, fine. I'll let you tell me what's going on when you're good and ready."

"What is that supposed to mean?" I ask, quicker than I probably should've.

"You tell me."

"I can't."

"You can."

"It was a mistake." I sit back up and run my hands through my hair, because this conversation is anything but relaxing.

"Um, what?" She shoots back up and slaps the sand excitedly. "I knew it! I knew the moment I saw the two of you in the backseat of my car that something had either already happened or was going to soon. I could just *feel* it."

Something happened between me and Micah alright, but just the idea of saying it out loud has my heart kicking into overdrive.

I'm so nervous that it feels like it's about to beat out of my chest and it's making it hard to breathe.

This is ridiculous.

"You can't say anything to anyone, got it? Because Xan will lose his shit if he finds out and I can't do that to their friendship."

She nods excitedly while reaching for the hair tie wrapped around her wrist and pulling her light hair into a quick ponytail. "I won't tell a soul. I swear. Especially Alexander because I know how he is when it comes to you and boys. I promise."

The fact that someone else other than Micah and I is about to find out that we've had sex makes it feel so much more . . . real. I almost can't handle it, but it's too late to turn back now.

"We had sex . . . outside . . . against his truck . . . in the dark . . . outside my brother's house."

The moment the words leave my mouth my whole body ignites into flames at the reminder of how hot and exciting the moment was.

Micah's hard body against mine . . . the V of muscles leading down to his long, thick dick . . . and most of all the way he felt inside of me as he *fucked* me hard, as if he wanted me to feel him inside of me for days. I never knew being backed against a truck could be so damn hot.

I can't even pay attention to Jamie's reaction because I'm too busy jumping to my feet and rushing over to the water to cool off. I'm so worked up by the pictures flashing through my head that my skin is scorched.

What the hell is wrong with me?
You've had your one night, Tegan.
That's all it was and all it can be.

I hear Jamie splashing in the water behind me, trying to get to me. When I turn around to begin making my way back to the sand, her mouth is hanging open.

"Holy shit, Tegan," she begins following behind me, almost

falling to keep up. "You can't just tell me things like that and then run away. That's crazy hot."

"That's the problem," I say quickly. "It was hot and amazing and I can't stop thinking about the way he made me feel, Jamie. It never should've happened and now I can't help but want it to happen again, even though it could very well mess up his and Xan's relationship. I hate it. I don't want to be that girl."

"Do you really think your brother would be that pissed if he found out you two hooked up? I mean, if it's more than just a random hookup then I'm sure he'll understand and be happy for you two."

"It *was* only a random hookup." I don't bother looking at her as I reach for my towel and shake off the sand before drying off with it. "So, yes, he'd be livid. You know Micah's reputation with women. He's a man-whore. Everyone knows he never commits to being in a relationship. My brother warned him to stay away from me for that very reason and he went behind his back and slept with me anyway. *We* went behind his back and I feel like total shit for it. He'll never trust him again if he finds out and he'll probably kick my butt and send me home early."

"Okay," she says calmly. "Then don't tell him and never let it happen again. You just admitted it was only a random hookup; just one 'anything goes' night. Problem solved."

She has no idea how much harder that is than it sounds. "How the hell am I supposed to just forget that he was inside of me and act normal when we bump into each other around my brother? Have you seen Micah?"

I begin making my way up to my brother's house and Jamie quickly grabs her towel to join me. "Good point. You're fucked."

I stop and give her an annoyed look. "You're not making this any better, so thanks for that."

"I'm sorry, but it's true. The only option is to avoid him at all cost for the rest of the summer. You don't want to end up being one of those girls that he's been with who becomes obsessive and can't stay away from him so he has to hide just to get them off his nuts. I've seen it and so has Alexander. It's happened to pretty much every girl he's touched."

The thought of all the girls Micah has randomly hooked up with for one night of the hottest sex of their lives has me feeling uptight and jealous. This is not how I'm supposed to feel. "How am I supposed to manage that when he works and stays with my brother almost ninety percent of the time?"

Once we reach the back of my brother's house we take a seat at the patio table and toss our wet towels down by our feet.

"I don't know." She shrugs. "Maybe find a different bar to write at and come stay with me on the nights he's here. My place is small, but I don't mind sharing it."

"Thanks, but I can't do that. That'll only have my brother questioning my reasons for not staying with him or coming to *Vortex* anymore. It'll all still come down to Micah in the end."

"Shit. I didn't think about that. You'll just have to woman up and keep that shit deep down inside as if it never happened. You're tough. I'm sure you can handle it."

"I hope so."

We're both sitting here in silence, lost in thought, when I hear the patio door slide open behind me.

Nervousness and excitement course through me at the thought that it could be Micah. I'm going crazy inside to see his sexy smile, but at the same time I know what that sexy smile and dirty mouth does to me. That's where the nervousness takes over.

Jamie looks up at the same time I turn around to see Parker step outside dressed in a pair of khaki shorts and a snug, white t-shirt.

He flashes us his charming smile, before closing the door shut behind him, giving us a nice view of his sculpted arms and back. "Hello, ladies. Mind if I join you?"

I don't know if this is good or bad timing, but maybe . . . just maybe he's the distraction I need right now, because I was so damn close to giving in and asking Jamie to come with me to *Vortex*.

"Parker, wow." Jamie stands up and looks him over, before throwing her arms around him for a quick hug. "You're looking . . . well, hot."

Parker's face turns red as he runs a hand through his hair. "Thanks, Jamie. It's good to see you too," he says with a small laugh. "You're looking great, as always."

"I know it," she says, with a confident smile. "But thanks for noticing. I don't know what's going on here with you and my friend, but I'll be in the pool listening while you talk."

"Really?" I laugh as she gives me a questionable look, before diving into the pool.

"Sorry, I didn't mean to bother you here at your brother's, but I haven't seen you at the bar in a few days and wanted to ask you something. Alexander let me in."

I motion to the chair Jamie was just sitting in. "No, you're totally fine, Parker." I smile as he takes a seat and the more I look at him, the more I realize just how handsome he really is. It's easier to notice when Micah isn't ten feet away giving me dirty looks.

But, I'm still not sure that's enough to get Micah off my mind.

"I've been thinking a lot about our date a few days ago and . . ." he leans in closer, before he reaches out and brushes my hair behind my ear. "I don't really feel like it was much of a *date* with your brother and Micah watching us like hawks. I was wondering if you'd come out with me to a party tonight so we can get to know each other without them making us both uncomfortable."

I catch Jamie nodding from the corner of my eye and mouthing *yes* repeatedly, so I cover the side of my face until she's out of view.

Some time away from my thoughts could be a good thing, but at the same time, going on another *date* has me feeling guilty for some odd reason. I don't really get why. It's not like Micah has been around, and it's definitely not as if we're going to end up being more than the one-night stand we had.

The only reason he was giving us dirty looks that night is because he's become overprotective like my brother asked him to be whenever he isn't around to watch me himself.

There's no other explanation, because jealousy is the last thing Micah could've been feeling.

Micah Beck jealous.

I'm positive that day will never come.

I don't even realize that I haven't answered him until he says my name, distracting me from my thoughts.

"I'll take a maybe if it'll somehow lead to a yes."

The hopeful smile he flashes me has the word leaving my mouth before I can really make a decision. "Okay."

He bites his bottom lip in this sexy little way as he stands up and looks me over. "I promise you won't be disappointed."

I catch myself swallowing, because even I can't deny that his little lip bite somewhat got to me. "When should I be ready?"

He pulls out his phone and takes a quick look at the time. "Can you be ready around seven? That's about two hours."

I nod and smile. "I can make that happen."

"Perfect." He leans in and places a kiss on my cheek, before wiping the wetness away with his thumb. It's sweet but still sexy in the way he does it. "I'll see you then."

Jamie is wiggling her eyebrows at me as he waves to her and

disappears back into the house.

She waits until he closes the door behind him before she jumps out of the pool and rushes over to grab her towel. "You went on a date with Parker and your brother didn't flip out? Why didn't you tell me this?"

"My brother is the one who set us up on a date. Weird, right?"

She shakes her head and laughs. "I don't get your brother sometimes, but I totally get why he did it. It's because he's worried you'll fall for Micah and get hurt. Why else would he be worried about hooking you up with some nice guy. He sees it too. He sees something happening between you two."

"Yeah, and maybe he's right by trying to give me a distraction. Maybe I'll thank him for this later. I mean, Parker is cute and he's sweet. The least I can do is give him a real date and see what happens from there, right?"

She nods, while running the towel through her hair. "As much as I'd love to see you and Micah together, and I mean together together, Parker might be the safe choice. You're right. Micah is a man-whore and there's no telling if you two will even hook up again. I say give Parker a fair chance. Forget about Micah for one night and have some fun. It's not like *he's* here trying to spend time with you or ask you out on dates."

She's right and I know it.

It sucks but it's true.

"Well, I already agreed to go out with him tonight. I'll give him a chance and take it from there."

"And . . ."

"And what?"

"You'll tell your good friend Jamie all the details, right?"

I roll my eyes and laugh right as Alexander pokes his head out the sliding door. "I'm heading to *Vortex* for the night. I trust Parker will be a gentleman, and if he's not you better tell me."

"I'm a big girl, Xan. I've already told you this."

"Dammit, Tegan. Just let me do my damn job," he says tensely.

"Fine. I'll let you know."

He nods. "Good. See you girls later."

"Later," Jamie says with a flirty smile. "I'll be coming in for a few drinks later, so tell your boys to be ready to grab the beers in the way back."

This has my brother smiling. "We'll be ready for you. We always are."

The thought that everyone will be at *Vortex* having fun and hanging out while I'm out at a party with Parker has me somewhat feeling regretful that I won't be there.

But at the same time, I know this is something I need to do, because if I join them and see Micah there I'll be too distracted to have fun anyway.

Maybe Parker is just what I need right now, and it looks like I'll be finding out soon enough . . .

Chapter Fourteen

Micah

I'VE SPENT THE LAST FEW days focusing on Sebastian as much as I can and making sure that he has everything he needs since his piece of shit parents are still nowhere to be found.

I know from experience that if he's left unattended for too long that he'll only get into trouble, and I won't be bailing his ass out of jail once he turns eighteen soon.

I learned the hard way when I was a kid, and even though I've been fighting hard to protect him because I never had that, Sebastian is about to see what tough love is all about if he keeps his shit up.

It's the first time he's had a phone his entire life, so I hope it doesn't end up being a mistake and that the little shit doesn't use it seek more trouble than usual.

Micah: Are you coming to help me at Express tonight?

Seb: I can't. I told Jimmy we'd hang at his place tonight.

Micah: And do what?"

Seb: Have sex with hookers and do blow off their tits before drinking until we pass out.

Seb: I'm kidding. That was last week.

His smartass response has me wanting to reach through the phone and choke the little asshole.

Micah: Keep your nose clean or you'll be dealing with me and I can promise that you won't like it. Got it?

Seb: Fine. Whatever. No hookers and drugs then.

I toss my cell down on my desk, before running my hands through my hair as my thoughts linger back to Tegan.

As much as I've wanted to stay at Alexander's place to see her, I feel it's better that I just stay the hell away from her right now before I fuck shit up more.

There's no telling what I'll end up doing if I have a chance to get her alone again and I need to stop being a fuck-up and betraying my best friend's trust. It's the only thing he's ever asked me not to do.

That's exactly why I need to go out tonight and get my mind as far away from Tegan as I can. Any distraction will do at this point, because nothing else is working.

Being here has me watching the table she usually works at, waiting for her to show up and work on her book. Now being at *Express* has me doing the same damn thing since she's written there too.

This girl has my head all screwed up right now and that's

something that's never happened before.

"Hey, brother." Alexander pokes his head into my door, causing me to look up from my desk. "You're good to head out for the night if you want. You've been here all damn day. Don't you have some other shit to do?"

"What can I say? These pricks keep me busy."

"Tell me something I don't know," he mumbles. He watches me for a few seconds, as if he has something to say, before stepping inside and taking a seat in the chair across from my desk. "Everything good with you?"

I cross my hands behind my head and look at him, trying to figure out how to answer his damn question. I'm stressed the hell out and he's the biggest reason why, but that's the last thing I'll be letting him know.

"Yeah. Why wouldn't I be?"

"Just trying to figure out why you haven't been to my place in a few days when usually you're there almost every day." He doesn't say anything else, but the suspicious look he's giving me is enough to hint what he's getting at.

"Just been dealing with the kid is all." It's not a complete lie. "His fucking piece of shit parents are still gone and I'm trying to keep his head on straight. I got him a phone, so I've been keeping track of him and letting him crash at my place."

"Good thing the kid will be eighteen soon. Maybe you can hire him in as a cook or some shit at Express."

I laugh, because having him work at a bar is the worst fucking idea ever. "Then I'll only have to worry about the kid more. He doesn't need a job where alcohol is easily accessible. I'd have to watch his every damn move and he'd probably burn the place down within a week."

"Okay. Bad idea. I'm tired and can't think for shit. I was going to sleep before I came in but I kept getting interrupted by visitors for my sister."

Visitors? Not one, but more than one.

For some reason I don't like the sound of that.

As far as I can tell she only hangs out with Jamie, so now I want to know who this other visitor is.

"Your sister been making new friends other than Jamie?" I ask, trying to sound cool about it.

He nods and stands up. "Yeah. Parker stopped by wanting to take her out tonight. I told her to let me know if he gets out of line. He's a good guy, but if he tries moving too fast with my sister I'll cut his balls off myself."

The mention of Parker's name instantly has me pissed off and wanting to cut his balls off my damn self. I have to grip my desk and squeeze just to keep my cool in front of Alexander.

"Yeah," I say stiffly. "Well, let me know how that goes."

"Alright, Man. I've got work to do."

The moment Alexander leaves my office I reach beside me for the bottle of whiskey and tilt it back, needing something strong to calm my nerves before I blow up.

I've never had a problem with Parker before, but now that he's trying to hook up with Tegan I hate the fucker and have daydreams about shoving my fist down his throat.

Just as I'm taking a second swig, my door opens to Colby stepping inside. He takes one look at me standing here tense with my jaw flexed and steps right the fuck back out of my office.

He's been here long enough to know when to avoid me and now is definitely one of those times.

Parker fucking Wright.

Vortex's pretty-boy-charmer.

He's the long-term guy you take home to Mommy and Daddy;

whereas I'm the one-night stand most women fantasize about, wishing their boyfriends would fuck them wild and rough like I could.

With a small growl, I tilt back the bottle one more time, before slamming the bottle down and cracking my neck.

Good thing Kalon has a party at his place practically every night, because I need a distraction more now than ever.

♪ ♩ ♪ ♩

ON MY WAY TO THE party earlier I got a call from Sebastian asking me to drive thirty minutes out of the way to pick his ass up from some kid's house whose parents are always gone like Seb's.

If it weren't for the fact that he was smart enough to call me before he got wasted and did something stupid, then I would've kicked his ass.

It makes me thankful that I didn't smash the whole bottle of whiskey before leaving *Vortex* like I really wanted to at the time.

What I slammed back before I left wasn't even enough to give me a buzz. It was more of the burn that I needed.

Now, it's the escape that I need, and Kalon's is always the best place for that.

Hopping out of my truck, I make my way around the back and immediately pour myself a double, before taking off to find Kalon.

I barely make it ten steps away from the drink table when someone clings to my arm and stops me from walking.

I know right away from the platinum blonde hair waving in the breeze that it's Gwen without even looking down to see.

"Fucking hell," I mutter, before tilting back the drink in my hand. "What the hell do you want?"

"Oh, come on, Micah. We're no longer at *Vortex* where you have to be a dick ninety percent of the time to show everyone who's in charge. We're at a party. Relax a bit and have fun."

I flex my jaw and tilt back the cup again as she attaches herself to me and begins kissing along my neck, clearly thinking I'm going to change my mind and fuck her into submission again. Not happening. "Why don't you do us both a favor and back the fuck up before I have to pry you from my body in front of all these people, Gwen."

She reaches up and cups my face, forcing me to look at her. "Look at me, Micah. Do you see me all over any other guys? I could have any guy here, but here I am wasting my time on you because I know you'll fuck me better than any of these *boys* can. So why don't you do us both a favor and come find me after you have a few drinks, yeah?"

With a small smile, she backs away, before spinning around on her heels and walking away.

It's then that I look past her to see Tegan playing beer pong with Parker, Kalon, and some chick that Kalon is probably banging to get over his ex.

She's standing next to Parker, dressed in a white tank top, a pair of short shorts, and those damn cowgirl boots that she looks irresistible in.

The fact that she's laughing and having fun with him has me tilting back my cup, emptying it completely this time.

It's taking everything in me not to go over there and rip her away from Parker to show him he hasn't got a chance in hell with her.

In fact, every part of me is dying to carry her caveman style into one of Kalon's spare rooms and fuck my way back into her thoughts before Parker can worm his way in any further and make her fall for his charm.

Why the hell does that send rage coursing through me?

"Fuck it."

I grab two beers and head toward the beer pong table. Looks like I'll have to show Parker to stay in his lane before he crashes and gets hurt.

If I know one thing . . . it's that he won't be leaving here with Tegan. Not as long as I'm around . . .

Chapter Fifteen

Tegan

AT FIRST, I WAS A little nervous when I found out the party we were attending was going to be at Kalon's house. The first time I came here I was with Micah, and even though he had his way of driving me crazy we had a lot of fun. I think it might've been the moment I realized I was beginning to really like him, even though I was fighting my hardest not to.

But Parker has been doing everything in his power to make me feel comfortable and at ease, and I'm just now beginning to loosen up a bit and push Micah out of my mind.

Kalon remembers me from last time, but he hasn't once mentioned Micah or asked why I'm here with Parker now.

It's as if he's used to most girls only making one appearance with Micah and that's exactly why my brother warned me to stay away.

"Do you got this?" Parker asks with an excited smile. "Just one more ball and we beat the champs."

"Oh, I've got this alright. I've been playing this game since I was fifteen." I smile and turn away from Parker's beaming face to concentrate on making this last ball in, but right as I get ready to toss the ball I make the mistake of looking up to see Micah walking toward us.

The sight of him in a pair of faded jeans and a snug black shirt hugging his sculpted chest to perfection has me dropping the ball before I get the chance to throw it.

"Oh, come on, Tegan. Something got you distracted?" Kalon throws his arms up and laughs, before reaching for the ball and throwing it up, catching it. "You've been a pro the whole night and now you can't even hold the ball. Here." He tosses the ball my way, but I don't even make an attempt to catch it, because I still haven't been able to pull my eyes away from the beautiful temptation in front of me.

After not seeing him for almost three days the sight of him has my heartbeat speeding up and my palms sweating.

Is it possible he's gotten even sexier than before?

Look away, Tegan . . . look away.

Just as I finally get the strength to look away from Micah, he looks up, his intense gaze locking with mine.

" . . . are you okay? Want me to go for you?"

I hear Parker talking to me, but I can't seem to make sense of much at the moment.

I shake my head, and even though I don't want to look away, I finally force myself to so I can grab the ball out of Parker's hand.

"I'm fine. I'm ready."

"Micah fucking Beck," Kalon hollers. "Well, shit . . . now I know why Tegan lost the ability to throw a ball."

The moment Kalon mentions Micah, Parker stands up straight

and pushes his shoulders out a bit as if to make himself look bigger.

It does nothing to bring him to Micah's level, though, and that knowledge has me reaching for the two cups in front of me left from our game and drinking what little bit of beer is in them.

"I didn't lose my ability to throw a ball," I say pathetically. "It slipped from my hand."

My entire body heats when Micah steps up in my personal space and leans in close to my ear. "Don't let my presence mess up your little date. I know I can be quite a fucking distraction, but I'm only over here to bring you a much-needed beer."

He steps back and holds out a bottle, refusing to pull his eyes away from mine until I take it from him.

"I needed to get away from the bar scene tonight," he says stiffly, before turning to face Kalon. "I was hoping to get some air, but I have a feeling that won't be happening now that I have someone to look out for."

His eyes meet mine as he says the last part, and I can't help but to be pissed off that he's acting as if I'm going to ruin his night by being here.

"Yeah, well you and my brother can piss off, because I don't need either one of you to look out for me like I'm a child." I tilt back the bottle in my hand, taking a quick swig. "So, why don't you run off and have fun so I can enjoy my *date*."

Micah's jaw flexes and his nostrils flare out as if he's the one who's pissed now.

Well, good for him.

How do you like it?

He hasn't been around in days and now he thinks he has the right to try and make me feel like shit for being at the same party as him.

I'm not having it.

"Let's go, Parker." I grab Parker's arm and walk away, before Micah can attempt to intimidate him and make him feel uncomfortable.

But from the stiffness of his arm I guess that he's already both. It's as if he's worried about me touching him, but I don't give Micah the satisfaction of releasing Parker's arm until we're on the other side of the pool and away from him.

"Please ignore Micah. Apparently he's had a bad night and wants to ruin ours too."

"Yeah . . ." Parker nods and takes a step back from me so we're not standing too close. "I'm not sure if that is the case, but I can't risk pissing your brother off and losing the management position I haven't even started yet. Are you sure he's okay with this? He said he was, but . . . I don't know. Did he send Micah here to watch us?"

I shake my head and clench my jaw. Everything was fun until Micah had to come over and ruin things. It's not as if I see Parker as anything more than just a friend, but he's a nice guy and shouldn't have to feel uncomfortable when he's with me.

"I'll take care of my brother, so let's not worry about him. It's not like we're kissing or anything. We're just hanging out and enjoying a nice night."

"That doesn't mean that I don't want to kiss you, Tegan."

His confession has *me* feeling nervous and uncomfortable now. Especially since Micah is clearly watching us, even though he's now talking to some guy.

As pissed off as I am at Micah, the thought of kissing another guy in front of him sends me into panic mode.

Parker steps in close and grips my hip, giving it a light squeeze. "What do you think Micah would do if I did?"

I swallow and let out a nervous laugh. "I'm not sure I want to find out."

"I can show you if you really fucking want me to."

Micah approaching us has Parker and I both taking a step back from each other, and before I can say anything he's pulling me away from Parker and into the house.

Everyone seems to be outside, so it's just the two of us, and everything about this moment is intense as he backs me up against the wall and places his hands above my head.

I suck in a deep breath and stiffen, unsure of what to expect, but the moment he lowers his head so his lips can brush over my ear, I find my entire body relaxing and leaning into him.

"If you want to be kissed then I'll be the one to do it. Do you got that, Tegan?"

I swallow and close my eyes as his lips move across my skin, making their way closer and closer to my mouth as he continues talking.

"My lips . . . my tongue . . . I can place them all over your body if you want." I let out a small moan as he swipes his tongue across my lips, before sucking my bottom one into his mouth with a sexy growl. "But I'll start with your lips because I miss the fucking taste."

Next thing I know his hands are pinning my wrists against the wall and his body presses against mine, showing me just how hard he is.

My entire body shudders with need as he grinds against me and I find myself wanting to reach out for his long hair so I can tug on it like last time.

"Fuck this, Tegan."

The words barely leave his mouth before his lips capture mine, him kissing me hard and needy.

We both grab at each other, losing control as his tongue swirls around mine with perfection. Because he's Micah Beck and every little thing he does with his mouth is flawless.

His hips push me up the wall and I tug his hair harder, causing him to move one of his hands down to wrap around my throat.

The light squeeze he gives it as he deepens the kiss has me moaning out, but louder this time.

We're so lost in each other that we don't even realize someone has joined us in the kitchen until we hear a throat clear.

"Fuck." I push on Micah's chest a few times before he finally backs away from me and runs his hands through his wild hair.

I go to wipe my hand over my mouth at the same time I look over to see Kalon grinning at us. "Aren't you on a date with another guy?"

"Shit," is all I can manage to say as I fix my clothes and fight to catch my breath.

But when I look over at Micah he's got his hands against the wall, his head bowed as he cusses aloud.

We both know we messed up, and apparently he regrets kissing me again.

"I need some air," I breathe out, before turning around and heading for the door as quickly as I can.

I don't even bother trying to find Parker at the moment. I'm not sure I can look at him, because I know that what I did was wrong. I might not look at this as a date, but I know he does and I just *kissed* another guy.

Talk about being completely confused.

It's been a few minutes since I stepped outside and I'm just beginning to calm down and catch my breath when I hear Parker calling out my name.

"Hey, Tegan. I've been looking all over for you. Are you okay? You disappeared with Micah and I didn't see where you guys went."

I nod and force a small smile.

I'm far from okay, but I can't let either of the boys know that.

"I'm good. We're good. He just wanted to talk for a minute about something my brother told him."

Parker smiles and finishes off the drink he must've gotten when I was inside with Micah. "Okay, good. I was worried for a minute that he was trying to steal my date."

I shake my head and swallow. "No. I'm sure Micah can have any girl here that he wants . . ." I look up in just enough time to see some blonde chick cling to him. My heart sinks at the sight. "In fact, he's with some trashy blonde right now."

Parker's smile widens as he looks over in their direction just as the blonde bimbo wraps her arms around his neck and kisses him on the cheek. "That's surprising. As far as I can remember he's already slept with Gwen. Once is usually his limit. It seems to be Micah's way when it comes to women. He's sort of a dirtball if you ask me."

"He's slept with her?" I whisper, mostly to myself. "You really think he's going to sleep with her again?"

"Who knows."

Seeing another girl all over him when he was just kissing me has my temper flaring, especially knowing that she's experienced him in the same way I have. All I can think to do is find another drink before I explode with jealousy.

"Shots. Let's do some shots."

"That sounds really good right about now," I say stiffly.

I force myself to not look Micah's way anymore because the jealousy that I'm feeling is making it hard to act normal. I know he's not mine, but seeing him with another woman is harder than I thought It'd be.

I don't like the feeling one bit. In fact . . . I hate it.

I've never wanted to punch a girl's face in before now.

Focusing my attention on Parker, I down a few shots and try

my best not to wonder what Micah is doing with that other chick right now.

But the more I try not to think about it, the more I end up thinking about it, and I find myself looking around to see if I can find them.

"Are you okay?" Parker asks with a cute little smile. "Have you had too many shots? I can get you some water."

I shake my head and smile. "I'm good, thank you. I'm just a little hot."

"A little hot?" He steps in close and runs his hands over my ass, before squeezing my hips with a small moan. "You've got me hot too. You have no idea how badly I want to kiss you right now."

Before I can refuse his kiss, his hands move down to squeeze my ass and his lips cover mine.

I barely even have time to react before he's yanked away from me and Micah punches him across the jaw, knocking him on his ass.

Parker looks up with surprise as he places his hand over the red area Micah's fist just left. "What the fuck, Man?"

"Touch her again and I'll kill you, Parker."

"She's here with me," Parker yells from the ground. "She's my fucking date. What the hell?"

Everyone around us stares as Micah picks me up and begins escorting me away from the party as if he's in control of me.

"What the hell!" I slap at his back as he walks us around to the front of the house and I don't stop until he sets me down next to his truck. "What did you do that for? Shit, Micah!"

He backs me against the truck. "Because his hands and lips were all fucking over you, that's why," he growls out in anger. "I should've fucking killed him then and there instead of warning him."

Angry, I push him away from me. "What the hell, Micah? I can take care of myself. I was going to stop him, but you didn't even give me enough time to."

"It's kind of hard to ask him to stop when your lips are on his. It looked to me like you were enjoying it."

"He barely kissed me. It lasted for a whole three seconds before you came along and punched him. Fuck, Micah." I grip my hair and begin pacing around the truck. "You punched him really hard. You might've broken his jaw. I can't believe you did that."

"I took it easy on him," he grinds out. "He got lucky. I saw the way his hands were groping all over your ass. You don't do that to a girl who's been drinking."

"Dammit, you should've let me handle him. I may be a little buzzed, but I know what I'm doing."

I stop and look at him as he opens the door to his truck.

"Get inside. I'm taking you home."

"You're unreal," I mutter, while stepping up into his truck. "And an asshole."

The last thing I want to do is face anyone at this party after the scene that Micah just made, which is the only reason I'm agreeing to leave with him right now.

Yes, Parker touched my ass and kissed me, which did make me feel uncomfortable, but Micah could've at least let me handle it before laying his ass out.

Parker is a nice guy and I know he would've stopped if I had asked him to. He just got a little excited and misread the situation between us.

"So I've been told." He slams the truck door shut and walks over to jump inside himself. "But that's part of the reason I turn you on so much. Admit it so we can all move past it."

I ignore him and turn away, but he's right. There's something about the way he takes what he wants and tells it how it is that completely turns me on.

It makes me want to punch him just like he just punched Parker.

And what makes it even worse is that watching him punch someone was somehow hot.

He's got me completely screwed up and the feeling is somewhat addictive . . .

Chapter Sixteen

Tegan

THE TRUCK BARELY COMES TO a stop before I jump out and slam the door shut behind me, feeling as if I'm suffocating.

The moment the fresh air hits me I feel as if I can finally breathe once again. Being inside Micah's truck felt like all the air was being sucked straight from my lungs. It was stifling.

The tension was too much for such a small space.

There were things left unsaid, but neither of us was sure if we should say them or not. At least I know *I* had things to say.

The sound of Micah's door slamming shut has me flinching and I take a deep breath, expecting him to close in behind me so we can argue our way to the house, but instead he takes off around back.

He doesn't even bother looking at me. He just dives into the pool, fully dressed, as if he can't get away from me fast enough.

This makes me angrier than I was before.

Why the hell should he get an escape? This is all his fault to begin with.

First he had the balls to kiss me and then act like it was a mistake, but God forbid someone *else* kisses me and he has the nerve to nearly knock him out.

He's so infuriating that I have half a mind to jump into the pool after him and rip him a new one for being such a pain in my ass.

But the moment his intense gaze meets mine from over the ledge of the pool, I decide it's not worth it and walk away.

Once in my room, I strip down to a t-shirt and panties and pull my laptop out, deciding to respond to my unanswered emails as a distraction. A few people have been asking me when *Still Breathing* is releasing and one person wants to know if I plan on writing a book for the supporting characters from my first release.

There's not nearly enough emails to keep my mind distracted from Micah and how much of an asshole he's being, so I log into *Facebook* and check my notifications.

An hour later, Micah is beginning to fade from my mind when a sponsored ad for *Express* pops us, stating that the grand opening will be in six weeks.

The ad has a photo of Micah sitting on the stage with his guitar, looking drop dead gorgeous.

"Well, apparently the internet is an asshole too."

Grunting, I slam my computer shut and crawl into bed, wishing I was tired enough to fall asleep.

I try everything from listening to an audiobook to binge watching *Shameless,* but it does nothing to stop me from wondering what Micah is doing downstairs.

We've been home for three hours now and I haven't heard a peep from him. It makes me wonder if he took off again and I just didn't hear his truck over the noise from the TV, but when I sit up and look out the window to check, his truck is still parked outside and my brother is pulling up on his motorcycle.

It has my nerves shooting off like crazy, because I have no idea if Parker told him about what went down earlier at the party.

Once he finds out that Micah went mad and punched Parker for kissing me, he's going to either be thankful that Micah was looking out for me or get suspicious that he did it for a whole different reason.

Hell, I'm not even one hundred percent sure of the reason he did it.

He was with another girl just minutes before, allowing her to kiss and hang all over him. I didn't like it, but I didn't go bat-shit crazy on the bitch either.

The memory has me angrily turning off the TV and slamming my head into the pillow beneath me.

I really need to get some sleep before my thoughts drive me crazy. Well, crazier.

It seems I've been crazy since the moment I set my gaze on Micah banging some chick nearly two weeks ago.

My brother takes his time coming upstairs and seems to be too busy taking a phone call to bother stopping by my room like he normally does, trying to make conversation on his way his.

I sigh in relief, realizing that he hasn't heard the news yet.

Maybe that will give me time to talk to Parker tomorrow and apologize for what went down.

I close my eyes and sit here in silence for a while, trying to clear my head and think about how I'm going to explain this all tomorrow.

I'm unsure of how much time has passed, but when I hear footsteps stop in front of my doorway I sit up and open my eyes. Micah is standing there, breathing heavily.

My heart stops mid-beat when he yanks his shirt off and comes at me, not stopping until he's reached the bottom of the bed.

A small moan escapes my throat the moment he crushes his lips against mine and crawls between my legs, pushing me higher up the bed with his hard body.

He kisses me hard and deep, his mouth needy and hungry against mine, taking me as if he has something to prove.

The excitement of that has me grabbing at his bare shoulders and digging my fingers in as he grinds his hips between my thighs, like he's desperate to feel me against him.

The truth is, I'm just as desperate to feel him against me. The way my heart and body are going crazy from beneath him, there's no hiding it.

There's only one thing stopping me from allowing him to take my shirt off when he reaches for it.

"Micah . . . no," I pant. "My brother is in the next room. What if he hears us? We can't . . . you should go."

"He's a heavy sleeper, and besides . . ." He runs his tongue over my earlobe, before sucking it into his mouth with a slight nibble. It sends a chill throughout my body. "I'll swallow your screams with my *mouth*."

I throw my head back and bite my bottom lip as his hand slides down my body, disappearing into the front of my panties. "Micah . . ." I halfway moan. "Shut the . . . shut the door."

"Shutting the door would involve me stopping and that's not something I'm ready to do yet." He slides a finger inside of me as deeply as he can, letting out a sexy little growl as he does. "You can't hide how badly you want me, Tegan. We both know you wanted me to fuck you right there in Kalon's kitchen and we both know I wanted to."

"Dammit, Micah," I moan out as he slides another finger inside, stretching me, before slowly pumping in and out. "We both know we should stop this."

But it feels too damn good.

His growl rumbles against my ear when he speaks. "And we both know we can't. So shut up and let me fuck you like you want me to."

He sits up and grabs my panties, sliding them down my legs, before quickly kicking his jeans off and standing before me, completely naked.

I swallow and grip the sheets as my gaze runs over his perfect body. Every dip of muscle makes me stupid and unable to think straight.

Not to mention his rock-hard dick that I could feel between my legs for a good day or two after he fucked me the last time.

And I have a feeling that this time it'll be rougher, because we both have some anger to let out.

"Lift your arms," he demands.

I do as told and allow him to strip me out of my t-shirt so that I'm lying before him, completely naked too.

"So fucking perfect." The way he tilts his head while running his hand up my bare thigh is almost animalistic. He looks me over as if he's ready to mark me as his.

And there's no way I'd be able to turn him down right now, because the idea of him doing that is oddly arousing and exciting.

He grabs my waist and roughly flips me over to my stomach before he slaps my ass. When I let out a little scream, he's quick to push my head down, burying my face into the pillow to muffle the noise.

I clench the sheets around me and moan into the pillow as he runs his tongue up my right ass cheek. For a moment I allow my body to relax, thinking that he's going to be gentle, but then he bites it so hard that I reach back and slap him across the face on instinct.

"Ouch! What the hell was that for, Micah?" My heart races as he steels his jaw and turns me back around to face the wall again.

I let out a gasp when he fists my hair and pulls my head back so he can speak against my ear. It's so damn hot the way he handles me and it's something I'm not used to. "For going on a date with Parker. I didn't like seeing you with him and I sure as fuck didn't like seeing his mouth and hands on you."

"Well, fuck you, Micah Beck." I turn my head sideways so our lips are brushing when I speak. "I don't belong to you."

"Oh yeah," he whispers, before running his tongue over my lips. "What if I want you to?"

My entire body shudders from his words. The idea of Micah owning me almost causes me to come undone on the spot.

"Then you'll have to show me," I bite out. "But I doubt that's what you really want or else you wouldn't have had some girl all over you tonight. I wanted to rip her hair out."

"I don't fucking want her," he growls against my lips. "I'll show you who I want, but I've got to keep that pretty mouth of yours under control."

With that he slams into me hard and deep, keeping his grip on my hair tight so he can swallow my moan with his mouth.

His body is hard as he moves behind me, his hips pushing me forward with each thrust, but his lips haven't left mine yet.

I'm thankful for that, because I know without a doubt that if it weren't for Micah's mouth on mine my moaning would've woken Alexander by now.

It's so messed up that the person we're both betraying is less than twenty feet down the hall, yet we're so fucked up over each other that we can't stop.

My body moves with his, my nails digging into his strong arms as he continues to hate-fuck me or whatever the hell this is that we're doing right now.

All I know is that it feels too good to care.

After a few more thrusts, he pulls out and flips me over, not wasting any time before spreading my thighs and entering me again with one deep thrust.

The mixture of pain and pleasure has me biting his shoulder as he lowers his face down to my breasts, kissing them as he fucks me.

I pull at his long hair as his mouth brushes over my nipples before he bites the left one and then the right one.

As he moves up to meet my lips again, the sound of my brother's door closing has Micah slapping his hand to my mouth to silence me.

I thought he was going to stop, but doesn't. Holy hell, I lose it when he continues to move in and out of me.

There's something about him risking it all because he's in too deep to stop that has me wanting him more.

With his hand still on my mouth, he leans in close to my ear, talking into it as he keeps his movements slow and steady. "Fucking hell, Tegan. He's going downstairs for something. Just don't make any sounds and he won't look this way."

We stay like this for a few minutes, both of us moving slowly and quietly, being sure not to draw any attention our way.

His slow movements are teasing my body in a way it's never been teased before and I can't handle it.

I need Alexander to go back into his damn room so Micah can go back to fucking me as if I don't matter.

Things are too intimate now and it scares me, because I don't want to take it for more than it's meant to be.

Just two people fucking out our frustrations.

No strings attached.

No emotions.

Just sex.

And he does just that as soon as my brother's door open and closes again.

As if he can't handle the gentle anymore either, he grips my throat and squeezes as he pounds into me over and over again, until I'm moaning out my orgasm and shaking below him.

It's almost as if me getting off was all he needed, because he thrusts inside of me once more before growling out his own release onto my stomach.

All it takes is a few seconds while we catch our breath before reality hits and I can see panic set in his eyes.

"Shit," he growls. "I can't think straight when I'm around you. That's why I've been staying the fuck away. But seeing you with Parker tonight had me losing my shit. I've been going crazy ever since I walked into the party to see you two having fun."

"I didn't really think you'd care, Micah. From what *everyone* has told me, you sleep with a girl once and never give her the time of day again. You haven't been around in days so I . . ."

"Because I *have* to stay away, Tegan. It's not because I want to." He sounds angry now. "You think I really want to stay away from you? Fuck no."

"I don't want you to," I admit. "But what we just did . . ." I stop to catch my breath once more. "We could've gotten caught and that wasn't even enough to make us stop. We came so close, Micah. Too close. I don't know what to do anymore. I'm so damn confused with you around."

I watch as he jumps to his feet and slips back into his jeans, before reaching for his shirt. His body looks stiff as he presses his hands against the wall to think for a second. "Fuck. I don't know what the hell is wrong with me. It was a dick move for me to come to your room and make the situation more difficult than it already was."

"Maybe you should leave then." An ache fills my chest the moment the words leave my mouth, but with the way I'm feeling right now I think it's best that I get some space when it comes to Micah.

I'm so damn confused, and him being here right now is doing nothing to help me think.

I seriously would've died if Alexander decided to look into my room to find Micah on top of me when he walked by to go downstairs.

"Yeah," he says stiffly, while walking over to wipe my stomach clean with his shirt. "I think that's best." He looks at me for a moment, the struggle of leaving obvious in his body language, before he turns around and exits the room.

The moment I'm alone I quickly get dressed and try like hell to convince myself that I'm okay with kicking Micah out of my room.

But the knot in my stomach and the emptiness that takes over now that he's back downstairs tells me otherwise.

I don't want Micah to leave and I don't want just one or two 'anything goes' nights with no strings attached.

I'm falling for Micah Beck and I'm not sure how long I can hide the way I truly feel . . .

Chapter Seventeen

Micah

I'M FURIOUS WITH MYSELF OVER the fact that I wasn't able to stop myself from fucking Tegan, even with the thought of my best friend possibly catching us. He would've beat my ass for touching his sister after he warned me not to.

Stopping wasn't an option for me at the time, because after seeing Parker place his lips where mine had just been, all I could think about was being inside her again.

I wanted her to *feel* me; wanted to be able to make her *feel* something that son of a bitch couldn't tonight.

She might've told me that she planned on stopping him from kissing her, but I couldn't give her the time she needed for that earlier, because the moment I saw his lips on hers, I saw red.

Who the hell was he to kiss her not even five minutes after my lips tasted and owned hers?

He didn't know...

"Shit, I need to think rationally."

I angrily toss my dirty shirt into the bathroom and sit on the edge of my bed, my head reeling.

I've never been overprotective and territorial over a woman before. Not to mention that I've never wanted to be with a woman more than once.

One night has always been my limit, because anything more and things get complicated. Feelings grow and attachments form and I just went and did that with Tegan.

It pisses me off that things have changed for the one person I was never supposed to touch in the first place.

My hands grip my hair as I try to figure out where to go from here. Do I pack up all my shit and leave before I'm able to fuck things up even more?

If I do that then Alexander will know I'm leaving for a reason, and I can't have him angry with both of us.

It's my fault that we're in this situation to begin with.

I'm screwing with family by letting my heart win over my damn head, but . . . I'm addicted.

To her.

To her taste.

To the way she wants to get to know me.

To the way she feels beneath my body.

I'm completely fucking strung.

Get some air. You just need some air, Micah.

I stand and walk over to the dresser, pulling out a pair of shorts to run in.

I can't sit here knowing that she's upstairs alone in her bed, covered with my scent.

Hell, I didn't even use a condom. I'm everywhere on her.

Once I hit the beach I run for hours.

Strung   171

I run until my muscles and chest aches.

It doesn't even matter that I'm supposed to be at *Vortex* in less than six hours. I know I won't be getting any sleep tonight.

♪ ♩ ♪ ♩

I MANAGED TO GO THE entire day yesterday keeping my distance from Tegan. It makes me feel like shit that I have to run away from her every time we have sex. I hate the space.

But it's the only way I can stop it from happening again.

It's the best thing for both of us, because every time we see each other we end up more drawn to each other than before.

After my shift at *Vortex* I left and came straight here to *Express* to work on putting together the tables that came in yesterday morning.

I was only able to afford six tables for now, but it's a start.

I'm in the middle of piecing together the third one when Sebastian walks through the door sporting an annoying grin.

"Hey, big guy. I figured you'd be here when I didn't find you at *Vortex*." He takes a seat at one of the finished tables. "You're always at one or the other. Shit, your life makes me sad. All work and no play. Well, outside of the bedroom at least. I've seen the girls you've left *Vortex* with and damn . . ."

I grunt and look over at him when his words trail off. "What the hell do you want? If you're not here to help then you can see your way out. I'm not in the mood for any shit today, and trust me, seeing your grinning face is almost enough to make me snap already."

I flip the finished table up to its legs, before moving on to the next table.

"You've been extra pissy and demanding lately. Have anything to do with that chick Tegan who told me you weren't at *Vortex* about twenty minutes ago? She was fucking slamming hot. Too bad she was with that pretty boy. What's his name again . . . shit . . ."

"Parker," I say stiffly.

He snaps his fingers. "Yes. That's the dude's name."

His words have me gripping the table in front of me. She's at *Vortex* right now with that fucker?

Why does it piss me off that not only is she there with Parker, but also that she decided to wait until I left to go there?

It shouldn't, but it does.

"I don't know what the hell makes you think it has anything to do with a girl," I bite out, trying my hardest not to look as if I'm ready to kill someone. When I look up he's still grinning like he can see right through me. I'm not going to entertain how I'm feeling right now. "Alright, what do you really want? I've got work to do and you're slowing me down."

"My parents are back." The smile on his face is no longer present. "They've been sauced since the moment they stepped through the door last night and my dad is extremely angry at life like usual. Mind if I stay at your place tonight and maybe even tomorrow?"

I shake my head and release a frustrated breath. I can't even begin to deal with his parents right now; not when all I can think about is getting to Tegan. "I don't mind." I reach into my pocket and toss him the key to my apartment. "Keep the door unlocked for me."

He stands and holds up the key. "Got it, Man. I've gotta go meet my friends."

"Don't let any of those little assholes into my apartment, got it?"

"I know the rules," he mutters. "You don't have to remind me every time. I'm not going to forget, shit."

"Hey, I've gotta make sure, because I don't want to have to

kick the shit out of some underage kid's ass for stealing my shit or touching something that doesn't belong to them. Just keep your friends out and we're good."

"Yeah, yeah. I'll see you later. They're waiting on me."

Once he leaves I spend the next thirty minutes finishing up the tables, before locking up and heading out.

I get into my truck with my mind set on going to my apartment and calling it a night, but I find myself pulling up at *Vortex* instead.

It's the last place I should be, but I can't help wondering if Tegan is still here. From the looks of the parking lot Parker is already gone, but that doesn't mean she is too.

It's a Thursday so it's pretty quiet, which would make it ideal for her to work on her book out back without too many interruptions.

I walk inside and Gavin nods at me from behind the bar. "What are you doing back, Boss?"

Ignoring him, I make my way around him and pour myself a shot, slamming it back. "I needed a drink and I don't have my place stocked up yet. Where's Alexander?"

He nods toward the stairs. "In his office with some chick. They've been up there for a while. Might want to knock first if you're headed up."

"I'm not." I reach into the cooler for two beers and pop the tops off. "Colby still out back?"

"Yes, sir . . . shit. I didn't mean to call you sir."

"Relax, Gavin." I grip his shoulder. "You act like I'm going to rip your head off or some shit. Just don't call me sir again and all is good."

He nods. "Okay, Micah. Thanks."

Apparently, I really scared the shit out of this kid when he first arrived, because he's been tense around me ever since.

I'm sure he'll be happy to know that soon enough someone like Parker will be his boss instead of an asshole like me.

When I step out back, I see Colby hanging around Tegan's table, but as soon as he sees me watching him he says something to her and walks over to join me.

"So . . . Parker came in a little while ago for some training and his face was all fucked up." He smirks. "Know anything about that?"

I take a swig of beer. "Is that what you heard?"

He laughs and steps behind the bar. "Nope. He said he got into a drunken fight the other night with some guy he didn't know."

"Is that right?" I look straight ahead, keeping my gaze on Tegan as she types away on her computer. "Weird. He must've touched something that didn't belong to him," I say stiffly.

Tegan looks up from her computer, her eyes locking on mine from across the patio.

My heart skips a beat as she shifts in her seat. I make her nervous just by being here.

Fuck, I like that I can make her nervous.

It means I affect her.

I just don't know if it's a good or bad thing.

"Bring us two more beers in about ten minutes."

Colby nods. "Will do, Man."

I make my way toward Tegan, not breaking eye contact with her until she closes her laptop and looks away. She's frustrated that I'm here.

Well, I'm just as frustrated at me being here too.

"How's your book coming along?" I ask, while taking the seat across from her and setting a beer down in front of her. "You look like you could use one of these."

She releases a long breath and reaches for the bottle. "Well, I have about six more chapters to write and they need to be done in enough time that I can send it to my editor in two weeks." She pauses to bring the bottle to her lips. "I was hoping to get some inspiration by coming here, but so far it's been a shit night."

I watch as she tilts the bottle back and all I can think about is how sexy her lips look. If it weren't for Alexander being able to see our every move from where we're sitting, I'd remove that bottle from her lips and run my tongue along them, getting another taste.

My cock twitches at the thought.

I clear my throat and tilt my bottle back, slamming half of it in one drink.

"Yeah, well maybe you're at the wrong place for inspiration. Especially since Parker was hanging around."

She huffs and takes another drink. "It was a lot fun explaining to Parker why someone who I'm *not* dating punched him in the face for kissing me. Luckily, he dropped the subject after I apologized to him and explained that you thought he was making me uncomfortable when he grabbed my ass so you were only trying to protect me like my brother asked."

"Well, wasn't he?" I ask. "If not . . ." I take a quick swig, needing a second to calm down. "Then I'll be sure not to disrupt your next date."

"I told him I wasn't looking for a boyfriend, so don't worry, there won't be any more *dates* for you to ruin."

"Was that the truth," I ask, leaning in close. So close that my breath hits her neck as I speak.

"What?" She swallows and her eyes close as I risk moving in closer until my lips are brushing her ear.

"That you're not looking for a boyfriend?"

"Well . . . um . . ." She seems lost for words, as if she doesn't know how to answer my question. "I can't think with you so close and you know it."

"And I love it too . . . the affect I have on you that no one else seems to."

She opens her mouth to speak, but stops when Colby sets two fresh beers down in front of us.

When I look up at him he shrugs and begins backing away. "I don't know shit and I'm not saying shit, but if Alexander watches those cameras half as hard as you do then I'd be careful. It looked like you two were kissing from where I was standing. Just saying . . ."

I flex my jaw as he walks away.

"You know what . . . I should go." Tegan stands and grabs her computer, packing it into a carrying case. "I can't work here and–"

"Come on." I stand and reach into my pocket, tossing down some cash for Colby. "I'll give you a ride."

"I don't need one," she says quickly. "Jamie is coming soon."

"Well text her and tell her not to." I place my hand on her hip and give it a squeeze as I move in close behind her. "You're not going home anyway."

I can hear her breathing quicken from my closeness, and it causes my lips to curl up into a cocky grin, loving the way her body reacts to mine.

"What about my brother?"

"Go to my truck and I'll talk to him if he asks any questions."

I expect her to fight me further on this, but instead she just nods and walks away, disappearing inside.

Once she's out of sight I stand here for a moment, trying to talk myself out of what I have planned, but I can't.

"Dammit."

I open the door and step inside to see Alexander talking to Gavin, but he looks my way just as I'm walking up to him.

"Are you giving my sister a ride home? I just saw her walk outside as I was coming downstairs."

"Yeah." It's not a lie. Just not the whole truth. "I'd rather she gets one from me than some stranger driving a shitty taxi."

"I'm trusting you'll keep her safe for me." His voice deepens as he pours himself a shot. "I saw Parker's face earlier and I'm going to assume that was your handy-work. Don't let me find out that it was for a reason other than you keeping an eye on her for me."

He watches me with narrowed eyes, while slamming back his shot.

"I'll keep her safe," is all I say, because if I say anything else then it'll be a lie. Me punching Parker had nothing to do with me being a lookout for him and everything to do with me being selfish.

"You're my brother, so I'm going to trust you. Don't let me down or I'll kill you."

I steel my jaw as he slaps my back and walks away.

He's going to kill me no matter what, because even if he doesn't find out today, tomorrow, or next week, the truth always comes out eventually.

And the truth is that I'm a piece of shit friend who's too damn selfish to protect his sister from the one person she should be protected from: me.

Chapter Eighteen

Tegan

WHEN I REALIZE WE'RE HEADED to *Express*, I can't help the smile that spreads across my face.

It's unstoppable.

Even though Micah has a tough exterior, I love that he's got a softer side he occasionally slips and lets show.

The only problem with that is the way it makes me feel whenever he does. It's hard to explain even to myself, and I've honestly given up on trying.

"Are we here so I can write?"

He nods and parks the truck, smiling with satisfaction as he pulls the keys from the ignition. "You seemed really inspired the last time you were here so I thought it would help. Plus, I'm not ready to go home yet. Not without seeing you for longer than ten damn minutes."

Learning that he wants to spend time with me has butterflies fluttering around my stomach as he reaches for my laptop and jumps out of the truck.

He's probably been working all day and night between *Vortex* and setting things up here, yet he took the time to bring me here so that I could write and we could spend some time together.

I'm not sure what to do with that, so I guess all I can do is go with the flow and try not to look too far into it.

My heart flutters with excitement when he opens the door and helps me down to my feet. Every time he touches me it's like my heart doesn't know whether to stop or skip a beat.

"We'll stay here for as long you need. I don't have anywhere to be. Just as long as I have you back before your brother gets home. He's already threatened to kill me once tonight. I don't need it actually happening."

"Wait. What?"

"Don't worry about it. Come on."

He places his hand on the small of my back and guides me to the door, unlocking it, and opening it for me to step inside first.

It's dark, so I stand in place as he flips on a few lights for us.

"Get your desk set up and I'll see if I have any beer left."

"You have more tables set up," I point out, while looking around. "It's looking great in here, Micah."

"Thanks. The tables came in the other day. I have about four more to order before the grand opening, but other than that and some decorating, this place is pretty close to being done." He walks toward the bar as I take a seat at the same table I sat at the last time I wrote and wait for my laptop to boot up.

A few seconds later he hands me a beer from over my shoulder and makes his way to the stage to grab his guitar and take a seat on the stool.

"We're doing this again?" I ask with a hopeful smile. "You

play while I write?"

"We're here for you, so yes."

Just like the last time he played music for me the words begin to flow, and before I know it I've written nearly three thousand words.

I've only got four, maybe five chapters left to write and I could probably pull it off right here tonight if he continues to play for me.

I likely could've pulled most of it off by now to be honest, if it weren't for me struggling to keep my eyes off Micah as he plays.

I find myself looking up at the stage every ten minutes or so, because it's impossible not to look at him with his guitar.

It's the sexiest thing I've ever seen.

"Eyes on the words . . . not my handsome face," he says with a smirk. "Do I need to put a paper bag over my head so you won't look at me?"

"Ha. Ha. Aren't we being cocky again." I pull my eyes away from Micah and look back down at the computer screen, fighting not to look back up at him. Especially since I know he's watching me right now as he plays. "Just keep playing . . ."

"You asked for it."

He stops playing the current tune and switches into a different song entirely.

I'm sitting over here trying to catch my breath, because I recognize the song the second the first lyric leaves his mouth.

I Found by Amber Run.

He's actually playing Amber Run. The slowed down acoustic version that I haven't been able to stop listening to for weeks.

That's why he asked me who my favorite band was, and the fact that he's playing them even though as of last week he hadn't heard of them, has my emotions all over the place.

I can't pull my eyes away from him as he plays and I find myself shutting my laptop, because there's no way I can *not* watch him.

Why does his voice have to be so beautiful and intoxicating?

Without even meaning to I close my eyes and get lost in his voice, knowing that I'll be forever screwed after this.

I'm drawn to him more now than ever and it's up to me to stay strong.

I have a feeling it's going to be a little harder after this.

By the end of the song my heart is beating so hard that I can practically feel it about to burst from my chest.

"You learned that song for me?"

He sets his guitar down by his feet and runs his hand through his hair, but doesn't say anything. He just looks at me, his gaze so intense that goose bumps cover my body.

"I don't know what to say right now. That . . . that was amazing. Thank you." I grab the beer in front of me and take a small drink. My throat suddenly feels dry and I feel hot. Extremely hot. "Can you play any more of their songs?"

He nods and reaches for his guitar again.

I'm shocked into silence when he begins playing another one of their songs.

What is Micah doing to me?

He's making me fall for him even more. That's what he's doing, whether he's trying to or not.

We're both silent after he plays the last song and he heads straight for the bar to grab two more beers, before making his way over to the table I'm at.

He looks around the room before he speaks.

"I've got to place my first liquor order next week. It's been a long journey but it's something I've wanted since I was eighteen. I used to sneak into bars and watch the musicians play. I remember imagining myself doing that someday and it brought me this peace I've never felt before." He pauses to take a drink, his eyes deepening as he stares up at the stage. "And since I never really felt as if I had a place of my own growing up, I decided then and there that I'd do what they were doing, except I'd do it at a place I owned. A place I can call my own."

I grab the bottle that he holds out for me and take a quick drink, while looking up at him. He's still looking at the stage, so I take this moment to admire him.

Micah Beck truly is a beautiful man.

His beauty has my heart doing flips inside my chest. I can't stop replaying his lips on mine, my hands in his long hair as our sweaty bodies move together.

I wasn't lying when I said I can't think straight around him.

His presence makes it impossible to think about anything other than him.

"You should be really proud. I know you haven't had things easy and what you've done here is amazing."

He looks down at me, surprised. "Your brother told you?"

I nod. "He told me about your mom and the foster homes you grew up in. He said you've been on your own since a young age."

His jaw tightens as if the memory upsets him. "Yeah . . ." He takes a quick swig of his beer as if he needs it. "It wasn't the best childhood, thanks to my mother running off. I had to steal to survive sometimes and I've seen the inside of juvie more times than I wish I would've, but that's why I'm working so hard for everything I have now."

I hate that he was abandoned and hurt by the one person who was supposed to love him the most. I hate that he had to struggle just to survive.

I stand up and cup his face, wanting him to look at me. "You're beautiful . . ." The words slip out of my mouth before I can stop them.

His eyes lock with mine and I can tell that he's fighting some kind of battle inside. "I don't know about that. I've been pretty ugly for a long time. I'm a selfish son of a bitch."

"Do you really believe that?" I question. "Look what you've been doing for Sebastian. Look what you've done for my brother and look what you're doing for me right now."

I watch his throat as he swallows.

"You saw me struggling and brought me to the one place you knew would help me. You didn't have to do that, but you did. Then the songs . . ." I lean in close, brushing my lips over his. "You learned them for me. That's pretty damn beautiful."

He closes his eyes and leans in closer, his heavy breath warming my lips. "You make me want to be better than the man I've been lately. It's fucked up the way I want you for more than just a one-night stand, when that's all I've ever wanted from a woman before, yet you're the one woman I can't keep or it'll ruin the one relationship that's ever meant anything to me. I hate it," he breathes. "I just want to make you mine, but I'm not good enough for you, Tegan."

I close my eyes when his hands tangle into the back of my hair and I find myself fighting to catch my breath. "You want me?" I question. "Because if that's what you're telling me, Micah . . . then I need you to kiss—"

His lips crush mine, cutting my words off, and before I know it he's grabbing my thighs and lifting me up.

His strong hands squeeze my thighs as we kiss, sending heat all throughout my body.

Just as I think he's going to take things further, he pulls away from the kiss and places his forehead to mine. "Let's get out of here, okay?"

I nod as he kisses my forehead and sets me back down to my

feet.

When we arrive at my brother's house, I begin making my way to the front of the house, expecting us to go our separate ways, but his grip on my hip stops me.

"Where are you going?" he whispers in my ear. "I told you I want to spend time with you."

I lean my head back as he brushes his lips over my neck. "I thought we were calling it a night. My brother will be home in less than an hour."

"No," he says softly. "We'll call it a night once you get tired of me. Are you tired of me yet?"

I shake my head.

"Good." He pulls the strap of my laptop bag down my shoulder and sets it down into the grass beside us, before turning me around to face him. "I put on a performance for you and now it's time to cool off. You know how I work."

He catches me off guard when he picks me up and begins running toward the pool. "Micah!" I laugh and hold onto his back. "What are you doing? Slow down!"

He ignores me, and before I know it I'm sinking to the bottom of the pool in his arms.

When he grabs my face under the water and kisses me, I swear my heart stops. This moment, this kiss, feels different than the rest.

Our lips are still touching when we resurface and his hands gently wrap into my hair and tug, causing my mouth to part for him.

"I can't get enough of you, Tegan." The way his lips move against mine when he speaks has me closing my eyes and moaning. Oh, how I love his mouth. "I know I'm not supposed to want you, but fuck, I do. More than I've wanted anyone before. I haven't been able to show you that, but I want you to *know* that."

I wrap my legs tighter around his waist as I grab onto his

hair and look him in the eyes. "I want you too, Micah. I came here thinking that all I'd ever want from you was one night of unattached sex, just to get you out of my system, but every time I'm around you I only seem to want you more and more. I don't know what to do. Even a date with Parker wasn't enough to make me stop wanting you."

He moves his hands down to cup my face and run his thumbs over my cheekbones. The mention of Parker has his jaw flexing, but I can see him trying to hold back his anger. "I never want to see you go on another fucking date with Parker or any other guy for that matter. You have no idea how hard it was to not lose my shit in front of Alexander the moment I realized *you* were Parker's date. You're mine." He sucks my bottom lip into his mouth, before releasing it with a growl. "No one else gets to taste your lips or touch you where I do. Got it?"

I nod and kiss him, wanting him to see that he's the only one I want. I'm so sick of pretending that I don't, and now that I know how he feels about me, I know there's no fighting it anymore.

"Tell me you're mine?" he demands against my lips. "I want to hear you say it, Tegan. Say it."

"I'm yours, Micah. I think I have been since the day I arrived."

"Fuck," he says, sounding breathless. "I love hearing those words."

His lips meet mine again and the way he's holding me truly makes me feel as if I'm his.

But as badly as I want this to mean that things will be easy and we can be with each other, I know that's far from the truth.

Breaking things to Alexander won't be easy, and I'm afraid that once he finds out it'll either be the end of them or the end of us.

I'm not sure I could handle either of those scenarios . . .

Micah

TEGAN WENT UPSTAIRS TO HER bedroom less than two hours ago and I'm already feeling the loss of her in my damn arms.

As much as I wanted her to stay downstairs with me, we were worried that Alexander would check for her in her room to make sure she was there once he gets home.

And the last thing we need is him finding out any other way than us telling him ourselves. Tegan decided that it'd be best to wait and tell him after *Express* is open and I'm gone, that way if he wants to kill me for a while he at least won't have to see me on the daily.

He's going to need some time away from me to get used to the idea and I get that. I get why Tegan wants to wait until then and as much as I hate keeping this from my friend, I want to respect Tegan and her wishes at the same time.

"Shit." Unable to fall asleep, I sit up and run my hands through my hair in frustration. I'm half-tempted to sneak into Tegan's room and sleep in her bed. "Fuck it."

I stand up and just as I go to take a step, Tegan appears in the doorway of my room.

She looks just as tired and frustrated as I feel.

"I couldn't sleep," she says, looking me over in my boxer briefs. "All I can think about is being close to you."

"Come here, baby." I grab her hand and pull her to me. My heart skips a beat the moment she melts into my arms as if that's where she's meant to be. "I want nothing more than for you to be close to me. You have no fucking idea."

I stand here and hold her for a while, this peace and warmth filling me that I've never experienced before. That's when I know there's no way in hell I'll be letting her sleep alone anymore.

I can't.

Not now that I know how she feels about me.

"Come on." I climb into my bed, pulling her down with me, under the covers. "We just have to wake up before your brother does."

She snuggles into my arms, wrapping her legs around mine as she buries her face into my chest. "Okay," she says on a yawn. "Now be quiet and hold me. It feels so good in your arms . . ."

I hold her tighter, my heart pounding as I listen to her breathing change. She's been in my arms for less than a minute and she's already asleep.

Why do I suddenly feel so damn soft and mushy around her?

In this moment, with her in my arms, I feel as if I'd do anything in the world for her and I've barely even known her for two weeks.

I've always heard that when you fall, you fall hard and fast, but before now I didn't believe that shit to be true.

Tegan Tyler has turned my entire world upside down without even trying, and now everything I've known for the last five years will come crashing down around me.

The first person I've ever truly trusted will never trust me again.

That only means I have to do everything in my power to prove that I'll never hurt Tegan, and I'm willing to do anything it takes . . .

Chapter Nineteen

Micah

*I*T'S BEEN TWO DAYS SINCE I told Tegan she was mine and she's snuck into my room every night to sleep in my bed since. After knowing what it feels like to wake up with her in my arms, I honestly can't imagine sleeping without her beside me.

We haven't even had sex since she's been in my bed, which makes it mean even more to me. We've talked and laughed and have gotten to know each other, with our bodies tangled together in the darkness of the basement.

It's something I never really saw myself doing and I can't see myself ever wanting to do it with anyone else.

She makes me feel different. She makes me feel that happiness truly does exist if you let it find you.

I've gone most of my life thinking that true happiness was bullshit. That everyone you meet will eventually leave you crushed and alone. When the one person who was *meant* to love you can't even manage to stick around, then why believe that anyone else will?

It's why I've kept my heart guarded. Because the memory of losing the one person I loved most in the world has haunted me since I was eight.

I never wanted to feel that helpless again, and I never wanted to be *enough* to anyone else to make them feel that way either.

But it's too late when it comes to Tegan.

I can't lose her. Not now.

We're already in too deep.

I've completely fallen for her and from the way she's been spending her time at *Express* with me for the last two nights, I know she's completely fallen for me too.

Being with her every chance that I get has become the norm for me and I honestly can't see things being any other way now.

It's close to time for me to put on my last performance here at *Vortex,* and that has all these mixed emotions running through me and shit.

I'm happy that I'll be opening my own place in a little over four weeks, yet I feel like I'm letting Alexander down in some way, because my performances have helped bring in a lot of his business over the years.

"I've been thinking a lot over the last few weeks." Alexander looks up from his desk, nudging me on. "What if I still perform here once a month?"

He smiles and tosses a stack of papers into a drawer. "Then I'd be happy as hell to have you, brother. You're always welcome here and you know it."

I nod and set my phone down. Sebastian just texted me to ask if he could come watch my last performance. I agreed as long as he sits with Tegan so she can watch his ass.

"The kid is coming to watch my show tonight. Think Tegan

would mind keeping an eye on him?" I ask him, as if I'm not planning on asking her myself. But Alexander has been less suspicious about his sister and I since I've been staying back at his place, and I want to keep it that way for as long as possible.

"I'll ask her." He looks up at the time. "She should be here with Jamie soon. I'm sure between the two of them they can keep him locked down at their table."

"Great." I stand up and slap his desk. "I'm going to check on the guys before I set up."

"Parker is coming in tonight," he says without looking up. "I wanted you to be able to focus on your last performance without the stress of running the bar while I'm stuck in my office for the first half."

The mention of Parker has my blood boiling, because I still haven't been able to stop picturing his lips on Tegan's. I'm a jealous son of a bitch when it comes to her.

"I've never had a problem with doing it before," I say stiffly.

He looks up at me. "You have a problem with Parker being around?"

"Nope," I say, grabbing for the energy drink in front of me and squeezing it. "I'll be out back."

Before he has a chance to say anything I exit his office and walk as far away as possible, before throwing my fist into the wall.

He may be getting my job once I'm gone, but there's no way in hell I'm allowing him to get my girl.

Once I compose myself, I make my way through the crowd, getting stopped by almost every girl I pass on the way. They all seem to know that it's my last performance and want a way to keep in contact with me.

Not a fucking chance.

By the time I finally manage to make it out back to setup the small stage, Tegan and Jamie are walking up from the beach.

Happiness fills me when her eyes meet mine, and she mouths *I've missed you*.

I setup as quickly as possible and discreetly get Tegan's attention again, motioning for her to meet me inside in the bathroom hallway.

Everyone is too busy trying to get drinks and find tables close to the stage right now, so I figured this will be the only place we can get a few moments alone.

As soon as she comes down the hallway I grab her by the waist and pull her to me, placing my forehead to hers. "You have no idea how hard it's been not being able to see you since this afternoon."

She smiles and wraps her arms around my neck. "It's only been like seven hours."

"Exactly." I move my hands up to cup her face, before I brush my lips over hers, causing her to release a small moan. "Seven hours is too long to not be able to taste you, Tegan."

She swallows. "Then taste me."

An animalistic growl sounds in my throat the moment our lips touch, and it takes all my strength not to make love to her right here in the hallway.

I haven't had a chance to show her that I can be gentle when I want to be, because I've been too focused on showing her that my attraction for her isn't purely physical.

It's so much more.

She's so much more.

"I still can't get over how weak in the knees I get when you kiss me," she whispers against my lips. "You make me weak, Micah."

"I hope that's not a bad thing." I kiss her again, but deeper this time, which has us both gripping each other as if we can't get enough. "Because I can't fucking stop."

"It's good," she says with a smile. "So good."

"Good." I smile against her lips. "I bet the hero in your book makes the heroine just as weak with his mouth too. Since you wrote him after me and all."

She laughs and slaps my chest. "You're still so full of yourself."

"Yeah, but now you have been too . . ." I lean in to whisper in her ear. "Twice."

"Really, Micah–"

I shut her up with my mouth, because it always seems to be the best way to quiet her when I decide to mess with her.

But I can't resist pushing her with my cocky mouth still, because even though she acted as if it annoyed her when we first met, I know it's what made her want me to begin with.

She's still wrapped up in my arms, our mouths locked on each other's when the sound of someone clearing their throat has Tegan pulling away from the kiss.

But seeing that it's Parker I refuse to release her from my arms until he's already past us, and disappearing into the bathroom.

"What the hell, Micah?" Tegan wiggles her way out of my arms and quickly fixes her hair in a panic. "Do you want him telling my brother about us?"

"No . . . shit," I mutter. "But I took one look at the asshole eying you over and I wanted him to see that we're together. I'll talk to him." I rub my hands over her arms to calm her down. "Can you go find Sebastian and make sure he sits with you and Jamie?"

"Micah . . . don't—"

"Don't worry, I'm not going to punch the guy. I'm just going to have a little talk with him."

I place a quick kiss on her lips and turn around to walk away before she can say anything else to stop me.

I guess old habits die hard and the asshole in me just came

out again. I might've messed everything up, but if Parker doesn't want to feel my wrath then I suggest he listen to what the hell I have to say.

I'll tell him the truth, and if that isn't enough to stop the guy from opening his mouth then I guess my fist will.

I just hope for Tegan's sake that it doesn't come down to that . . .

Chapter Twenty

Tegan

MY HEART IS STILL RACING from me and Micah getting caught making out just a few moments ago. I feel sick at the idea that Parker might run off and tell Alexander. I don't want him to find out that way.

I take a seat at the table with Jamie and sit here, trying to make sense of everything as she side-eyes me.

"Everything okay?" She leans in to touch the back of her hand to my forehead. "You look pale all of a sudden. What the hell happened in there?"

"Nothing," I say, shaking her hand off my forehead. "Cool it. I'm fine."

"Oh, bullshit, honey," she huffs. "Tell me now before I go inside and find Micah to ask him my damn self."

I shift in my seat and wave Sebastian over when I see him emerge from the crowd, hoping he'll be a good excuse to change the subject. "Not now. We have company. I'll tell you all about it once we leave. I promise. But I can't right now."

"When we leave?" she asks quickly and sits back in her seat, looking as if she's about to lose it. "You know I can't wait until we–"

"You're with us, Sebastian," I say, cutting her off and giving her a look to tell her to shut the hell up. The last thing I need is another person asking questions about Micah and I, and if this woman doesn't shut her mouth that's exactly what's going to happen. "Looks like we're on Sebastian duty tonight, so pick a seat or we'll all get in trouble."

The kid laughs and pulls out a chair to join us. "What happens if I get into trouble? Do one of you fine ladies tackle me until I behave? Because that's a kind of trouble I don't mind being in."

Jamie and I both laugh, but I do mostly because the kid reminds me of Micah. "I think you've been spending a bit too much time with Micah."

He shrugs and takes a sip of his soda, looking up at the stage and then around him as if he's preparing for something. "Where is the big guy? I'm so used to him dragging me out that it's a little hard to enjoy this rare moment without flinching."

"There he is," Jamie says with a huge smile. "Oh my goodness is he looking finer than usual or is it just me?"

I swallow nervously as I watch Micah step through the crowd alone. It has me worried that he got into another fight with Parker and left him in the bathroom bloodied.

That is, until Parker steps out just a few seconds behind him and makes his way to the bar.

His face doesn't look any more bruised than it was a few moments ago, so I'm going to take that as a good thing.

At least I hope.

"You two are into that whole long-hair look, huh?" Sebastian runs a hand through his short, blonde hair. "Maybe I will grow it out after all. It'll look pretty badass with my surfboard. What do you ladies think?"

"Uh, hell yeah." Jamie turns her attention from Micah to Sebastian. "How old are you again, kid? Are you legal?"

"Eighteen," he says with a lift of his brow.

My eyes widen at Jamie when she smiles. "He's seventeen, Jamie. Don't even think about it."

"Only for three more months." He runs a hand through his hair again and winks at Jamie. "You're only what . . . two years older, maybe? Three months ain't shit to wait. Just saying."

"Actually, she's three years older. Almost four, so calm it down, playboy. I'm sure there's plenty of girls your age around."

"Oh, please, ladies. Those girls can't handle Sabastian Masters. I need a *woman*."

Jamie and I both laugh at the same time, which has Sebastian throwing his arms up and slapping them to his somewhat muscular chest. "Well, it's true. Don't laugh until you go for a test ride." He lifts his brows at Jamie. "Sup, girl?"

"Ignore him." Micah says from over my shoulder.

The moment he moves around so I can get a better look at him my stomach twists into tiny knots. I want to ask him what he said to Parker, but I can't with these two around and it's driving me crazy.

Micah places a fresh soda in front of Sebastian, before setting two beers down for Jamie and me. "If you ladies have any issues with the kid let me know and I'll stop my show to drag him out of here myself."

"Oh, come on, Dude!" Seb leans back in his seat and places his hands behind his head, attempting to look cool. "The chicks are digging me, so don't even worry. Just run along to the stage and play us some music to better set the mood."

Micah flexes his jaw and flicks Sebastian on the forehead. Then he leans in close and looks him in the eyes. "Just sit there and keep your eyes on the stage unless you want to lose them."

Sebastian grunts and rubs his forehead. "Don't hate, big guy."

When Micah pulls his eyes away from Sebastian they meet mine, just long enough for him to nod as if to tell me that his conversation with Parker went well.

I release a breath and place my hand over my chest in relief, watching as he walks up to take his place on the stage.

Not even five seconds after he grabs his guitar and takes a seat on the stool my phone goes off in my back pocket. I reach for it to see a new message from Whitney.

I've been so wrapped up in Micah that I've almost forgotten about Whitney and my parents. I haven't talked to them in days and now I'm realizing that I've shut them out without meaning to. I feel like total shit.

Micah glances up at me while he tunes his guitar, but before I can get too wrapped up in him and what's to come, I open my best friend's message and read it.

My heart sinks as I read the words.

Whitney: I can't believe you've been gone for over two weeks and we've only talked once. Too busy for your bestie?

Tegan: I'm a crap friend and I'm sooooooooooo sorry. There's no excuse and I promise I'll call you after Micah's performance. Please don't hate me.

Whitney: Soo . . . Micah is the hottie's name? And you better call me. You still have like ten more weeks before you come back home and I miss you.

Tegan: I will. I promise, and I miss you too. XOXO

The mention of going back home has me looking up at the stage, trying to figure out how I'm going to leave Micah at the end of summer.

The thought hasn't even crossed my mind over the last two weeks because I've been too worried about keeping things between us a secret.

I promised my parents I wouldn't move yet, but Micah is making me rethink all the promises I made before I showed up here in California.

How am I going to leave him? Can I even do it?

How am I ever going to get on a plane and say goodbye knowing that he most likely won't be able to come visit me often? Not with *Express* about to open up. It'll keep him busy just like *Vortex* has with Alexander since he opened it.

But how can I break my parents' hearts and tell them that I can't come back home?

Then they'll be left with both of their children living over two thousand miles away.

I feel sick as I sit here and fight the thoughts in my head. I feel like no matter what I end up doing I'll be hurting someone I care about. And I've already hurt Alexander . . . He just doesn't know it yet.

"How's everyone doing tonight?" Micah's deep voice draws my attention back to him.

"Oooh . . . he's starting." Jamie gets all excited and hits me as if I'm not already watching him.

"I have ears, you know."

"Shhhh . . ." she shushes me, keeping her eyes on him as he speaks again.

"First off, I want to thank you all for coming to my performances over the years. I appreciate it, and it saddens me to say that this will be my last performance here for a while."

"No!" the crowd shouts.

"Why?" is tossed around the room.

Micah smiles and adjusts the microphone to answer the screaming fans. "Because I'll be performing at *Express*. I'll have my own place to run, so unfortunately, I won't be around here much. You're more than welcome to still follow my performances, but don't forget to show my boy Alexander some love. Tweet about Vortex and continue to spread the word."

He's about to start playing when a random person yells from the back of the crowd. "Will you be playing shirtless?"

He laughs and shakes his head. "Sorry, ladies."

A few random girls scream that it's okay and I can hear others close by talking to their friends about how they can't wait for *Express* to open.

I'm happy for him. I truly am, and seeing that so many others are supportive of his upcoming bar I can't help but to smile as he begins playing for them.

It's best to put all of my thoughts and questions aside for now and just enjoy the strumming of his guitar as he begins humming into the microphone.

I still have over two months to figure everything out, and surely I can do it by then, right?

It takes me a few seconds to figure out what he's about to sing, but the moment he begins singing, I recognize it from listening to music videos on *Youtube*.

It's called *Oceans* by Jacob Lee.

The lyrics are beautiful, and every time I hear the song I only seem to love it more. It's one of those songs that are so pretty and peaceful that you can just close your eyes and play it on repeat.

Except I can't close my eyes right now, because as usual I *need* to watch Micah as he performs.

I need to watch him as he pours his heart and soul into singing. And what I love the most is that I haven't even heard him sing his own music and I can only imagine how much passion he's going to put into those once he plays them for everyone.

I have a feeling it'll be enough to have me drowning in a puddle of tears in front of him.

"I've never heard this song before," Jamie says quietly. "It's so beautiful."

"Extremely beautiful," I whisper back, keeping my eyes on Micah's facial expressions as he stays zoned in.

I'm enjoying the night with Jamie and Sebastian, us mostly staying quiet so we can listen to Micah, but as he announces his last song my brother scoots out the chair beside me and takes a seat. "Might want to blink before you hurt your eyes, little sis."

Sebastian laughs. "I thought I was the only one who noticed."

"Hey, I'm watching just like everyone else here is," I say defensively. I grab for my beer and take a quick drink, trying to act cool. "It's his last performance here for a while, so it's kind of important. That's all."

"Is it?" Alexander asks. "Is that why he's barely looked at anyone in the crowd besides you? Or am I just imagining that too?"

"Well, she is his girlfriend, right?" Sebastian asks, causing me to stiffen.

"What the fuck, Tegan?" Alexander stands up, but I grab his arm to calm him down before his temper causes a scene.

"No," I say quickly. "Sebastian only thinks that because Micah asked me to keep an eye on him."

"That better be the only reason," he grinds out.

Sebastian and Jamie both look at me with wide eyes, surprised at how upset my brother has gotten at the idea of us dating.

"My bad for making assumptions." Sebastian takes a sip of his soda and runs a hand through his hair. "I'm not used to Micah asking a girl to look out for me. I didn't mean to rile anyone up."

Alexander relaxes his shoulders and takes a seat again. "Don't work me up like that again, got it? I don't want to hear shit about you and Micah ever again. I can't handle the mess that would make and you know it."

"And you won't have to," I lie, my heart racing. "Now can we just enjoy the rest of the show?"

My brother nods, and when I look back at the stage Micah looks tense, but is doing his best to get through his last song.

He doesn't make eye contact with me again until right before he sets his guitar down and stands up.

Everyone is clapping and whistling for him. I hate he has to walk right past our table as if I don't exist in order to make my brother believe that there's nothing going on between us.

My heart sinks as random girls jump up to hug him and flirt with him on his way into the building. As much as I try to look like it's not upsetting me, I'm pretty sure that anyone with eyes can see it just as much as I feel it.

"You okay, little sis?" Alexander grabs my shoulders and bows his head to look down at me. "I'm only keeping you away from him for your own good. I know you guys have spent a lot of time together since you've gotten here, but I can promise that he'd run at the first sign of commitment. I've seen him with more women than I can count over the years and none of them have meant more to him than a one-night stand he could get off with. He's damaged when it comes to love, Tegan." He pauses to make sure Jamie and Sebastian aren't listening to us. Once he sees that they're wrapped up in their own conversation, he continues. "If he ever hurt you I don't think I could forgive him. And to be honest, I care about Micah too much to lose him as a friend. I hope you understand how much I love you."

"I do." I can barely hear myself over the sound of my heart pounding, but I do my best to get the words out anyway. "And I love you too. You've always looked out for me and it means the world to me. But . . ."

"But what, Tegan? What if he can change?" He grips my shoulders tighter and shakes his head. "He can't, because deep down he's scared of being abandoned by another woman. He has mommy issues. So please . . . *please* tell me that there's nothing going on between you two. I don't want the two most important relationships in my life ruined."

I want to tell him the truth, regardless of the consequences. It hurts so bad lying to him, but I can't yet. Especially after seeing the pain in his eyes at even the possibility of a *Micah and me*. Right now he has hope. I don't want to take that away.

He's truly worried that we'll both get hurt. He may not come out and say it, but he's scared for Micah too, and the possibility of it not working out. He's scared for all of us.

Now I'm sort of scared too.

I'm scared that my brother is going to hate us both for lying to him and I'm scared that maybe . . . just maybe he could be right about Micah.

What if he can't change?

What if the thought of me leaving him has him hurting me first?

I'm not sure I can handle my heart being broken by Micah, because I'm scared that it'd never fully heal.

Not after knowing what it feels like to be in his arms.

Not after getting a taste of what it's like to be his.

I want Micah Beck, and not just for today or tomorrow or even for the whole summer.

I want him for as long as I can keep him . . .

Chapter Twenty-One

Micah

WALKING PAST TEGAN AFTER MY performance and having to pretend I didn't want to wrap her up in my arms and kiss her in front of everyone felt a whole lot shittier than I thought it would.

As soon as I made it upstairs to my office, I punched my desk a few times, needing to let some frustration out.

It's been close to thirty minutes since Alexander and Tegan had a little conversation before she left, and I can't stop thinking about what he said to her. Not knowing what is driving me crazy over the possibilities.

I'm pacing around my office, still worked up, waiting on a text or anything from Tegan when the door opens and someone steps inside.

"Everything good, Man?" I raise my head to see Alexander standing in the doorway, watching me with hard eyes. "You seem a little upset about something? Anything you want to talk to me about?"

I run a hand through my hair and steel my jaw, while shoving my phone into my back pocket. "Nothing you want to hear. It doesn't concern you."

He steps further inside and closes the door behind him. "I can see the way you look at my sister. What I can't figure out is if that means you've already touched her or that you want to, but either way, I better not hear shit about you two hooking up. I've never given you shit about your personal life. This is the only fucking request I have for you. She's my family. Blood is thicker than friendship. I hope like hell that you don't break my trust and five years of friendship over pussy because you can't keep your dick in check. That's the only one that's ever been off limits."

"So you thought it'd be a good idea to bring Parker in the fucking picture?" I step closer to him and look him in the eyes when I speak. "Why . . . because he had a good life growing up? Parents who looked out for him and bought him things, fed him, and all that good shit that I didn't have? Does that make him better than me? Or is it because he doesn't feel the need to keep everyone at a distance in fear of getting hurt? What makes you think I'm not good enough for her? That I can't love someone when I find the right one? Am I that big of a piece of shit to you? Because you keep calling me a friend but you're not acting like one."

"Fuck you, Micah," he grinds out. "You know damn well that it has nothing to do with your fucked-up childhood and everything to do with the numerous women you've hurt since I've known you. I don't want my sister added to that list. You want to know why?" He steps in closer so that we're almost nose-to-nose. "Because I'll be the one picking up the pieces after you sleep with her and then crush her like you've done every woman you've ever laid eyes on.

You could have any and every woman your dick wants to sink into, so don't make me *hate* you because you decide to choose my sister out of thousands of other willing women who mean *nothing* to me."

Fuck. My heart is beating so hard that my chest is hurting. I hate that he believes I'll only hurt Tegan. He hasn't seen the way I am with her. I hate that he thinks I can't change. The part that I fucking hate the most is that I've already sunk my dick into her twice and I have to hide it from him in order to keep our friendship intact.

"Maybe I want to change. Maybe I just need the right girl. For someone standing here judging me I don't see you in a serious relationship."

He laughs and shakes his head in frustration. "You've had twenty-five years to find the right girl, Micah. Are you sure you're even looking? Think about it. You haven't had one girlfriend. Not one fucking girlfriend since I've known you. At least I've tried. At least I've given my heart to a woman before, and so has Parker. So, yeah . . . I brought him into the picture. I did it because I knew that he wouldn't hurt Tegan. If anything she'd hurt him. That might've been an asshole thing for me to do, but I'll do anything to protect my sister from someone like you who has the capability of crushing her world completely."

His words have me running my hands over my face in anger. There's so much I want to say right now but am holding back because I don't want to upset Tegan by giving us away.

We need more time together, so I can prove to her first that I can change. That I'm committed to her and I never plan on hurting her. Once she believes it I'll spend all my damn time proving it to him if I have to, but right now she comes first.

"I've gotta get out of here before I lose my shit. Stop worrying about Tegan getting hurt by me. She hasn't given me the time of day anyway." I brush past him and grab my keys. "I'll be at *Express* if you need me. I've got performances and shifts to schedule."

He nods, but doesn't say anything as I exit my office.

After his shit tonight, I need some time alone to think.

♪ ♩ ♪ ♩

IT'S BEEN A FEW DAYS since my performance at *Vortex,* and ever since Alexander had his conversation with Tegan it feels as if she's been keeping her distance from me.

Even though we've still been spending time together at *Express,* she's only crawled into my bed to sleep with me once since that night.

It's pretty obvious that she's worried I don't want her there or that I'll hurt her if she gets too close.

I don't blame her for being cautious around me, but it kills me that she's acting different, that she's afraid of us . . . of me.

The last thing I want to do is hurt her and I need her to see that. That's exactly why I'm standing in the dark hallway, about to do something I've never done before.

I'm about to give her a piece of me that I've been afraid to give to anyone before, but I need to show her how much she means to me and that she's not one of *those* girls her brother has told her about.

I stand here briefly, staring at her closed door with my hands in my hair.

My heart has never beat so fast before. I'm truly terrified right now, but still I push the door open and step inside, gently closing it behind me.

From the rhythm of her breathing I can tell that she's sleeping, so I crawl into her bed and kiss her neck.

The moment my lips meet her skin she lets out a slight moan and whispers my name in the dark.

"Micah . . ."

I kiss her neck again, before crawling above her, settling my body between her legs. "I can't stand you not being in my bed," I say against her forehead. "It feels so damn empty without you."

She opens her eyes to look at me, and I can see the worry in them. "I wasn't sure you wanted me in it still and I didn't want to make you feel pressured."

"What the hell, Tegan? Of course I want you in it. I'd want you in it every night if I had the choice."

She reaches up to twist a strand of my hair between her fingers as she studies my face. "I'm afraid of getting hurt by you, Micah. Everyone is putting stuff in my head. I'm falling and I'm falling fast and hard. It terrifies me and I don't know what to do. This is so much more to me than a fling like I thought it'd be, so I feel like I need to be careful when it comes to you."

I grab her hand and kiss it, before placing it on my bare chest, showing her just how hard and fast my heart is beating in this very moment. "Do you feel what you do to me, Tegan?"

She nods.

"I'm terrified too, babe. But it's not because I'm afraid I'll hurt you. I'll never fucking do that. It's because I'm afraid you'll hurt me. That's the only way I'm walking away from us. Got it?"

"I won't," she whispers. "I won't hurt you. Not on purpose at least. But . . ."

"But what?" I cup her face and look into her eyes to show her that I'm listening. I hear every single word she's speaking. It's not just going in one ear and out the other like it's always done in the past. I don't want to ever miss anything she says. "Talk to me. Tell me."

She releases a small breath and moves her hand up to run over my bicep, focusing on the tight muscle as she speaks. "You're opening your bar soon and I promised my parents I wouldn't move away yet. What happens once summer is over?"

My heart sinks at the mention of her family. I almost forgot that she didn't actually live here. The selfish part of me wants to tell her to stay anyway, but because I don't want to be selfish when it comes to her, I say the only thing I can at the moment. "We'll make it work, Tegan. I'll take care of everything when it comes to us. I'll do anything it takes to make us work. You have my word."

"I trust you," she whispers.

As soon as the words leave her lips I capture them with mine, kissing her soft and sweet to show her that I'll be gentle with her and take care of her.

With our lips still pressed together, I slowly lift her shirt up her body, only breaking the kiss long enough to pull it over her head.

Even that is too long to go without tasting her lips.

As soon as our lips meet again, I pull her up to her knees and gently tug her bottom lip with my teeth as her hands work on removing my jeans.

I'm so incredibly hard and horny right now that I feel as if I could bust just from the feel of her hand when it runs over my length. I've never needed to be inside a woman more than I do at this very moment.

Within seconds I'm laying her back on the mattress and spreading her legs so I can move in between them. With our eyes locked together, I enter her in one deep thrust.

We both moan into each other's mouths as I still my movements, giving her body time to adjust to mine.

"Move . . ." she whispers against my lips. "I need to feel you, Micah. Please."

I move on her demand, taking her slow and deep, our bodies molded together and covered in sweat as I give her the most important part of me: my heart.

No other woman has ever experienced me in this way before and I want her to be the only.

I run my hands through the top of her hair and gently kiss her neck, making my way up to whisper against her ear. "Are you on the pill, baby?"

She nods and grips onto my triceps with a moan when I push in deeper and stop. "Yes . . ."

"Good," I say against her neck. "Because I'm going to come inside of you."

I move my mouth along her neck, over her jaw and up to meet her lips as I continue moving in and out of her.

Her hands are all over me, gripping at me as if she wants me deeper, but I'm already as deep as I can go, so I pick up speed, which results in her nails digging into my back.

"Micah . . . faster . . . keep going," she pants.

Her demands have me gripping onto her waist, moving at a steady rhythm. As badly as I want to take her fast and hard, moving slow and with meaning feels way too good to change it up now.

I want her to *feel* me and not just physically.

♪ ♩ ♪ ♩

Tegan

THE WAY MICAH MOVES INSIDE of me is torturous, because I can feel *every last* inch of him. My body can hardly handle taking all of him, so I find myself begging for him to move faster.

The way he's looking at me, kissing me and even holding onto my hair while he tries his best to be gentle is so different than any time before this.

It's as if he's giving me a piece of him that I know I'll never want to give back.

The thought has it hard to breathe and every part of me is coming undone each time he enters me. He's holding me close, so damn close, as if he's trying to protect me.

I swear he owns me. He's claiming me as his and not just for one night. For *so* much more.

His long hair covers us, his scent surrounding me each time I inhale, and I'll forever remember Micah Beck's taste and smell. It's imbedded in my memory for life.

Each time he enters me he does it with meaning, and I find myself holding onto him as if I'll fall off the bed if I let go.

I can't think. I can't breathe. All I can do is feel.

And ever since he told me he's going to come inside of me, my skin has been on fire with need, because there's nothing hotter to me than Micah filling me.

I want him inside of me. Every last drop.

When his thrusts become a little harder, a little needier, I dig my nails into his arms and tilt my head back with a moan.

He catches my moan with his mouth and moves inside of me as deeply as he can.

"I'm close to coming inside of you." His breathy words hit my lips as he speaks. "I need you to come for me, baby. Right . . ."

He buries himself deep inside of me and my body obeys, unable to hold back any longer. Not even five seconds later Micah pulls my bottom lip into his mouth and holds it captive as he comes inside of me, filling me with his release.

"Shit . . . baby . . ." he breathes into my neck, before reaching up to cup my face. "You're shaking."

He's right. My entire body is shaking and not just because of the orgasm he gave me. It's because of what he gave me along with it.

"I can't help it," I whisper. "I just feel so . . . I don't know, Micah. I've never felt this way before. Ever."

He leans in and presses his lips over mine, kissing me gently, before he speaks. "That makes two of us."

After we both take a few moments to catch our breath, Micah pulls out of me and cleans me up. I expected him to go back to his room, but instead he crawls back into my bed and wraps me up in his arms.

We lay here in silence for the longest time, just holding each other. He kisses me every once in a while to let me know that he's still awake, until we both eventually fall asleep.

And it ends up being the best sleep of my life, because I know in this moment that Micah is truly mine . . .

Chapter Twenty-Two

Tegan

I'M COMPLETELY ZONED IN ON writing the last couple hundred words needed to finish my book when I hear a tap on the wall, followed by my brother's laughter.

"You all good in here, little sis?" I look over just as he's stepping into my room, covered in sweat from his afternoon run. "I've been awake for a few hours now and haven't seen you leave this room once. Have you even moved from that spot all afternoon?"

I smile up at him. "Nope!"

"Nope as in all isn't good or nope to not moving?"

"To not moving. I'm so close to finishing this book that I don't want to move until I type those two fabulous words: the end."

"Oh yeah . . ." his words trail off as he takes a drink from his bottle of water. "How close are you? Close enough that you'll be finished today?"

I nod.

"Good. Then you won't mind taking a short break to hang with me on the beach until I leave for *Vortex*." He motions for me to get up as if I have no choice. "Come on, before I tell Mom and Dad you won't hang out with me."

He gives me the same pathetic look I used to give him when we were kids before I tattled on him for not playing with me.

"Really, Xan?" I close my laptop and laugh. "You probably would tell on me just to get back at me for all those times I ruined your fun."

He motions again for me to stand up. "Hell yes, I would. And I don't think you want our parents flying out here to make sure you hang with your big brother, so get out of that damn chair before I call them." He can barely keep a straight face, but tries anyway.

"You're still a pain, you know that?"

He smiles over his bottle, before taking a quick drink while backing up. "I'm going to change really quick. Meet me out back." He slaps the door and rushes off to his room.

It feels like it's been forever since I've been able to spend some alone time with Alexander, so of course I don't mind taking a break for him, but I couldn't resist giving my brother a hard time just to see what kind of mood he's in first.

He appears to be in a good mood, which most likely means that he still has no clue that Micah and I have been spending every night in each other's beds.

We've been enjoying our time in the sun for over an hour now and surprisingly he hasn't had to rush off to work yet for anything and I'm thankful, but at the same time I feel as if I'm walking on eggshells around him, waiting for him to ask me about Micah.

It's been just over a week since Micah put on his last performance at *Vortex* and Alexander had his little talk with me about staying away from him.

He hasn't brought him up since and I can't figure out why. It's not like he doesn't know that I've been spending a lot of my time helping Micah at *Express*. He just doesn't know about all the *extra* activities.

"You don't suck at Frisbee as much as you did when we were kids," he teases, while reaching out to catch it. "You can at least get it to go further than your feet."

"Ha. Aren't we funny." I flip him off and then take off running for the blue plastic when he throws it. I catch it and attempt to throw it back, but it barely makes it ten inches in front of me. "Don't even think about laughing, Xan."

"I stand corrected. You're not better."

I roll my eyes and run over to our towels to get a drink of water. He follows, reaching for his too.

"So how do you like it here so far? It's beautiful, right?" He tilts back his bottle, almost emptying it, before he continues. "I knew the moment I got here that there was no way in hell I was returning to Wisconsin. I miss you and our parents, don't get me wrong, but I'm meant to be here, owning a bar on the beach. I've never been happier."

I smile and grab the Frisbee from him. "I don't blame you for not wanting to move back, Xan. I never have . . ." My words trail off as I make my way back over to my throwing spot. "It's gorgeous here. And not to mention quiet and peaceful. I love Whitney, don't get me wrong, but she's the loudest person I've ever met. She wants to party practically every night and so do our friends. And when it's not them dragging me away from my writing, it's our parents needing me for something. I just need some time alone to think sometimes. The beach, the bar, and even the back patio . . ." I point toward the house, "are perfect places for me to escape for a while."

"You don't need that whole party scene every night either.

You've got something great started with your books and I'm proud of you. As long as you can keep your head in them and not get distracted. Speaking of distractions . . ." He catches the Frisbee as I toss it to him. "Have you talked to Mom and Dad lately? They've called me a few times, but I haven't had much free time to sit down and talk to them."

"I've talked to Mom five times this week," I grunt. "She's still upset that I didn't call much when I first got here and she won't stop bringing it up."

He laughs and tosses the Frisbee up, catching it as it comes down. "You know how Mom is. She doesn't want to lose her baby girl yet. She's spent most of our lives smothering us and she's afraid of losing that soon with you too."

When he doesn't throw the Frisbee back I walk toward the water, getting my calves wet. Alexander follows, doing the same. Well, more like his ankles since he's so tall. "Can I tell you the truth, Xan."

He nods and looks down at me. "I love it here so much that I'm not sure I can keep the promise I made to our parents about waiting three more years. I want to move here."

I can't really read his facial expression as he stands there in silence and it's making me nervous.

Please don't mention Micah. Please . . .

"If you can promise me that it has everything to do with loving the beach and having some peace and quiet to work and not because of Micah, then I'll talk to our parents for you and explain why being here is good for your writing."

I swallow nervously and look down at the water, because I'm not sure if I can look my brother in the face and lie to him.

This lie has already been going on for three weeks too long and I'm not sure I can do it anymore.

I've completely fallen for Micah and keeping us a secret is the hardest thing I've ever had to do.

There's been so many times that I've wanted to run into Micah's arms and kiss him when we're at *Vortex* to show everyone that we're together, but I have to stop myself every time.

It's getting harder, because it's obvious that Micah wants to spend his time with me just as much as I want to spend it with him.

If for some reason I don't make it down to his bed by the time he's ready to fall asleep he comes crawling into mine, as if he can't sleep without me in his arms.

And truthfully, I've been finding it hard to sleep away from him also. But some nights, by the time my brother has gotten home I'm so exhausted from writing that I end up crashing before I can go down to Micah's room.

So the fact that he comes to me says a lot.

Micah isn't the same one-night-stand-guy I met over three weeks ago . . . The same one I witnessed screwing some random girl against the sliding glass door downstairs and then kicked to the curb.

He hasn't so much as even looked in another girl's direction, and I'm hoping that my brother has noticed it too. Anyone can change if they want to.

Because I'm not sure how much longer I can go without telling my brother the truth, and even though he doesn't speak of it, I know it's eating Micah up inside too.

"Xan, I–"

"Shit. One sec," he says while reaching into his back pocket for his phone when it goes off. "I'll be right back."

I can't believe I'm about to tell him the truth, but maybe now is the best time to do it. Maybe I can talk him down from being mad at Micah with it just being the two of us if I just explain how much we care about each other.

All these thoughts keep running through my mind of the different ways I can start this conversation, but every single one makes my stomach hurt.

It takes my brother a few minutes to come back over, but when he does I can tell our day of spending time together has ended.

"I'm sorry, but I have to get to the bar. Parker called and said that Micah just fired Ryan for serving drinks to some underage kids and he's in his office looking to fill his spot. They're shorthanded now." He points at me as he begins walking backward toward the house. "But we'll continue this conversation later if you're serious about wanting to stay here. Will you be awake when I get home?"

"I'm going to help Micah and Sebastian tonight at *Express,* so I'm sure I can stay awake for a couple hours once we call it a night."

His jaw flexes at the mention of me being with Micah again, but I refuse to lie to him about hanging out with him. "We'll talk later."

I nod and watch as he rushes up to the house to change.

Well . . . so much for getting it all out in the open.

I walk over and grab the Frisbee and the two towels we brought with us and begin walking back the house.

I won't be seeing Micah for another few hours and I want to finish this last chapter so I'm able to go back to the very beginning and read it over, before sending it to my editor.

But the moment I pull out my laptop all I can think about is Micah and Alexander and how soon they might not be speaking to each other because of me.

The thought of the two of them hating each other has my chest aching and my stomach twisted into knots. Especially since I'm the one to blame.

I hate it. I hate it so much.

But I think I need to tell Micah when I see him tonight that I'm going to tell my brother the first chance that I get.

That way Micah can be prepared to deal with my brother's wrath. I've seen it before and it's far from pretty.

I just hope I can keep the guys from killing each other once the truth comes out.

I don't think I can handle watching two of the most important men in my life hurt each other.

It would crush me.

But the hiding and going behind my brother's back ends tonight.

Because there's no way I can hide my feelings for Micah any longer. Not when I'm quickly falling in love with him . . .

Chapter Twenty-Three

Micah

TODAY WAS A ROUGH DAY at *Vortex,* because all I could think about was getting out of there so I could spend time with Tegan. It had me anxious and uptight all day, practically chewing everyone's ass off that stepped foot into my office.

It didn't help that thirty minutes before I was scheduled to walk out the door two of Sebastian's asshole friends showed up with fake IDs, thinking I wouldn't notice them in the crowd.

They were sadly mistaken. Thanks to Sebastian pulling this shit on me for the past two years, I keep a close eye on everyone who steps foot into this place.

The little shits were barely able to take their first sip before I snatched them both by the back of their necks and threw them out on their asses.

I was heated, so they're lucky I didn't do more damage. The only thing that calmed me down about the situation was that

Sebastian wasn't with them. He seems to be doing better lately and I hope he keeps it up.

I ended up firing Ryan's incompetent ass on the spot and had to spend the next hour going through applications to find him a replacement.

I told Parker that I could handle the situation, but like an idiot he called Alexander anyway and took what little free time he had to spend with his sister away. It pissed me the hell off and apparently it pissed him off too, because he was not happy when he arrived.

It felt as if he was taking it out on me with the way he kept giving me dirty looks every time he stepped into my office for updates on Ryan's replacement. The way he was sizing me up confirmed he had something on his mind, almost like he thought I was trying to keep him away from Tegan myself.

I may be worried about him finding out about us before we're ready to tell him, but that doesn't mean I don't want Tegan to be able to spend time with him while she's here.

Even if that means him finding out and coming at me to kick my ass. I'm not going to lie. I deserve an ass beating for what I've done, and when the time comes I'll take it.

A lot has changed over the last week between Tegan and I, ever since I showed up at her room in the middle of the night.

I'm not the same guy I was weeks ago, and that moment proved it to not only her but myself too.

I'll do what I can to prove it to Alexander too.

"You going to tell me how you got the money for those new shoes?" My attention veers to Sebastian's new pair of Nike shoes the moment I step behind the bar, where he's helping stock the liquor. They're not the same pair I paid for.

He shrugs as if it's no big deal. "I got a job washing dishes at the diner around the corner."

"Don't lie to me, Sebastian." I drop the stack of applications I've been searching through and get face-to-face with him. I can always tell when the kid is lying, but I'm a little off my game right now thanks to my head being all over the place. "You better not be selling drugs again or I'll kick your scrawny ass."

He laughs, reaching into the box for another bottle to stock. "Chuck got me the job last week. I swear. He loaned me a hundo until I get my first paycheck. Trust me, big guy."

"I try my damned hardest to, but until you prove to me that I can trust you I won't be able to. Trust isn't given, it's earned. Got it?"

He slaps my shoulder and lifts a brow. "Got it. Now calm it before you bust out of that shirt like the Hulk. You can even stop by and check on me. I know you're dying to."

I'm the last person who should be schooling someone on trust right now, and looking over at Tegan as she sits there writing is a harsh reminder of that.

How the hell am I supposed to expect a kid to be truthful with me when I can't even be truthful with my best friend?

"I'll be doing that this week." I grip his shoulder and smile. "I'm proud of you, kid."

"Hell, I am too sort of. It being my first legit job and all. Which reminds me. I need a favor."

"What? A ride? Sure."

He shakes his head. "No. A place to stay so my asshole parents can't steal my money for drugs and booze. I want to be better than them and I know you'll help me get there."

"Yeah . . ." I look him in the eyes. "You already are. We'll discuss you staying with me later, now that you're almost eighteen."

"Hell yeah," he says excitedly, before turning his attention to Tegan. "How's that last chapter coming along over there? Did you add me to the story yet so the ladies can meet me?"

Tegan laughs and looks up just in time to catch me slap Sebastian upside the head. "Leave her be so she can concentrate."

"Damn, big guy. Remember what I said. Calm it." He throws his arms up. "Can't blame a guy for trying to make an appearance in a book. My name needs to get out there."

Tegan looks up from her computer and laughs. "Sorry, Sebastian. Maybe my next book. This one is practically done," she says with a proud smile. "All that's left to do is go over it from the beginning before I send it to the editor and it's ready to go."

She stands up and starts walking toward us.

"Are you serious?" I set the stack of applications back down before I come at her and pick her up, grabbing her legs to wrap them around my waist. "I'm fucking proud of you, baby. So, when do I get to read about me?"

I can't help but to tease her still, even though she's already mine. It's just who I am with her.

"Who says I've been writing about you?" she asks against my lips. "You've had that little idea in your head since the day you were snooping over my shoulder. A little cocky, are we?"

A deep laugh rumbles in my chest as I move my hands down to grip her ass. "I think we both know that I'm much more than a *little* cocky."

"Oh, come on you two!" Sebastian complains from beside us. "Do you ever give it a break? I've got virgin eyes over here."

"No," I growl. "Close your virgin eyes and ears if you don't like it. You're gonna have to get used to it being like this twenty-four-seven when you're around me and my girl. Especially if you're staying at my place."

I move my hands up to wrap into the back of Tegan's hair, before brushing my lips over hers, as if Sebastian isn't watching us.

I could really care less.

He's known about us for almost a week now and I'll never forget the look on his face when I called Tegan my girlfriend in front of him. The kid was speechless, and I've never heard Sebastian shut his mouth for longer than two seconds before in the entire time that I've known him.

It took him at least two minutes before he burst into laughter and then asked me to repeat myself as if he was convinced he was hearing me wrong.

Just like everyone else, he knows my reputation of being a one-night-stand-guy. He's never seen me with the same girl twice.

"So, I'm still your girl?" she teases, tugging on my bun. "Because Parker—"

I slam my lips to hers, cutting her off before she can get another word out. I'm sure she can tell from the roughness of my kiss and the deep growl coming from inside my chest that I'm showing her just who she belongs to.

I can't deny that I'm all alpha male when it comes to Tegan and I'll take down anyone who tries to take her away from me.

I get so wrapped up in our kiss I almost forget that we're not the only two in the room, until Sebastian clears his throat.

"Okay, you two have fun. I've gotta run."

I look over as he's typing something out on his phone and rushing to get out of here. "Where the hell are you going in such a hurry? I thought you wanted to help out and make some extra cash?"

"Chuck is outside for me. I'll help tomorrow. Cool?"

He's lucky I'm desperate to spend some alone time with my girl or else I'd give him a harder time about leaving his job unfinished. "Tomorrow. I call and you be ready. No excuses, Seb. We've got a lot of shit to discuss. Rules and all that."

He smiles. "Okay, cool." He nods and blows a kiss at Tegan.

"Later, babe."

She laughs as I lift her up and set her on the bar. "Later, kid. Stay out of trouble."

The moment we're alone she wraps her legs around my waist and squeezes. "Kiss me again and call me your girl."

I tangle my hands into the back of her hair and lean in to brush my lips over hers. I wait until her eyes meet mine before I speak the truth. "You're my girl for as long as you'll have me."

She wraps her arms around my neck and nips at my bottom lip teasingly. "Well, we've already had sex three times. I think one more time and I'll be good."

I tug at her hair and grind my hips between her legs, showing her how hard I am for her. "Oh yeah? I knew you were only using me for my body so you could write that book of yours. But are you sure once more will be enough?" I pull her bottom lip into my mouth and suck it, before I release it and run my tongue along it. "Because if that's the case then I'll be sure to make it the best sex of your life, so that I can change your mind. I don't want anyone one else having you. You're mine."

"Mmmm . . ." She moans against my mouth and tightens her hold on my waist. "You've already given me that three times, Micah. Unless you know some new tricks then—"

I crush my mouth to hers, unable to hold back any longer. This woman has no idea what her mouth does to me. And if she's going to give me a damn challenge she better be ready for me to accept it and win.

With a deep growl I release her hair, before I yank my shirt over my head and toss it aside, moving right back in to kiss her.

I own her lips with my kiss, because I want to possess every part of her, including her damn heart.

Her breath is heavy against my lips, showing me just how

badly she wants me to take her right now, but when I go to reach for her jeans she places her hand on mine to stop it.

"What's wrong?"

"You need to promise me something first." She looks worried as her eyes land on mine again.

"I already told you that I'm yours, Tegan. I'm not going to leave you. I promise." I grab her face and kiss her nose. "I'll promise you anything you want. Just say it."

"I believe you, Micah. It's not that. My brother—"

"We're telling him tonight," I say quickly. "I want the same as you and I can't lie to him anymore. But for now . . ."

I capture her mouth with mine, kissing her hard and deep. She has to think that I'm desperate right now with the way I'm moving my body against hers as if I'm going to lose it if I don't get inside of her soon.

But not showing her how much I need her is torture for me. It's been almost a week since we last had sex, because I wanted to show her that sex isn't all it's about for me. Making love to her was the first step in showing that and taking time away from sex was the second.

I'm hers. All fucking hers, and it's time I make her feel that again.

I move my hand down again to undo Tegan's jeans. I barely get the button undone when out of nowhere, Alexander's angry voice comes from beside me.

"You motherfucker." He grips my shoulder and pulls me back, and before I'm able to react Alexander's fist slams into my jaw repeatedly, not stopping until Tegan screams at him to stop.

I steel my jaw and regain composure as he reaches for Tegan's arm and starts walking away.

"Don't touch me, Xan!" she yells in her brother's face, while shaking his hold on her. How dare you hit him like that without even giving us a chance to explain."

Guilt takes over as Alexander takes a step back and reaches for the nearest bottle of liquor, as if he needs it like air, his face still shock-ridden.

"Xan, we were planning on telling you—"

"I don't want to hear your excuses, Tegan. You knew how I felt about you getting involved with Micah, and yet you did it anyway. I thought you had a little more respect for me than that after everything. Aside from that you lied to my fucking face over and over. I need one goddamn minute!"

I stand here, my gaze focused on Alexander as he turns away and tilts the bottle back, taking a long drink.

I brace myself for more. I can only imagine what we looked like to him. I'm sure it's all he can do right now not to kill me after walking in on me shirtless, between his baby sister's legs.

"We need to talk," I say, grabbing for my shirt to put it back on. "We've been wanting to tell you for a while—"

"For a while? What about all those fucking conversations and threats, Micah?" He takes another drink, before slamming it down onto the bar so hard the bottle breaks, liquor spilling.

When he turns around, his hard eyes land on me. From the anger present in his stare and shaky arms, I can tell he's fighting with everything he has not to punch me again. "We've been friends for almost five years. Does that mean nothing to you? I trusted you and made you my manager. I've been a good fucking friend to you, and I've never asked for anything except that you work beside me at my bar and keep an eye on things when I'm not around. You've been my only real friend since I moved here. You were like a brother to me. Until now I would've trusted you with my fucking life. In all that time I asked you not to do *one* thing. The one thing that would fuck me up and break my trust. You went behind my back and did it anyway. You went after my only sister. I can't even stand the sight of you right now." His nostrils flare as he eyes me over. "Give me one good reason why I shouldn't kill you."

"Xan." Tegan steps in between us, looking worried that Alexander will lose it and blow up on me again. "He didn't do this alone. It's my fault just as much as it is his. Don't you dare put all the blame on him. I'm not a kid anymore. I can make my own damn decisions without your consent."

"Move, Tegan. I'm not speaking to you right now," he growls, putting his arm out to get her at a safe distance from us. "I wanna know why my best friend stabbed me in the fucking back." He rolls his neck, while cracking his knuckles. "I'm waiting, asshole."

My jaw tenses as I stand in place and run my hands over my face. I've been prepared for this moment for a while now and I'm ready to take another blow if it helps keep his anger aimed at me and not her. "I don't have a good fucking reason. I went after her because I was a selfish son of a bitch who couldn't stay away, even if it meant fucking things up with my best friend. *I* did this. *I* went after her, so don't be mad at her. Hate me, but not her."

"You're right," he says, walking toward me. "You are a selfish son of bitch, and always have been."

I stand tall, knowing what's coming next. I take it like a man as my best friend's fist connects with my already sore jaw.

It stings like hell, but I make no attempt to move out of his way or come at him.

A real man takes responsibility for his actions.

"What the hell, Xan?" Tegan rushes over and pushes her brother's chest, but he barely even moves. "Hit him one more time and I won't speak to you ever again. Do you hear me?"

His jaw flexes as he runs his hands over his face, before grabbing the ledge of the bar. "How long have you been trying to sleep with my sister? Don't fucking lie to me."

"A few weeks."

"Three fucking weeks." He punches the top of the bar a few times, before speaking again. "Since she got here. That's messed up and you know it."

"Xan, that's enough! I've seen how you get. Now stop before it's too late and you say or do something that you can't take back. I care about Micah and I want to be with him. It's not your choice and there isn't a damn thing you can do about it, so stop right fucking now."

I try to focus on Tegan's words to calm myself down, but Alexander breaks my concentration by shoving me into the bar and getting in my face. "I practically raised her. I've witnessed her broken-hearted more times than I wish I had. The last thing she needs is to have it broken again by some man-whore who doesn't even know the meaning of commitment. It's only a matter of time until you're bored and ready to move on."

I push him off of me and try to reason with him. "Do you think I'd risk our friendship if it wasn't serious? I fucking care about her and I'd prove it to you if you'd give me a fucking chance. Now back off."

"That's bullshit and you know it." He shoves me again and I get up just to be shoved for a third time.

"Dammit, Alexander, stop! You're fucking pushing it now," I bite out, fighting with everything in me to keep my cool.

I don't want to fight my best friend when I know I deserve the beating, but I can only take so much before I snap.

"You're done," he says, rubbing his hands over his face to calm down. "We're done. I don't want you around my sister. I want your shit out of my house and bar by tomorrow." He turns his attention to Tegan, who looks torn over what to do. "There's no changing my mind, Tegan, so don't even try. If you stay here with him then I want you out too, because you're opening yourself up to get hurt and used by the biggest player I've ever known. Don't come crying to me when it happens. I will not pick up the pieces this time. I warned you. More than once at that."

"Xan, he's not going to hurt me. Do you hear yourself?" She walks over and gets in his face. I've never seen her this angry before, and I don't like it one fucking bit. "We were planning on telling you about us tonight. I tried at the beach before you ran off. You weren't supposed to find out this way. Don't give me ultimatums. That's not fair."

He shakes his head and looks between the two of us. "My best fucking friend and my sister, both lying to me behind my back for weeks like it's a game. For fucking weeks! Do you know how that feels? Do you know how much that hurts? It fucking kills me. This is exactly what I wanted to avoid. There is no good ending here." He turns his attention back to me. "All I wanted was to protect you both, but if I have to choose between the two, protecting Tegan is my number one priority. If I have to cut you out of my life in order to do that then I will. You may think you care about her now, but what about a month from now? What about in a year? I will never trust you not to *hurt* her, because at some point it's inevitable. That's how you're wired."

"Then maybe you don't know me as much as you think you do." I take a step forward, looking him in the eyes. "If you did then you'd know that when I care about someone I put my all into them. And that's what I plan on doing with Tegan if you would just give me a fucking chance to do that."

"Maybe you can do that with the kid. I've seen you do it, but it's different with him. He's not someone you're trying to sleep with. As soon as some easy chick comes around, wanting your dick, you'll realize like you always have that meaningless sex is your thing and then where does that leave my sister? Broken and crushed." He turns back to Tegan, who's standing there, looking hurt and confused "Let's go."

"Dammit, Alexander," I growl. "Don't make her choose. It's not fair to her. I tried to talk to you like a fucking man before. To find out your reasons for distrusting me with her. Give me a fucking chance to show you how much she means to me before making her walk away. You know damn well that's what she'll do because she'll always choose you first and that's how it should be. You're her family."

"I can't, Micah. You're not like the assholes that broke her heart in the past that she was able to get over in a few weeks. They were *nothing*. There's something about you that leaves girls hanging on after being with you. I've seen it day in and day out. It's been three weeks. I'm not taking the chance of seeing what happens if it goes on any longer."

"Tegan is different," I say, pissed off more now than when he punched me. "I don't give a shit about my past and the women I've been with. None of them have been her. I'm not the same asshole I was before she came along, but you're too wrapped up in being pissed off at me to see that. I haven't touched or even looked at another woman since I've slept with your sister."

"You fucked my sister?" The mention of me sleeping with Tegan has his fist flying into my jaw before I can dodge it. I pop my jaw. Did he really fucking think she hadn't given it up to me yet and that I've been chasing her this whole time? We're grown. "I'm really going to kill you now, asshole."

"That's it!" We both look at Tegan as she rushes over to her brother and pushes him back a few steps. "I'm going to be with

Micah and you can't stop it from happening. All I hear about are your whoring ways too. The booty call after our lunch date and the office sessions. You've told me and I've heard. People talk. Why do you think you're better than him? And who are you to force me to choose between the man I care about and my family? You're my brother, Xan. My damn brother. You may be pissed right now, but you'll get past that once you give us a chance. That's all I'm asking for."

"I can't do that, Tegan, so don't fucking ask me to. We're not talking about me right now. If you don't want to listen to me and stay away from Micah then I need to walk away right now before I kill him, because I can't look at either of you without feeling betrayal in my chest."

"I've fallen for her, Alexander. It was never supposed to happen, but it did. Don't fucking walk away from her as if you're going to cut her out of your life because we want to be together. That's bullshit and *you* know it."

"Do us both a favor and stay away from her, Micah. You know it's best for her. Think with your heart and not your dick for once."

"That's what I'm doing for the first fucking time ever! Jesus, that's what you're not understanding." I punch the bar, before gripping it, wishing I could rip the fucker apart.

"Yeah, well it would take something huge to make me believe that, like a miracle, and I doubt that will happen." When I look up he's talking in Tegan's face. "I'm out of here. You can stay with that asshole for the rest of the summer if you want, but when he rips your world apart don't come running to your big brother to mend your broken heart. It won't be fucking happening."

Tegan stands there shaking as her brother walks away, leaving her like she's about to fall apart.

I want to go to her. I want to wrap my fucking arms around

her and tell her that I'll protect her.

But it's my fault this is happening. I should have tried hard to stay away.

The thought of their relationship being ruined because of me has me saying the last thing I wanted to be saying tonight, but I did this, and if anyone is going to suffer it needs to be me. Not them.

"You need to go with Alexander." I grip the bar tighter, until my fingers feel like they could break. "Repair things with your brother. I'm not worth it, Tegan."

"Micah." She reaches for my arm. "What the hell are you saying? I don't want to leave you. Did you not hear me tell my brother that I want—"

"I'm saying that you need to leave, Tegan," I growl, shaking her grip on my arm. "I will not stand here and let him cut you out of his life over an asshole like me. Go."

My chest aches more with each demand that leaves my mouth. The words are physically crushing me.

"Just go before he leaves, dammit."

"Fine." She pushes my arm and then my chest when I turn to face her. "You want me gone, then I'm gone. I guess you can't handle it when things get tough. Fuck you, Micah! Fuck you for making me fall for you."

"Tegan . . ."

"No. You don't need to explain shit to me. I'm gone." She rushes over to the table to grab her laptop. "Maybe I should've listened to my brother. You're fighting real hard for us. *Real* hard."

I stand here, frozen in place, watching as she walks out the door.

Everything inside of me aches at the idea of losing the two people I care about the most. I really fucked up this time.

Grinding my jaw, I swing my hand across the bar, knocking

over a couple of bottles of liquor along with everything sitting atop. Limes, straws, and cocktail napkins go flying.

The sound of the bottles breaking doesn't faze me one bit, because the only fucking girl I've ever loved just walked out the door and I have no idea if I'll get another chance with her.

I may not be fighting for us, but I'm fighting for her. I wouldn't be a man if I allowed her and Alexander's relationship to be ruined because of me. It'll only end in regret. I won't do it.

All I can do right now is give them time to work things out and maybe, just fucking maybe, she'll come back to me and Alexander will give us a chance.

But he said so himself; it's going to take something huge for him to ever believe that I won't hurt Tegan.

I don't know how the hell to do that other than walk away from her right now and let them heal.

This fucking kills me.

Not only have I just lost the friendship of the only person who's been there for me, but I've possibly just lost the only girl I've ever fucking wanted for good . . .

Chapter Twenty-Four

Tegan

I FEEL SICK TO MY stomach as I stand here at the airport about to board a plane back to Wisconsin.

It's been three days since Micah told me to walk away from him and I haven't felt the same since. I don't think I've ever truly known what a broken heart feels like until now.

I haven't been able to sleep at night and I've barely left my room at my brother's until I had to leave for the airport this morning.

As hard as I fight to keep Micah off my mind, he's lingering there and all it's doing is hurting me.

I never expected to fall in love with the naked guy running around my brother's beach house.

But I did.

As far as I know Micah has already gotten everything from *Vortex* and Alexander has given him a week to get everything from the house since he has a lot of stuff there.

It feels so empty without him around and no matter what I do, if I stay, I'll only be reminded of Micah and how he's no longer around.

There's been so many times that I've wanted to pick up the phone and call him just so I can hear his voice, but I can't get past the hurt of Micah sending me away like he did.

That's not how things were supposed to go down. It wasn't supposed to end with me walking away and losing him.

But we both knew that my brother wasn't going to change his mind. We were living in a fairytale if we thought otherwise. As much as it hurts, I believe Micah did it because he trusted it was the best thing to do at the time.

I'm still not sure if Alexander and I are completely good with each other, but I just can't be there anymore.

I'm doing what is best for everyone.

"Are you sure you want to do this, Tegan?" my brother asks, reaching for my bags. "I know things have been a little messed up for a few days now, but that doesn't mean you have to leave."

"I can't stay, Xan." I look up to meet his eyes, mine feeling heavy. "Being there is only a reminder of how you and Micah are no longer talking because of me. And I can't sit there, dying inside because I want to be with a man that I can't have. I'm too emotionally *exhausted* to fight when it'll never end with your approval."

His eyes are filled with guilt as he watches me grab the bags from him. "I'm only protecting you and you know it, Tegan. As much as I wish I could believe that Micah Beck is capable of a relationship, when you've known him as long as I have and have seen as much as I have, I just . . . I can't. I'm sorry for that."

"Yeah, well I'm sorry too." I swing my bags over my shoulder, before looking back up at him. "But maybe you should at least thank him for making me walk away from him. He's the reason I left with you that night. I was willing to take my chance that you'd eventually forgive me, but I'm guessing he wasn't willing to take that same chance and risk the two of us never speaking again."

My brother's jaw flexes as he runs his hands up and down his face. It takes him a moment before he's able to speak. "He made you leave that night?"

I nod and release a breath. "My flight is about to leave. I should get going." I give my brother a quick kiss on the cheek and walk away, before I can change my mind about leaving.

I just hope that maybe Alexander knowing what Micah gave up for us is enough for them to eventually work things out.

I may not be able to have a relationship with Micah, but maybe I can begin to heal if I know that my brother can again.

♪ ♩ ♪ ♩

I DIDN'T BOTHER TELLING MY parents or anyone else for that matter that I was returning today.

The truth is, I just want some time to be alone, before falling back into my old life.

I'm sure Whitney will be shocked once she comes home to find me here, but I'm hoping to tell her as little as possible so that I don't have to think about it.

Today is the last day I'm able to work on my book before sending it off to the editor, so I spend most of the evening doing re-writes and changing things that just don't feel right anymore.

Still Breathing pretty much ended up turning into mine and Micah's story, as hard as I tried not to let that happen, so it only feels right that I change the story to fit what really happened.

A lot of my readers may end up upset, but not everyone is lucky enough to get a happily ever after.

After typing out "The end" I hit send on the email and close down my laptop.

The editor will have the story for three days and then it's going to straight to the formatter who will have it for two.

I plan to hit publish in five days.

I should be excited, but I feel anything but. I expected to be celebrating this moment, not sitting around depressed in a pair of old pajamas, hiding away from the world.

But things don't always go as planned.

I get comfortable in bed, well, as comfortable as I can, and turn on the TV as a distraction. Unfortunately, it doesn't distract me as much as I had hoped and I find myself checking my phone every so often as if I expect to hear from Micah.

I'm sure if he was going to call or text that he would've done it by now, but a girl can only hope, right?"

When my phone goes off twenty minutes later I get a small surge of hope, but when I open the message it's only Jamie responding to my earlier text. Even though I don't feel like talking to anyone, I send her a simple text to let her know that I'll explain everything to her in a few days.

After tossing my phone aside, I turn over a few times and fight to get comfortable, but it's impossible. Being here doesn't feel the same as it used to.

My bed used to be my escape from the world. The place I went to when I wanted to hide out and write, and now all I want to do is be in a different bed.

I know I was only away for a little over three weeks, but *here* doesn't feel like home anymore.

"Tegan . . . are you home?"

Whitney's voice comes from the kitchen, so I sit up and lean against the headboard.

"I'm in my room," I mumble.

Her face is beaming when she walks in, but quickly turns into a look of confusion once she notices my appearance. "Oh, honey. What the hell happened to you?" She takes a seat on the edge of my bed. "You look like you haven't slept in days."

"I haven't," I admit. "I messed everything up and I haven't had a moment of silence in my mixed-up brain since. I'm driving myself insane, Whit."

She gives me a sad face. "Do you want to talk about it?"

"Not really," I say softly. "I think what I need is a week-long nap before I'm ready to talk about things. I'm hurting right now and need to figure things out. That's all."

"I hate this." Whitney throws her arms around me and the moment she pulls me in close, I lose it, and the tears begin to fall.

I'm so mixed up; confused and angry at the moment, and it's been building and building for the last three days. I can't hold it in any longer.

I don't want to be weak. I don't want to feel broken from the loss of Micah, but I do.

I know it'll take time to get used to being without him, but the truth is I don't want to get used to being without him.

I don't want to get used to not feeling his strong arms around me or feeling his lips brush against my neck whenever we're close.

Micah Beck isn't someone you can just learn to get over. He's someone that you learn to love, and once you do you never stop.

"I'm sorry, sweets," she says, consoling me as she rubs my head. "Are you sure you don't want to talk about it?"

I shake my head and pull away from her grip. "No, I just need some sleep. Exhaustion is kicking my ass and making everything worse than it really is. I promise." I force a smile to make her feel better. "I'll be better once I get some sleep."

"Alright," she breathes. "I'm not going anywhere. I'm here

when you want to talk. Okay?"

I nod. "I know. Thank you."

"That's what friends are for, and just know that if this has anything to do with the sexy guitar guy then I'll fly to California and kick his ass myself."

Her threat has me smiling. "I don't doubt that."

She smiles back and looks toward the door when Ethan calls her name. "Get some rest, babe."

I watch as she stands up and exits the room.

And like a fool, I reach for my phone and pull up the picture I took of Micah the first night I watched him perform.

The sight of him sitting there with his hair flowing around him while he plays his guitar has me throwing my phone across the room in anger and hurt.

I may have told myself that the only reason he pushed me away was because of Alexander, but I'm not so sure I'm fully convinced that was the only reason.

Maybe, just maybe, he doesn't feel the same way about me as I do for him. If he did it wouldn't be this easy for him.

It's that thought that has me wishing I never went to California in the first place, because the idea of Micah not loving me back hurts worse than anything I could ever imagine . . .

Chapter Twenty-Five

Micah

TONIGHT IS THE GRAND OPENING for *Express,* yet I don't feel nearly as excited as I thought I would when I look around at the final setup.

Ever since I forced myself to tell Tegan to walk away, I've felt like a huge part of me is missing. It's been eating at me, making it hard to fucking sleep at night.

Opening *Express* and giving myself something to call my own has been my number one priority for as long as I can remember, but now I'm not so sure that's it's the most important thing to me anymore.

When Tegan was around I saw a future where she'd spend her nights with me at the bar, writing her books, while I performed weekly shows. And when I wasn't performing I'd sit back with her and watch the other performers, us both enjoying the place together.

I still want that.

I want that so fucking much that it hurts.

I've bowed out and given them both time, but I'm not so sure I can stay away any longer. I was hoping that since tonight is the big night for *Express* that Tegan would've come by to wish me luck at least, but I haven't heard from her in nine days.

The thought has me gripping the bar and hanging my head. I don't know what the hell to do to make things right and it's slowly killing me.

"Holy shit! Have you seen the crowd outside?" I raise my head to see Sebastian walking toward me, holding a package. "I had to fight my way through it just to get inside. It's mad out there. I almost lost this," he says, holding up the box.

"There were close to eighty people out there the last time I checked." There's no emotion in my voice. No excitement, and I can tell from the look on Sebastian's face that he notices too.

"You good?"

I hold out my hand. "Yeah, I'll take that."

Knowing what's inside the package has my heart about to beat out of my chest.

I knew Tegan's book was due to release yesterday, so I jumped online and expedited my order, getting it here as quickly as possible.

I've been curious about the story ever since her face turned red when I asked her if she was writing about me.

He hands it to me, keeping his eyes on me as I look it over. "What the hell is it?"

"A book," I say stiffly.

He laughs and readjusts the stack of napkins. "Oh yeah. I forgot you like read." His smile fades when he looks up to see my facial expression. "Is it hers, Man?"

I nod and hide the package under the bar next to the register.

Now I'm thinking about her even more, and the fact that she isn't here has me wanting to do something out of character for me. "I need you to get Donovan and Jasmine clocked in and behind the bar to work, no later than six-thirty. The door doesn't open until seven and the first performance doesn't start until eight. I'll be back."

"Whoa." Sebastian watches me with wide eyes as I reach for the book and head for the door. "Where the hell are you going and since when do you trust anyone else to run things? Especially me."

"I have somewhere I have to go first." I stop at the door long enough to turn around. "I trust you to get things started. I'll be back before we open."

He opens his mouth as if to say something, but before he can I step outside. The group has grown since the last time I was out here and even that isn't enough to stop me from leaving.

A few girls whistle as I rush by them, but I don't slow down. I just keep on walking until I'm jumping into my truck and headed to Alexander's.

I barely have time to stop the truck before I'm jumping out and running to the front door, hoping with everything in me that she's here and not at *Vortex* with Alexander.

When no one comes to the door after a few seconds, I knock again, desperate to get to her. I almost consider pulling out Alexander's house key that I never gave back, but decide that he'd probably really kill me this time.

"Fuck it."

I reach for the key and right as I'm about to stick it in the lock, Alexander answers the door, dressed all slick as if he has somewhere to be.

I can tell from his pissed off expression that he's not happy with me showing up, but I don't really give a shit about that right now.

"What the fuck are you doing here, Micah?"

"Where is she?" I run my hands over my face, anxious to get to her. "I need to see her, Alexander, and I'll remove you from my path just to get to her right now. I don't give a damn anymore, so don't test me."

With his jaw steeled, he steps outside and closes the door behind him. "She's not here. I'm surprised you don't know that already. I figured you would've contacted her by now."

My heart stops at the mention of her not being here. "What the fuck does that mean?" I look up as he's running his hands over his face. He looks torn. "Where the hell is she? Tell me. Now."

"She's gone." He releases a long breath, looking me over. "She left almost a week ago."

Panic sets in, and before I can stop myself I'm grabbing at Alexander's shirt and getting in his face. "Tell me where the fuck she lives? I need to get to her. I'm sick of your shit."

He shoves me away from him and fixes his shirt. "Down the block from my parents. She . . ."

"Text me the address." I take off running for my truck, needing to get on the first available flight to Wisconsin.

"What about the grand opening for *Express*? What the fuck, Man? It's in less than an hour."

That shit is not even enough to stop me at this point. I jump into my truck and head for the airport, because I don't want to do this without her.

It's not that I can't. It's that I don't want to.

Because this night doesn't mean shit without her by my side— the girl that was there when it was just a mostly empty building and dirt on the floors.

Express can open any night of the fucking week, but making her wait for me to stop being a dumbass and come to her can't.

I just hope I'm enough for her to come back with me . . .

Chapter Twenty-Six

Tegan

TO GET ME OUT OF the funk I've been in since I arrived home, Whitney decided to invite a few friends over for a bonfire at our place tonight.

Everyone's been listening to music and drinking around the fire, enjoying the nice night, but all I've been able to think about is Micah and how tonight was the grand opening of *Express*.

I want so badly to know how it went—is still going—but I'm stuck here instead of where I really want to be, all because I made a mess of things.

The thought has me more down tonight than I have been since everything first fell apart over a week ago.

I've been such a wreck that I haven't even checked the sales for my new release, when usually I check it obsessively.

When I released my debut novel I must've spent the first month clicking that damn refresh button, counting every single sale that popped up on my dashboard.

None of that matters with this release, and it sucks, because just months ago that's *all* that mattered.

Until I met Micah and fell for him like a fool. Now he's the only thing that matters, and knowing that I'm missing the biggest day of his life hurts so damn much.

I was supposed to be there to see the proud look on his face when the door opened. I was supposed to be there to see him perform on his *own* stage in front of people for the first time. I'm missing it all and it's killing me inside.

I came so close to buying a plane ticket this morning so I could stop in for a few minutes, but since I didn't have any plans of letting him know I was there I decided it would only hurt me more.

Not going was probably a smart decision that I'll thank myself for later.

"Tegan!" I look up from my spot on the porch step when Whitney yells across the yard at me. She's sitting on Ethan's lap, but plops down into her own chair. "Get over here with us and stop being a party pooper. Come on!" She slaps the chair next to her. "Don't make me tell you again."

Releasing a frustrated breath, I take a sip of my beer and stand up. I've been avoiding everyone for hours, so the least I can do is sit by them and pretend to be involved.

Pretending is something I'll probably have to do for a while, so I might as well start tonight. Put on that damn happy face and wear it as best I can.

"It's been over a week now, babe." She grabs a S'more from Ethan and hands it to me as I sit down. "Eat this and live a little. I hate seeing you like this. Either call him or forget about him. But this . . . what you've been doing since you got back needs to stop. You're miserable and you're making me miserable too. It's not fun."

"It's not that easy. I can't just call him, Whit."

"Why not? Because your brother will be pissed off? Or is it because you think this Micah guy doesn't want you to? Explain it to me. You haven't given me much to go on. All you've done is mope around the house, watch TV, and eat snacks like they're going out of style. That's not like you at all."

"It's complicated, okay." I take a bite of the messy treat, giving myself a moment to think. "I don't know if he wants me to call him. The fact that he hasn't called me yet could mean that he's moved on already. What if my brother was right all along?"

"He's a player, huh?" She takes a drink of beer, before she moves her chair in closer. "Players can change, babe. Are you forgetting that Ethan was a "player" before we started dating? All these playboys need is for the right woman to come along and shake them up a bit. Your brother doesn't know that because he's a player too. He just hasn't found the right woman to shake him up yet. Tell me this . . ."

I take another sip of beer and look over at her. "Yeah?"

"Do you love this guy?"

"Yes." My answer is automatic. "So much that it hurts to be away from him. It's killing me and I don't know what to do. I've never experienced this kind of pain before."

"Then take a chance and call him. It's worth a try at least, don't you think? If love weren't a game of risks it wouldn't be so hard. Or rewarding."

I think about her advice for a few minutes, coming to the realization that she's right. I'll never know if he loves me back if I don't at least try. I've been so scared of him not returning my feelings for him that I've spent the last week convincing myself that the reason I can't call him is because of my brother and his friendship.

But I can't do this anymore. I need to at least know if he feels the same. Even if he doesn't.

Then maybe I'll be able to move on with my life and stop being so damn miserable—as Whitney pointed out.

"I'll call him tomorrow."

What the . . ." She reaches into my pocket and snatches my phone out, nearly making me drop my beer. "Call him now. Why wait until tomorrow?"

I shake my head, staring down at my phone. "I can't tonight. It's the grand opening of his bar. He–"

"That's a bullshit excuse and you know it, Tegan. He could be there, miserable as shit and staring at his phone the whole night because he hasn't heard from you. Maybe hearing from you will make his *big* night even bigger. Now . . . please . . . do us all a favor and call him."

She holds my phone up, not giving in until I take it from her hand and stand up. "Fine. I'll call him."

My hands shake as I scroll down to his name. Just seeing his name on the screen is enough to send my heart into overdrive.

I swallow and hit the call button.

There's no turning back now.

Either he'll answer it and I'll get to confess my undying love for him or he'll send me to voicemail. Either way, it's time I move on with my life and this phone call is going to determine which direction I'm going to go.

With each ring of the phone my heart beats faster and harder, until it feels as if I'm choking on it. Or maybe that's just the vomit trying to work its way up.

Why am I so nervous?

When the phone goes to voicemail after only a few rings, my throat and chest begin to burn, but I hold the tears back and turn around to face Whitney.

"It went to voicemail," I choke out.

"Okay, babe. Maybe he didn't hear it because of all the—"

"After a few rings, Whit. That means he declined my call." I shake my head and force a small smile. "It's fine though. I got my answer and that's all I needed."

"I'm so sorry, babe." She replaces my empty cup with her full one. "You need this more than I do. Drink up."

I look down at the cup, about to take a drink when *I Found* by Amber Run catches my attention. It's one of the songs Micah played for me at *Express* that night and all it does is make me feel sick to my stomach.

"I don't think so. This . . . song . . . I can't." I hand it back to her, anxious to get away. "I think it's best if I go to bed and call it a night."

"No, stay out for a while. You need this."

"Maybe I do, but I don't want it right now. Thanks, but no thanks. I'm going to bed."

After a few seconds she finally huffs and takes a step back. "Okay, I get it. I don't like it but I get it. I'll check on you in a bit then."

I don't say anything. I just walk away, because all I can think about is getting alone as quickly as possible, before my emotions get the best of me in front of everyone.

Our friends seeing me a mess over Micah is the last thing I want or need.

Hurrying up the steps, I reach for the door and step inside.

The sight of Micah standing in front of me, holding my book in his hand steals my breath straight from my lungs.

"What are you doing here, Micah?" I fight to catch my breath as he eyes me over. "Your bar . . . the opening?" I question.

I swallow as he takes a step forward and holds the book up.

"This ending is bullshit, Tegan," he growls. "This isn't how the fucking story is supposed to end. It can't."

I suck in a breath as he steps closer and cups my face. "How is it supposed to end then, Micah? You tell me, because I don't have a clue. So, tell–"

His lips crash against mine and he kisses me with desperation that confirms he's missed me just as much as I've missed him.

All I can do to avoid falling over is grab onto his shoulders and hold on for dear life as I go weak in his arms.

After a few moments he pulls away, both of us fighting for air as he presses his forehead to mine. "I rescheduled the grand opening for three weeks from now. The bar means *nothing* to me compared to you, Tegan. I've known that all along, but as I was standing there waiting for the door to open, I didn't feel shit. I didn't feel happy or accomplished. I just felt . . . empty. I knew there was no way I'd be going along with the grand opening without you there by my side." He pauses to take a breath. "I had no idea you left California or else I would've shown up here days ago. It's killed me not being able to see you. But I knew we couldn't be good until you and Alexander were. That's the *only* thing that made me strong enough to push you away that night. But I can't fucking go without you any longer."

I swallow as he runs his thumb over my bottom lip.

"Please give me another chance, because I can promise you that I'm not leaving here without you. I don't care if it takes me proving to your brother for weeks, or hell, even months before he's okay with you coming back with me." He lifts me up and wraps my legs around his waist. "You're mine, Tegan Tyler, and I've known that since the first time you opened your mouth and gave me a hard time."

I smile and wrap my arms around his neck. "I've missed you

so damn much, Micah, and I wanted to be there for you tonight. I did, but I was afraid you didn't want me there. I didn't want—"

"I love you, Tegan."

His confession stuns me speechless for a few seconds, and when I finally speak my voice is barely a whisper. "You what?"

"I fucking love you," he says against my lips. "I have for a while now, and you leaving has only made me love you more, not less." His eyes meet mine with nervousness. "Do you love me, Tegan? I need to know."

"Yes," I whisper. "Yes, I love you, Micah. I'm in love with you and I want to be with you."

"You have no idea how fucking happy that makes me." He kisses me again, giving my bottom lip a slight tug.

"Wait." I move away from his mouth, just now realizing that I never told him where I live. "How did you know my address? Did Alexander . . ."

He nods and sets me down to my feet. "I got him to text me the address on my way here."

A small smile takes over, because I know my brother well enough to know what that means. "He trusts you again, Micah. It's the only way he would've given you my address. Trust me on this. It'll take a little time for him to come around, but he will."

He smiles back and kisses me once more. "Does that mean you'll come back with me? I don't care if it's only for the summer. I just want you with me."

"Oh my God." Micah and I both look at Whitney when she steps through the door with her mouth wide open. "He's here. In our kitchen. In Wisconsin. Not there in California at his bar. This is big." Her mouth curves into a huge smile. "He loves you," she nearly squeaks out. "I knew it!"

"I do." Micah smiles against my lips, kissing me again. "A hell of a lot."

"Well, it's nice meeting you and all, but with the way she's been moping around for the past week, hurting over you, I should kick your ass." Her smile broadens. "But I won't because you two look happy and I don't want to ruin it."

Micah looks down at me and rubs his thumbs over my cheeks. "I deserve to get my ass kicked and I'd gladly take another beating for you. I'm sorry, baby. You better believe that letting you walk away for a second time is the last thing I'll ever let happen. I promise."

I wrap my arms around his neck and pull down until his lips meet mine. "Good. Because if you tell me to walk away again I'll slap you."

He laughs against my lips. "You know where that will lead, right?"

"Okay . . ." Whitney holds her cup up to us. "I'll be outside drinking this tasty beer so you two can catch up . . ." She clears her throat. "In private. I'm glad you're here, guitar guy."

"Me too," he says, tangling his hands into my hair. "Now I need to make up for lost time."

Before Whitney has a chance to walk outside Micah is lifting me up and carrying me through the house with his lips against mine.

I grab the doorframe when he almost passes my room, so he backs up and steps inside, closing the door behind us.

Within seconds we're both fully naked, our bodies tangled together as he makes love to me.

It's rough at first, both of us unable to be gentle. But by the second round it's sweet and gentle, the two of us taking our time on each other's bodies.

Everything with him feels perfect right now, and I know

without a doubt that there's no way I'm not getting on a plane with him once he's ready to go home.

As much as I hate to hurt my parents, I belong with Micah and I'm not letting anyone keep us apart this time.

It's time I think of myself and do what makes me happy, and there's nothing that makes me happier than being with Micah.

We love each other and I have to believe that everything will work itself out in the end, because I know we're meant to be together.

Him coming here proves that . . .

Epilogue

Micah
Three weeks later

I STAND HERE WITH A satisfied smile on my face as I take in all the bodies filling the room.

Express is at its capacity and there's still a small line of people waiting for others to leave so they can come in and watch the performers lined up for tonight.

I couldn't be more thankful that Tegan has been here by my side since the doors opened a few hours ago, because I seriously don't think I could enjoy this moment as much without her here to experience it with me.

Stepping behind the bar, I grip her waist and lean in to speak against her ear. "Thank you."

She laughs and turns around to face me. "For what?"

"For being here. It means so damn much to me. *You* mean so damn much to me." I move my hand up to caress her cheek. "And I appreciate you working the bar for a while. You really didn't have to."

"I wanted to," she says, wrapping her arms around my neck. "Everything needs to be perfect tonight and I really don't mind. It's sort of fun."

"It is perfect." I swipe my tongue across her lips, before kissing her. "You being here assured that."

"I know," she says with a cocky grin.

I laugh and kiss her again. The more she's with me the more I wear off on her and I love it. "I should go greet some more guests before my performance."

"Okay, babe." She moves her hands down to grip the top of my shirt, before she pulls me in and playfully nips my bottom lip, and then kisses me. "You've got ten minutes before you're up. Don't be late or I'll have to punish you."

I smirk, before running my tongue over my lips. "I have a feeling that I'm going to love you being in charge."

She watches me with a playful smile as I hurry away and get lost in the crowd, wanting to make my way around to as many people as I can before my show.

"Thank you for coming." I smile and shake the hand of another guest, welcoming them to *Express*.

I've shaken too many hands tonight to count and I still haven't made it around to everyone.

I'm just about to hold my hand out to greet the next person when I look up to see who's standing in front of me.

Alexander is standing there dressed all sharp in a blue button-down shirt and a pair of black slacks.

As happy as I am to see he decided to show up for the opening, I don't know what to expect from him.

We haven't spoken much since I returned home with his sister, so I assumed he still hasn't come around to the idea of us dating yet.

"Micah." He holds his hand out and I take it, giving it a firm shake.

"Thanks for coming."

He nods and releases my hand. "I see you have my sister working for you."

I look over at Tegan to see her watching us from behind the bar with a small, hopeful smile.

"Yeah." I can't help the smile that takes over as she blows me a kiss, before turning away to help a guest. "I hired her as management. I wanted someone I could trust, and well . . . you know me."

He nods and reaches for his glass. He watches me over the rim as he takes a drink. "She seems happy. Really happy."

"And I plan to keep her that way. I don't care what it takes and I want you to know that." I meet his eyes, wanting him to see the truth in them. "I fucking love her and I'd do anything for her. Whatever it takes. I want you to fucking see that."

"I know." His lips curl into a small smile as he sets his glass down. "I realized that the day you showed up at my doorstep when you were supposed to be *here* opening the damn place you've worked so hard on. I know more than anyone how long you've worked to get this place up and running. You wouldn't have walked away unless you truly loved my sister." He pauses to look over at her again. His smile broadens as he watches her laughing with someone. "I was a hothead. I needed some time to be pissed off at your dumbass for going behind my back. I didn't want to give in too quickly. I'm not a pussy."

I chuckle and grip his shoulder. "I think your fist slamming into my jaw about ten damn times proved that you aren't. The fucker still hurts if moved just right."

He grins and hands me one of the shots in front of him. "Sorry about that, Man. I lost my shit when I saw you two together. I just want what's best for her, but now I know that's you."

We tilt back our shots at the same time, and just as we set them down Tegan wiggles her way in between us with a smile. "I see you boys are playing nice," she says, wrapping her arms around me. "This has totally made my night."

Alexander releases a breath, while looking us over. It's the first time since the night he caught us that he's seen us together. "I suppose you two do look nice together. I do kind of already like him. But I'll still kill Micah if he hurts you." He cracks a smile, which has Tegan moving to give him a hug.

"It's that time," she whispers, after moving back in to hug me. "Are you ready?"

I nod and kiss the top of her head. "Yeah." I drop my hands down to cup her face, and then move in to kiss her long and hard. "As long as you're watching me, babe."

She nods and moves in close to Alexander as I walk away and head toward the stage.

My heart is racing with a mixture of nerves and excitement, because tonight I'm performing a song I wrote for Tegan when she was gone.

I want her to feel every word of the pain I felt without her in my life.

And now that she's here, there's no way in hell I'm ever allowing her to leave me again.

I may not have ever experienced love before, but I'm damn sure that not everyone gets as lucky as I am. I plan to hold onto this feeling for as long as I can, because I already know what losing her feels like and it's something I never want to live through again.

Tegan Tyler is mine and I'll spend every day making sure she knows that . . .

♪ ♩ ♪ ♩

Tegan

EXCITEMENT FILLS ME AS I watch Micah make his way through the crowd and up to the stage. Jealousy is the last thing on my mind, even though random girls still make attempts to get his attention.

It's different now, because I know that he's mine, when before I only wanted him to be.

He doesn't offer the girls a second glance as he grabs his guitar and takes a seat on the stool. He looks down at his guitar while he tunes it, before looking up to see if I'm watching him.

I smile to let him know that I am. It's always been impossible for me not to.

After staying in Wisconsin for a few days I took Micah over to my parents' place to meet them and break the news that I was moving to California.

They were upset at first, but after seeing how happy Micah made me I think they finally warmed up to the idea of me leaving with him.

Apparently my brother had talked about Micah to them over the years, telling them all good things about how he's had his back and really helped *Vortex* get going in the beginning.

I'll admit, I was a little annoyed that even my parents knew about him when I didn't, but I guess it ended up being a good thing in the end, because my parents were quick to trust him with me. They ended up loving him, which made me extremely happy.

I was hoping that by the time we arrived in California Alexander would be ready to talk to Micah and work things out, but he found ways to avoid him for the past three weeks.

He hasn't even been to Micah's place to see how I like it there. He's made me come to him every time I want to see him.

When I saw that my brother made an effort to show up for

the grand opening I had hopes that he'd talk to Micah, and when I saw that they finally were happiness and relief filled me. I knew he'd eventually come around, but I didn't know how soon and the wait has had me anxious.

"I'm still proud of him, just so you know. Still a little pissed too, but proud as hell." I look away from Micah to give Alexander my attention as he continues. "I've never seen anyone work harder than he does and that's always impressed me. I'm actually happy that he has you to help him, to be honest. Trust has never come easy for him, so I was wondering who he'd get as management." He laughs and takes a sip of his drink. "I figured he'd attempt to run the whole damn place himself. It wouldn't have surprised me in the least, and he probably could've pulled it off. If anyone could it'd be that dick."

I smile and bump him with my shoulder, happy that he's willing to give Micah another chance. "He's pretty amazing, right?" My heart jumps with excitement when I look over to see that Micah is watching me. It reminds me of when he played at *Vortex,* and I don't think I'll ever get used to that feeling. "I love him, Xan. He treats me good and I'm so damn happy when I'm–"

"I know, Tegan. I'm sorry for being an overprotective asshole." He grabs the back of my head and looks down at me. "All I want is for you to be happy. It's obvious that Micah is what makes you happy. I can see now that I was wrong. I'm choosing to trust that he'll keep it that way, because I've never seen him this happy or *crazy* before when it comes to a woman. The asshole about ripped my head off to find out where you were. I never thought I'd see that day."

I laugh when he does. "I didn't know that story, but I'll have to ask Micah about it later."

"Did I miss it? Please tell me he hasn't played yet?" Jamie shows up beside us, appearing out of breath. "It's crazy in here, and if it weren't for Sebastian working the door I don't think I would've made it past the line outside. Wow."

"You didn't miss him. He's about to play." I look behind her for Sebastian, but can't see him anywhere. "Isn't Sebastian coming in for–"

"Hell yeah, I'm here." Sebastian's voice comes from behind me, almost scaring the shit out of me. "The ladies wouldn't stop flirting with me at the door." He grins, taking a spot next to me. "There's no way I was missing this though, so I had to tell them I'd be back."

I roll my eyes and laugh as Sebastian winks.

"How's everyone doing tonight?" Micah asks into the microphone, causing the whole room to go quiet. "Everyone enjoying the music so far?"

The crowd screams with excitement, which has Micah laughing into the microphone. "I'm gonna sing an original song tonight, so I hope you all enjoy. It's something I've never done before."

The room goes quiet again as Micah begins strumming his guitar, and like always I can't take my eyes away from the stage.

He's sitting there, dressed in a pair of old faded jeans and a black t-shirt, yet he still has the attention of everyone around. It's his talent that brought everyone here and not him being shirtless.

Him playing shirtless at *Vortex* was just an extra treat for everyone, but for me it takes away from the most important part. I love that here it'll be all about his amazing voice. The introduction to the song plays and before I know it I'm lost in the stanza . . .

"I should go to sleep now, but all night you've been on my mind.

Tossing and turning, I never thought we'd run out of time.

My head is ready for some peace, from the thoughts that never cease.

I haven't found any since you walked away.

Because I miss you more than I know how to say.

There's an ache deep in my heart, pain in my chest.

My girl's long gone and my mind will never rest.

It's just past four AM . . ."

Listening to the lyrics has *my* heart, because I know right away that his song is about me. He must've written it over the week I was back home in Wisconsin. I hate that he had to feel those things for even a second.

I swallow back my emotions and glance over to see Alexander looking at me. He wraps his arm around my neck and offers me a small smile, because he knows too now just how much Micah hurt when I was gone.

"I'm not ready to do this without you, my world is torn in two."

With each word that he sings I find myself getting closer to the stage, my eyes locked on him as he pours his heart out.

I've never heard such raw emotion in his voice before and it's ripping my damn heart out that I'm not next to him right now, showing him that I'll never leave him again.

Right as I reach the end of the stage, he stands up and swings his guitar over his shoulder, coming at me as if he *needs* to get to me.

He doesn't even bother finishing the song. He just walks off the stage and pulls me in as he crushes his lips against mine so hard that it about smothers my breathing.

It's as if the song reminds him too much of the pain he felt when we were apart. It does the same for me too.

I wrap my hands into his hair and kiss him back, harder than I've ever kissed him before.

We're so lost in each other that we almost forget we're not alone, until there's a loud whistle followed by some cheers of excitement.

Micah pulls away from our kiss and places his forehead to mine. His eyes meet mine as he moves his hands up to cup my face. "I love you so fucking much, baby, and I never want to know what it's like to lose you again."

I shake my head. "You won't have to." I stand up on my tiptoes and brush my lips over his. "I love you, too. And that song . . . It was beautiful. I loved it, but I don't want to hear another sad song from you ever again. I can't handle it. Promise me."

He flashes me a cocky smile. "So, you loved my song?"

I laugh and hit his chest. "Is that all you took from that?"

He shakes his head.

"Then promise me," I say firmly.

"You've already promised me you'll never walk away again." He rubs his thumb over my lip. "That makes it easy to keep my promise to you. Do you really need to hear it?"

I nod. "And I need you to promise me the same."

He smiles against my lips. "I'll promise you anything you ever want, Tegan. Trust me."

"I do," I whisper.

And it's the truth.

I love this man with all my heart, and I know without a doubt that he feels the same way.

And I know for a fact that things can only get better from here now that everyone accepts us being together.

He is mine and there's no one else I'd rather give myself too.

Because Micah Beck is addictive to the last drop and I'm completely in love with him . . .

The End

Acknowledgements

FIRST AND FOREMOST, I'D LIKE to say a big thank you to all my loyal readers that have given me support over the past few years and have encouraged me to continue with my writing. Your words have inspired me to do what I enjoy and love. Each and every one of you mean a lot to me and I wouldn't be where I am if it weren't for your support and kind words.

Also, all of my beta readers, both family and friends that have taken the time to read my book and give me pointers throughout this process. Thank you all so much.

Thank you to my boyfriend, friends and family for understanding my busy schedule and being there to support me through the hardest part. I know it's hard on everyone, and everyone's support means the world to me.

Last but not least, I'd like to thank all of the wonderful book bloggers that have taken the time to support my book and help spread the word. You all do so much for us authors and it is greatly appreciated. I have met so many friends on the way and you guys are never forgotten. You guys rock. Thank you!

About The Author

VICTORIA ASHLEY GREW UP IN Rockford, IL and has had a passion for reading for as long as she can remember. After finding a reading app where it allowed readers to upload their own stories, she gave it a shot and writing became her passion.

She lives for a good romance book with tattooed bad boys that are just highly misunderstood and is not afraid to be caught crying during a good read. When she's not reading or writing about bad boys, you can find her watching her favorite shows.

CONTACT HER AT:
www.victoriaashleyauthor.com
www.facebook.com/VictoriaAshleyAuthor
Twitter: @VictoriaAauthor
Intstagram: VictoriaAshley.Author

Books by
VICTORIA ASHLEY

STANDALONE BOOKS
Wake Up Call
This Regret
Thrust
Hard & Reckless

WALK OF SHAME SERIES
Slade
Hemy
Cale
Stone
Styx
Kash

SAVAGE & INK SERIES
Royal Savage

PAIN SERIES
Get Off On the Pain
Something For The Pain

ALPHACHAT SERIES (Co-written with Hilary Storm)
Pay For Play
Two Can Play

LOCKE BROTHER SERIES (Co-written with Jenika Snow)
Damaged Locke
Savage Locke

Printed in Great Britain
by Amazon